T0304991

Sunbirds

Sunbirds

PENELOPE SLOCOMBE

JOHN MURRAY

First published in Great Britain in 2024 by John Murray (Publishers)

1

Copyright © Penelope Slocombe 2024

A CIP catalogue record for this title is available from the British Library

Hardback ISBN 9781399817240
Trade Paperback ISBN 9781399817257
eBook ISBN 9781399817271

Typeset in Sabon MT by Manipal Technologies Limited

Printed and bound in Great Britain by Clays Ltd, Elcograf S.p.A.

John Murray policy is to use papers that are natural, renewable and recyclable products and made from wood grown in sustainable forests. The logging and manufacturing processes are expected to conform to the environmental regulations of the country of origin.

Carmelite House
50 Victoria Embankment
London EC4Y 0DZ

www.johnmurraypress.co.uk

John Murray Press, part of Hodder & Stoughton Limited
An Hachette UK company

For Luis, Finlay and Emilio

Author's Note

Although it is hard to find official figures, dozens of foreign travellers have reportedly disappeared or been murdered in the Kullu region of northern India since the early 1990s. In 2003 an article in the *Guardian* estimated that there could also be as many as nine thousand foreigners living illegally in the surrounding hills.

Your children are not your children.
They are the sons and daughters of Life's
longing for itself.

Kahlil Gibran, The Prophet

Part One

I

ANNE

With Anne there is no good place to start, so it might as well be here. A phone booth – flimsy and hot – at the back of a cyber-cafe in a hill station in the Himalayan foothills of India, where she sat very still, watching a line of ants march up the wall. The receiver pressed tightly against her ear, counting the rings, hoping her husband wouldn't pick up. The answering machine kicked in after the twelfth ring: her own voice, recorded some ten years earlier, telling her to leave a message. And just before the mechanised beep, in the background, the kitchen door, sun-light splinting off the windowpanes, the Atlantic lapping at the garden wall, her son's voice: *Mum?*

Anne put the phone down without leaving a message. Heat was prickling her skin, sweat sticking her shirt to the small of her back. She ran a hand over her hair and tried to remember, not for the first time, if it had, in fact, been sunny that long-ago day when Torran had burst into the kitchen and interrupted her recording. She'd meant to redo it but never had. And now she called to hear herself as much as her son: herself but not herself, that other woman she used to be. Lost to a day that may or may not have been sunny and would, but for the record-ing, have slipped away, as unremarkable as all the others.

In the booth, the ants continued their steady march. A never-ending line winding lazy like a river to disappear through a crack where the wall met the ceiling. It was late afternoon – midday in Scotland – and she did think about calling back, leaving a message so Rob wouldn't worry. But there was nothing to be said and no new leads. She wondered if he intentionally avoided her calls, if he was standing even now in the dim hallway of Taigh na Criege, staring at the phone. Anne watched the ants and then slowly reached a finger to the wall and flicked a tiny body out of line.

The air outside was fresh after the humidity of the phone booth. Beyond squat concrete shacks and tangled telephone wires, the sun was setting in a violent blaze of red and pink. Anne followed the ridge as the trees fell away and the town began to assert itself amid the cries of street vendors and the growl of scooters. Tourists browsed the pashminas and jewellery spilling from shopfronts while young travellers lounged in low-lit cafes, playing chess and smoking pipes. Incense and frying spices filled the air, not quite masking the scent of pine and mouldering rubbish, which curled around the edges of everything.

Past the Hanuman temple, Anne stopped to buy chai from a man sitting cross-legged on a table by a battered pan, humming tunelessly as he stirred milk and spices. She took the clay cup he gave her, wrapping her fingers around it as the sun sank behind the mountains. A sea of clouds rose from the valley, a chill slicing through the day's lingering heat. Soon the rains would come, and Anne knew she should think about heading south.

Beside her, a couple of blonde girls, pale as ghosts, performed the pantomime of ordering and paying in a language they didn't understand. The old man continued to hum through their nervous chatter, deftly plucking the change from an outstretched hand.

Anne drank the last of her chai and returned her cup. The taller of the girls smiled at her as she turned to go, and she smiled back, hesitating before walking away. They looked fresh off the plane; there was little chance they'd know anything about her son.

She joined the flow of pedestrians and cycle rickshaws down the hill to join the Mall Road, stepping over sleeping dogs and around playing children. Men stood outside restaurants waving menus and calling to her as she passed – a few she knew and acknowledged with a nod as they greeted her by name. But she was distracted and didn't stop to talk, her mind returning again to the conversation she'd had that afternoon with the headmistress of the Girls' College, and to her offer of a more permanent arrangement. Anne was unofficially volunteering there, still on a tourist visa, ready to leave at a moment's notice. But the days passed and still she was here and nothing changed.

Turning towards the Upper Mall, Anne paused again as the last of the light faded over the Garhwal range to the west, the valley already full of night. She'd glimpsed something today, sitting across the large mahogany desk from Mrs Chatterjee, sipping the English Breakfast tea she'd been offered from a China cup: the possibility of another life, a profession – of sorts – something she'd never had. But with it would come an acceptance, an admission she wasn't willing to make.

The lights of Dehradun were blossoming below, and Anne glanced at her watch; the speed with which day turned to night still took her by surprise. In Taigh na Criege the summer sunsets lasted forever and when he was a child Torran would never sleep. And who could blame him for wanting to stay up when the sun still danced above the sea? Lost in the memory of his Paddington pyjamas, his long-armed monkey dragging across the floor, she nearly didn't see him, though he walked straight past her, so close their arms almost touched. Torran. Not the boy but the man he was now.

She stood completely still, unable to catch a breath, and he continued away from her, his pace neither fast nor slow, that familiar bounce in the roll of his feet.

Blood rushed through her like the roar of the sea. And still he was walking, was disappearing into the crowd, and yet her body wouldn't move. She opened her mouth to call for him but there was no sound.

And then someone bumped into her from behind, propelling her forwards, and she was off, half running towards him, her hand reaching, her pulse thrumming, her heart refusing to acknowledge what her mind already knew.

But still she sped up, pushing through a group of young women, ignoring the indignant honk of a scooter, scattering a family of monkeys squabbling in the road. And even as her heart drummed against her ribs, she knew.

It wasn't him.

Broader, taller, older, darker hair, but still she had to be sure, because how much can a person change in seven years? Her hand was on his arm and he turned in surprise, half frowning and half smiling, and very much not her son. She took a step back and then another, the rushing turning to a ringing in her ears.

He raised an eyebrow. 'Can I help?' And then, looking more closely. 'Are you OK?'

But Anne was retreating.

'Wait,' he said, reaching for her arm. His fingers were a question on her skin before she pulled away.

He said something more, but she was already walking and didn't hear what it was. The growl of the sea still in her ears, she kept her eyes fixed before her, ignoring the curious stares. Up ahead a cow wandered down the middle of the road, a thick string of saliva trailing from its mouth, its dark eyes unblinking and inexplicably sad.

Hotel Broadway was tucked down the end of a side street off the Mall Road. There were no streetlights and she hurried past the glow of the tailor's workshop, raising a hand to the tailor's son, who sat behind an old Singer sewing machine in the open doorway. She felt better here, away from the crowds, cool air filling her lungs.

Her pace slowed as the hotel came into view. With its green roof tiles and painted shutters, it looked like something you'd find in the Swiss Alps rather than the Himalayas. The valley fell away sharply beneath it, leaving the hotel clinging to the side of the mountain as if afraid it might be shaken off.

Up the stairs and through a tiled sunroom full of wicker furniture and red geraniums, Anne's simply furnished room smelt perpetually of damp. She pulled the door closed and stood in the darkness, waiting as the shadows arranged themselves. Across the room was a large bay window, the lights of the town shimmering along the ridge.

Torran had sent them a postcard of that view when he'd stayed here in the spring of ninety-seven. Anne had pinned it with the others on the board in the kitchen. The hastily scrawled message so typical of those last few postcards: inconsequential, unable to offer the comfort or meaning she would later search them for, poring over every word, whispering them as she fell asleep.

Greetings from Mussoorie – hill station of Princes! Staying at a cool little place called Hotel Broadway – of all things! The warm weather has yet to arrive. Thinking of heading south.

But he hadn't, of course. He'd travelled further north to Manali and then he'd disappeared. Just like that. And what do you do when your only child, at eighteen, rises early one summer morning and, leaving all his worldly possessions, walks out of his hotel room and vanishes into thin air? Perhaps you search. And when you can search no more you stop, where you are, and you wait.

But Manali wasn't somewhere Anne could be, with its towering peaks, whispers on the streets, sense of threat and posters of all the other missing travellers. So why not Mussoorie, with its old-world charm and the rest of the world spread out beneath you. That postcard had been the last, and Anne told herself that if there was some message hidden within it, it would be this: that Mussoorie was the place he would know to look for her.

On the wall by the door, Anne had hung a large map of India and stuck pins in it. Plotted routes and possibilities with brown string. There were photos and newspaper clippings and, on a rickety table, copies and translations of the police files, their own investigation notes, missing person posters and flyers, all stacked neatly in cardboard boxes, now gathering dust.

Anne surveyed the dark outline of the map, all the words and images she knew by heart. And why did she keep them there still? She'd had nothing to add for the longest time and it was all a pretence anyway, a futile attempt to feel like she knew something. That she had all the pieces of the jigsaw and if she could only arrange them in the correct way, the whole picture would come into focus.

She thought again of the man on the street who was not her son, of Mrs Chatterjee's offer, and had a sudden urge to tear everything down, to be rid of it. Taking a step forwards, she reached out her arm, dizzy with the possibility of a change.

But as quickly as the impulse came, it was gone, and she found herself turning in a half circle, back to face her own transparent image in the glass.

No, she told the darkness, *Not now*. The darkness wrapped its arms around her. *If not now – when?*

II

BEFORE

Things fall apart gradually. The stronghold, once unconquerable, begins to weaken the moment it is complete. The ground beneath it erodes, the walls crumble. Little by little, year by year. Long before the damage is visible from the outside, the whole structure is compromised. By the time the cracks appear, it is already too late.

Anne feels Robert's withdrawal long before he walks into their bedroom and takes his case, which she'd placed beside her own on the bed, and puts it back in the cupboard. She hears him cursing at the fall of objects as he shoves it between the hoover and the ironing board. Then his feet on the stairs and water running in the kitchen below.

She looks at her own empty case, three dresses folded neatly beside it, her hand still resting on the blouse she was about to pull from the top drawer of the chest by the window. Outside the sea is lapping the shore listlessly, grey drizzle falling on brown earth. Autumn giving way to winter.

Downstairs the tap goes off. She listens for the kettle's whistle but there is only silence. And then cupboard doors, the clink of glass bottles. She glances at the clock; it is not yet noon.

She could go down now and join him, begin the conversation they've been avoiding for so long. Open herself up in the hope that he will too. Ask him what is going on, even though the simple act of removing his case has already made it abundantly clear. Perhaps that is all it would take: an acknowledgement.

Yet those moments when we stand at a crossroads often pass us by unheeded, and only in retrospect do they acquire significance. That's what Anne will tell herself later, at any rate.

9

That she couldn't possibly have known at that moment that the whole house was about to crumble, its integrity irrevocably breached.

She hears the living room door open and close. The clock's indifferent ticking. A gust of wind throws sudden life into the rain and it raps against the glass. Anne lifts the blouse from the drawer and smooths the wrinkles over her arm. She wonders if she should take one jumper or two. She makes a mental note not to forget a thick pair of trousers for when the temperature drops in the mountains.

III

ESTHER

They met in the Elephant House on Edinburgh's George IV Bridge. It was a rainy day in June and the big windows at the back of the cafe were so steamed up that Esther could only trace the faint outline of leafy trees against a charcoal sky.

Evie Sinclair was late. Esther ordered, and set up her tape recorder on a table in the far corner, taking out a fresh pad of paper and a pen and arranging them in front of her. She looked up when the door opened, but it was only a couple of teenagers, not the middle-aged woman she was expecting. The waiter brought her coffee and she took a sip and wondered if Evie would come. She'd been vague on the phone, claiming she had information on an old story, but she wouldn't elaborate. If Esther hadn't just sent off an article and found herself without any new commissions, she probably wouldn't have bothered to meet her.

She'd just finished her coffee and was contemplating going outside for a smoke when Evie arrived. She knew it was her from the way the woman scanned the room, holding the door open as if she might slip out again. Esther raised a hand. Seeing her, Evie smiled, letting the door swing closed behind her.

'You must be Esther,' she said when she reached the table, and Esther stood to shake her hand, but Evie waved it aside as she undid her wet coat and hung it on a chair. 'Oh, I don't go in for handshaking, I'm afraid. I would give you a hug, but people seem to find that strange. Especially when they don't know you.' She gave a girlish laugh. 'Are you a hugger, Esther? You don't look like one, if you don't mind me saying.'

'No, I'm not,' Esther said, as she sat back down.

After Evie had settled herself and a waiter had taken their order, there was a momentary silence as both waited for the other to begin.

'I came across your article,' Evie said eventually, bright eyes observing Esther closely. Her skin was the weathered brown of someone who has spent long summers outdoors and she wore her white-blonde hair in two long braids.

'The one about the Kullu Valley and the missing people.' She held Esther's gaze as she spoke, as if to read something there. 'An old article. It was in *New Traveller*. Look, I have it here.' She took the magazine out of a canvas bag and laid it between them on the table.

It was the Winter 1997 edition. The cover showed a picturesque mountain scene: lush valley, translucent river, majestic snow-capped peaks; the headline, 'Missing at the End of the World', written across it. Esther knew it well. It had been her first cover story and the article that launched her freelance career. The story that had brought her so much opportunity, and so much trouble.

'Where did you get this?' Esther lifted the magazine, flicking through the pages to the article where Torran Carmichael's grinning face stared up at her. 'It's almost seven years old.'

Evie's smile wavered. 'I've been clearing out my parents' house. It was in a box.' Her gaze drifted to Torran's photo. 'My father died this spring.' Evie clasped her hands together on the table. 'But my mother died a while ago. Not long after that article was published, in fact. I wasn't there: I hadn't been there for a long time. Too long. Never take your parents for granted. One day they'll just be gone and there's nothing you can do about it.'

She had a way of talking that was at once light and commanding, as if her words meant nothing and everything at the same time.

'And the article—'

'When did *you* last speak to your mother?'

Esther could feel Evie's eyes on her as she stared down at her blank notepad. She felt the need to write something under the intensity of Evie's scrutiny but there was nothing to write, so she scribbled in the corner instead, as if testing her pen.

'No mother. But we're not here to talk about me.'

'I'm sorry,' Evie said.

'Don't be.'

The waiter returned with their drinks, and Esther watched as Evie stirred three lumps of sugar into her tea. She caught Esther's eye. 'My doctor's worried I'm getting diabetes, but after years of drinking chai, one develops a sweet tooth.' She raised the cup to her lips, blowing on the surface as steam rose around her face. Then she replaced the cup on the saucer without drinking. 'Do you have children, Esther?'

'No.'

'I never had children of my own either. Although you've still got time, of course.' She motioned to the magazine, still open on the table. 'My niece tells me his father writes children's books.'

'He does. At least he did. They're very popular.'

'It's an intimate portrayal of the family.'

Esther shifted in her seat. Evie's words seemed rehearsed, and Esther wasn't sure she liked where she was going with them.

'You must know them well.' It wasn't a question, and after a moment waiting for Esther to say something, Evie continued. 'And you went to India? To research this?'

Esther put her pen down, glancing at the door as a group of Japanese tourists came in, rain hats sparkling.

'It was a quick trip,' she said, thinking of the short week she'd spent in Manali and the Kullu Valley, the unreliable accounts from other travellers, the suspicious locals, the officials who'd closed ranks, the towns and villages that closed their doors and their eyes. 'No one was interested in talking to a journalist.'

'You didn't get many answers?' Evie didn't sound surprised.

'No, I just came away with more questions.'

'It says almost two dozen Western travellers disappeared from around Manali in the nineties.'

She still didn't meet her eye, and Esther was beginning to suspect Evie was wasting her time.

'At least. Yes.'

Evie nodded slowly, as if settling something in her own mind. 'Well, I can't help you with all of them, but I might be able to help you with this one.' And she touched her finger to the photo of Torran.

Esther felt a spark of excitement she was careful to hide.

'Are you going to turn that on?' Evie nodded towards the tape recorder.

'Do you mind?'

She was silent, looking again at Torran's picture. When she finally spoke, it was as if to him.

'Some stories need telling. What harm could it do now?'

Esther sat very still, finger hovering above the record button.

'It says there's an upcoming book. About the disappearances. About Torran.' Evie pointed to the end of the article. 'But I went to the library, and they told me there is no book.' Her blue eyes were wide and childlike, but there was something calculating too.

'It didn't work out in the end.'

'That must have been a disappointment. For you. And for the family.' She picked up her cup, eyes fixed on Esther's face.

Torran's eyes were on Esther too and she closed the magazine, pushing it back across the table. The door opened again, and she thought about leaving. Just standing up and walking away.

'Don't you want to know what happened?' Evie said, pulling her back to the moment, perhaps sensing her unease. 'For your story. For his parents.'

Esther thought of Anne and Robert the last time she'd seen them, diminished but still hopeful. Though that was years ago. Before the article.

'Go on,' she said.

Evie put her cup back down and glanced at the tape recorder.

'But before we begin, I need your word.' She leant towards Esther as she spoke, her voice low and urgent. 'That you won't go to the police – in India. At least not yet. And that you'll tell his parents. Tell them to go soon.' She hesitated. 'Tell them they must go soon. Time is running out.'

IV

ANNE

Morning found her on the balcony, as it usually did. Up before the sun as the days grew shorter. She slept little and rarely dreamt. Wrapped in a Tibetan blanket, she watched the first light of day stretch across the sky in sharp fingers of purple and gold.

She had woken to a host of memories lingering over her bed, leaving her shaken and anxious. Sometimes it was Torran and sometimes it was his absence that haunted her when she awoke, and that morning she was thinking about the early days of the search, when they'd had so much hope, so much certainty he would come back to them. The naivety to believe that in a country of one billion souls, it would only be a matter of looking and their son would be found: an elaborate game of hide-and-seek that had got out of hand. And Anne ached for the people they'd been, for the blind faith that had propelled them from one false lead to the next.

The disappointment, despite its inevitability, never lessened over time, and she knew that if someone came with new information now she would drop everything. She'd have no choice. But she was drifting on a crewless boat, at the mercy of the wind and tides, when she longed for the shore. She thought again of the previous evening, the man who had walked – just a little – like her son, who had turned to look at her and not been him, and she hated him for it.

Karl had been the first man who wasn't Torran. Living in a cave near McLeod Ganj, a hill station further north that was home to the Dalai Lama – a good omen, surely. Some Dutch backpackers had seen him on a hike and called it in. They couldn't be sure, but he'd looked like the picture on the posters. It was Anne and

Robert's second trip to India. October, only a few months after Torran's disappearance. They'd have him home for Christmas.

It had been a six-hour hike from town, and they'd hired a local Tibetan guide, little knowing when they shook hands with Dawa just how often they'd require his services in the coming years, how much they'd come to rely on him.

That morning, as they followed him through breathtaking valleys, beneath towering mountains, Anne had almost let herself see the beauty of this far-flung place her son had led her to. She'd laughed with Rob, and they'd talked of other things, things unburdened by fear and sorrow.

They'd fallen silent as they neared the cave, but even as she held her breath, she'd felt the weight return. And when she saw the emaciated figure, still too far away to even tell the colour of his skin, she knew.

Karl was nothing like their son. And he wasn't happy to see them. He responded tersely to Rob's questions, pale eyes too big in his thin face. He told them his name was Shiva, that he'd lived for three years on nothing but air and the glorious light of Brahman. Traces of cockney seeped through the spiritual fervour in his voice. When Rob asked about his family he turned abruptly into the cave, emerging moments later with a passport in a Ziplock bag which he thrust at Rob, telling him to take it; he had no use for it any more. Then he sat, crossed his legs and closed his eyes. Anne walked away as Rob continued talking. But the man only laughed, the sound vibrating off the rocks, and refused to utter another word.

In the end Rob had copied Karl's details to pass to the authorities and left the passport by the entrance to the cave. Catching up with Anne, he tried to speak but she shook her head, and when he took her hand she felt a pull so heavy she feared he would drag them both under.

And if she'd known then what lay before them, the sightings that would take them from Pune to Calcutta to Kathmandu – if she had known then – perhaps she would have sat down right there on the ground, cross-legged like Karl, closed her eyes and refused to go on.

Now, despite the warmth of the blanket, she was glad when the sun rose above the eastern hills, bringing a subtle but palpable heat. She took a breath and let it out as a sigh, dismissing the memories as the shadows lifted. From unseen places birds were singing. The scent of chai and porridge rose to meet the pine and eucalyptus. The rhythmic beat of a gong sounded out across the valley, calling worshippers to prayer.

Stiff from sitting, Anne rose to stretch. Giving the valley one last glance, she turned towards her room and saw with a start that the balcony adjacent to hers was occupied.

As if conjured by her memories, the man she'd seen on the street – the latest Karl – was leaning against the metal railing, gazing out across the Dun Valley, feet bare on cold tiles. His hair – so much darker than Torran's – still ruffled from sleep. He didn't acknowledge her presence, though he must have seen her, and she felt suddenly exposed; their balconies were so close she could have reached out and touched him.

Anne tried to settle to marking the essays she'd set her students, but her eyes kept wandering to the window, to the day unfolding beyond. She had a stack of new posters waiting to be put up, to replace the sun-bleached ones that rendered her son transparent, a ghost staring back at her wherever she went.

The sun was high when she left the hotel, her bag full of posters, the essays abandoned on her desk, and she was grateful for the grounding of the heat, for the faint breeze that cut through it. She'd taken to wearing a traditional *salwar kameez* – cool and comfortable and cheap to have made – and when she draped the long *dupatta* over her head, she could almost pass unnoticed through the crowds.

She followed the Mall Road around Gun Hill and through the Tibetan market before turning north towards Happy Valley, a verdant, wooded area popular with walkers and visitors, heading towards the colourful Buddhist monastery and the Tibetan Refugee Centre.

As she walked, Anne concentrated on her steps, the sound of her boots on the concrete, the feeling of the ground upon impact. She'd once been good at sitting still. As a musician she was used to it; playing with an orchestra involved a lot of sitting and waiting for your call. Rob's constant need to talk and move had first amused her and then inevitably annoyed her. He used to joke that she was his anchor, his lighthouse, his rock, the still point in life's storms. Always sea-related – living on an island would do that to a person. Eventually, everything revolves around the sea.

And then Torran disappeared and overnight she found she couldn't abide the stillness: she had to keep moving or everything that had happened would catch up with her.

So focused was she, on her steps and her memories, that she almost didn't see it. But something made her look up as she passed under a shaded grove of deodar and eucalyptus and there it was, right beside her, balanced gracefully on a low branch. The bird didn't fly away when she turned, but cocked its head and lifted a delicate leg, tucking it beneath its body. Anne stopped.

It was the shape and size of a blackbird, but the feathers around its head and down its back were an iridescent blue, flushing to purple across its breast, otherworldly among the greens and browns. The bird tilted its head to one side and then the other, watching her through unblinking eyes. Watching her as she watched it. Their eyes locked.

Anne felt the pulse of the moment, of their being together, suspended in a breath. And then, as in answer to a call, the bird threw her one last piercing look and vanished into the trees. She stood staring at the space where it had been. Still caught in the moment. And then the crunch of footsteps on the rocky path and the sound of a human voice pulled her back.

'We've got to stop meeting like this.'

Anne blinked at the dark outline against the sun. The young man who was not her son was standing in front of her, his voice warm and lazy as the day.

She smiled, despite herself. 'Did you see that bird?'

The man looked in the direction she indicated but shook his head. She felt irrationally disappointed in him and, with a tight smile, tried to walk around him, but he didn't move.

'You headed somewhere nice?'

'No,' she said, and he laughed good-naturedly, stepping aside to let her pass.

'But it's such a beautiful morning.' He spread his arms as he spoke.

'Yes,' she said, trying to make her words as light as his. 'I hope you enjoy it.' And she started walking again.

'Where are you going?' the man called after her, and although she had every intention of continuing on, she found she had stopped. She turned to look at him and he grinned again so that it was almost impossible not to smile back.

She thought of the posters in her bag and the map on her wall, the usual round of hotels and restaurants, the endless expressions of pity, the awkward glances, the shaking heads. Her own pale reflection in the window the night before.

'I'm going for a walk,' she said on impulse, gesturing towards a path that she knew but had not followed for a long time.

The man looked at her until she glanced away. There was a small line between his brows. 'You want company?'

Until that moment she wouldn't have said she was lonely, but now it seemed obvious that she was.

He stepped towards her cautiously and she wanted to laugh but instead forced herself to meet his eyes.

'All right,' she said, and the line between his brows disappeared.

'Great.' He shoved his hands in his pockets. 'I'm Liam, by the way.'

'Anne.'

There was an awkward pause and then they both started walking at once, footsteps falling perfectly in time.

V

ESTHER

In the end there was nothing for it but to go. She'd called Taigh na Criege half a dozen times the evening after she met Evie and again the following morning, but only got that old message of Anne's. Hearing her voice from so long ago filled Esther with an unease she didn't care to contemplate. She could have sent an email and waited, of course, but Evie's urgency propelled her forwards and after dropping some shopping off for her dad and asking his neighbour to check in on him, she caught the train to Glasgow and from there on to Oban.

It was a long time since she'd travelled that way and she watched the familiar hills and lochs flash past, trying not to think about what sort of reception she'd receive from Anne and Robert after all this time.

Evie had been right about that, at least: Esther did know them well. Once.

Rain was falling when the Mull ferry docked at Craignure and the people waiting to board were huddled against the weather like bedraggled sheep.

The bus followed the coast for several miles before the road narrowed to a single track and turned inland. Green hills rose to rocky mountains, strewn with granite boulders and tinged with purple heather. Pine tree plantations sheltered in deep valleys, drystone walls cutting patterns across their slopes.

The bus left Esther beside a metal gate tied with orange twine. The wind was rising, sweeping the rain in sheets like an advancing army, falling sharp against her face. She watched the bus disappear into the grey with a vague sense of foreboding and then bent to open the gate, fingers clumsy on wet metal. Up ahead the track faded into clouds that seemed to have been pushed from the sky to wander the earth. Turning back towards the road, she saw three sheep huddled in the lee of a drystone wall, regarding her with solemn eyes.

The house kept itself hidden until she was almost upon it, peeling away from a wall of cloud and the granite slope. The wind gusted as she passed Robert's old camper van, ripping the hood from her head. Esther struggled to pull it back, leaning into the wind to move forwards. She couldn't hear the sea, but she could smell it on the rain.

In the shelter of the house the wind dropped instantly, almost throwing her off balance. She stood, catching her breath, steeling herself for what was to come. Before her the red paint of the porch door was faded and flaking. Inside, old coats and life-jackets hung above a crowded shoe rack. A sheep's skull sat on the low sill, sun-bleached and smooth, coiled horns still intact.

Home.

The word came unbidden and unwelcome. Taigh na Criege had never been her home. Not really. Though she'd lived there for over five years. Still, as she pushed the door open, without knocking, the familiar scent of damp waterproofs and tomato plants caught at the back of her throat. She pulled the door closed and faltered, eyes fixed on the tiny yellow flowers already giving way to fruit. That morning she'd thrown away three dead stalks from her father's kitchen window, soil dry as dust. Her father who used to fuss tirelessly over his plants, pinching out new growth to encourage the fruit to ripen. Yes, even he had been good at caring for things once.

The thought held her and she was still staring at the plants when the inside door opened, flooding the porch with light, and turning she saw Robert, just as his look of surprise slipped into a scowl.

VI

ANNE

They could hear the water long before they reached it, pounding the rocks like thunder, swollen from early monsoon rains further north. As they neared the bottom of the falls, they passed a group of French hikers heading back towards town, and a Tibetan family shortly after. So Anne was surprised, when they emerged from the wooded path, to see the clearing deserted. They had the place to themselves.

Liam went to stand in the spray while she wandered to a favourite rock where she could sit with her feet in the water and look up at the thirty-foot drop.

Taking off her boots and socks, she laid them out in the sun and rolled up her trousers. She poked her toes in the water, clenching her teeth against the cold, and slowly lowered her feet and calves until they were submerged.

Beneath the surface her limbs were pale and foreign, light and insects skimming over them. She closed her eyes, feeling the sun on her skin, the faintest touch of spray.

Torran had been to this waterfall. There were several pictures of it on the reel of film in the camera he'd left behind in his hotel room. She and Rob had brought the photos the first time they'd visited, pacing around until they'd found the exact spots from which they'd been taken. Standing side by side, they'd silently scrutinised everything, as if some meaning could be found in the way he'd chosen to frame the rocks and trees and water. But the place kept its secrets and, in the end, there were only two things Anne knew for sure: he would have loved it here; he would have gone swimming. She felt for his presence now, his reflection in the memory of water.

23

A shadow crossed her face and she opened her eyes.

'Sorry,' Liam said, stepping to the side. 'Mind if I sit?'

'No.' She shuffled to make space, grabbing her socks and stuffing them in her boots.

Liam slipped out of his sandals and sat down beside her, lowering his feet into the water. He inhaled sharply.

'Cold?'

'Refreshing.'

They were silent. The sound of water filled their ears.

Then Liam turned to her, eyes narrowed. 'You ever swum in here?'

She shook her head. 'It's cold,' she said again, turning back towards the water.

He laughed. 'Only at first.'

'I don't know if it's safe.' She vaguely remembered something in the guidebook about deep underwater currents, although the pool looked calm and the river it drained into was shallow here, its current broken by large boulders.

'Well, Anne' – Liam turned back to her from surveying the water – 'I'm game if you are.'

She opened her mouth to protest and then stopped. It was hot and humid. She could feel the sweat gathering at her temples, the thin material of her tunic sticking to her skin.

'Come on.' He stood, feet dripping shadows against the rock. She saw the drops clinging to the dark hair on his legs, catching the light and rolling away. 'It'll do you good.'

Anne frowned up at him. 'What do you mean by that?'

His face was serious and kind. 'Nothing.'

She hadn't mentioned Torran, but the possibility that he knew anyway bothered her.

'I don't have my swimming costume,' she said, looking away.

Liam shrugged and raised his hands in mock defeat.

'It doesn't bother me. And I'm pretty sure no one else will object.' He raised an eyebrow as he motioned around the empty clearing.

Anne felt the stirrings of a recklessness she had once, briefly, possessed. Because what did it matter anyway? What did she have to lose? She was so tired of herself.

And it could have happened: rising to her feet and pulling the damp tunic and underwear from her skin, hair tumbling down around her shoulders, clothes abandoned to the sun-dried rock. An impulse she didn't quell but acted upon. The shock of the cold that would not register at first, the blissful numbness as she glided towards the depths of the pool. No feeling or sound, only light and shadow until her lungs might burst. And then the inevitable rise, the siren song of the world pulling her back, breaking into insect buzz and heat. That feeling that perhaps she could let go, if only she had something to hold on to.

'Anne?' She turned to see Liam still squinting down at her, hand outstretched. 'Are you coming?'

But she shook her head and turned her gaze to the far bank where two crimson butterflies flitted in and out of the trees. A moment later cool droplets hit her skin as Liam dived into the water.

'You don't know what you're missing!' He was in the middle of the pool, shouting over the pounding water.

She thought of the summer days jumping from rocks and swimming in coves around Inch Kenneth, seaweed tugging her ankles. 'I can imagine.'

He disappeared under again, staying down until the ripples he'd created were lapping the shore, and then resurfaced, further away. He turned, treading water, hair slick against his face, watching her.

'Where are you from, Anne?'

'England. But I've lived in Scotland for thirty years.'

He nodded, water running down his neck. Worried what he would ask next, she stood.

'Changed your mind?' He started swimming towards her, arms wide in a lazy breaststroke.

'No,' she said, glancing over her shoulder towards the path. 'I should get back. It's so hot.' She thought with longing of her room, its damp shadows. It was too much – his company. She was too exposed.

'Well, there's an easy way to fix that,' he said, laughing, and before she could step back he had scooped the water in his hands and hurled it towards her.

She gasped at the shock of it on her skin. Liam only laughed louder and splashed her again and she stumbled backwards, caught between annoyance and relief. And she found herself laughing too, as he continued to hurl water, laughing so that it hurt, and she couldn't stop.

She looked wildly around for something to return the attack but of course there was nothing. Nothing except his clothes, which she darted towards and held above her head. 'I'll throw them in!'

He stopped splashing and gave a cry of indignation. 'You wouldn't dare!'

'Wouldn't I?'

They stared at each other and then she lowered the bundle, suddenly embarrassed. She put the clothes back on the rock. Liam was still now, watching her, and she was seized by a wretched self-consciousness. The longing to be noticed; the fear of being seen.

VII

ESTHER

'So my prodigal niece returns.' Robert put a steaming cup of tea and a tumbler of whisky on the table in front of her, poured a generous measure of the Bunnahabhain for himself and raised it distractedly in Esther's direction before taking a thirsty gulp. Pulling out the chair opposite, he sat down heavily, whisky glass in hand. 'It's been a long time.'

The kitchen was warm and cheerfully lit and almost exactly as she remembered it. Robert had hung her sodden raincoat to dry above the Aga, where it dripped rhythmically, the water hissing as it evaporated. Tessa, their old Border collie, was curled on a cushion by the stove, observing her through half-closed eyes. Esther wrapped her fingers around the cup until it became too hot to hold. Robert was watching her too.

'I didn't know if I'd be welcome.'

Robert scratched the stubble on his cheek and sighed. 'You're still family, Esther.'

'Dad's not been well,' she said, although in truth he'd been no worse than usual.

The hard look in Robert's eyes softened. 'Aye? I'm sorry to hear that.'

She looked away quickly, fixing her gaze on the table, the ridges and grooves in the tired wood.

'And your mum? Does she know?'

Esther shrugged. 'No idea. Why?' She looked up then, trying not to sound too interested. 'Have you seen her?'

'No,' he said, and Esther saw the shadow that crossed his face whenever he spoke about Lucy. His favourite sister, her mother. 'She never answers my calls.'

27

Robert took another sip of whisky, rolling the amber liquid in the glass so that it left a translucent film in its wake, like waves retreating across the sand.

'I've been trying to get hold of you.'

'Aye, I got your messages. I've been meaning to call you back.' Esther wondered if this was true.

'Where's Anne?' she said, glancing towards the hall. 'It's probably best if I talk to you together.'

Robert's laugh was hollow. 'You've been away too long, Esther. Anne's been gone over three years.'

'What?' Esther looked around the kitchen stupidly, as if Anne might be lurking behind the pantry door. 'Where is she?'

'India.'

She stared at Robert, but he wouldn't meet her eye. 'Without you?'

It seemed incredible that Anne could have been there all this time and Esther knew nothing about it. For the first time it really dawned on her how completely she'd been cut out of their lives.

He grunted, looking down at himself as if to confirm his presence. 'So it would seem.'

She took a sip of whisky, the peaty liquid burning her throat. Outside, the day had darkened to premature night; it was just gone five, but it felt much later. Rain battered the windows, the glass rattling in its frame. Esther's coat continued its rhythmic dripping. It was almost twenty years since she'd left, but the familiar sounds and smells were disorientating.

Behind Robert was a wall covered in family photos, most of which Esther had never seen and wasn't in. Torran at various ages, a black-and-white wedding shot, half a dozen different sunsets over the sea. Although she'd never met her in person, Esther recognised Torran's high-school girlfriend Fiona, standing on a rock beside him, arms around his waist. She'd gone with him to India but left for Australia after two months when they'd decided to go their separate ways.

There were only two photographs Esther had seen before. The first was the one of Torran released to the press after his disappearance. One of a series found in his camera, the last known pictures of Torran. Taken in front of ornate iron railings at a lookout point in Mussoorie. In the one framed and hanging on the wall he was facing the camera, eyes unguarded, squinting against the sun. But Robert had shown Esther the others when they first returned from India, eight or nine in total, taken in quick succession as Torran dropped his pose and turned away. If you flipped through them you could almost catch Torran's movements, like a child's flip book. His gaze falling to his feet, his hands leaving his pockets as he wrapped his arms protectively across his chest. In the last shot he had turned completely to face the eastern horizon. Robert and Anne had never managed to track down the person who'd stood at that viewpoint with their son and taken those photos.

The other picture she recognised was of a much younger Robert and Anne – he in his early twenties, she barely eighteen – standing in front of Taigh na Criege, Robert's curly hair hanging past his shoulders as he beamed at the camera, one arm slung casually around Anne's waist. Although almost as tall as him, Anne seemed diminutive, delicate beside his broad frame. Her black hair fell straight and shiny around her face, and though she was smiling her eyes were serious. Unlike her husband, Anne was not looking at the camera, her gaze on something just beyond the camera's reach.

Robert stood and walked over to the photo, stooping slightly to look into the face of his younger self. 'We'd just moved here. No running water, no electricity – but such big plans for the place. God, we were young—' He stopped, a smile finally breaking across his face. 'I don't need to tell you this. I'm sure you've heard it all before.'

Esther smiled too. 'You may have mentioned it once or twice. It was a lot of work – apparently.'

Robert almost laughed. 'Aye, it was.'

He examined the photo for a moment longer and then straightened, downed the last of his whisky and reached for the bottle to pour another. He motioned towards her glass but Esther put a hand over the top. She could still feel that first sip roiling in her stomach.

Robert leant against the counter. 'But enough of that.' He dismissed the wall of photos with a flick of his hand. 'What's all this about, Esther? Why are you here?'

VIII

EVIE

Evie Sinclair and her best friend Ronda arrived in Kathmandu in early summer seventy-five. A bus from the airport took them and a few dozen other young Westerners directly to Freak Street, that fabled place of legal marijuana cafes and gurus offering enlightenment on every corner.

And it was just as they'd imagined: long-haired hippies in rooftop cafes smoking chillums; all-night conversations about peace, spirituality and self-discovery; the tranquil faces of orange-robed monks; the incense and the shrines; the cheap restaurants with jukeboxes playing 'Purple Haze', 'All You Need Is Love' and – the anthem of that long hot summer – Bob Seger's 'Katmandu'. There were the freaks and beatniks that tumbled wide-eyed from 'magic buses' driven overland from Europe, full of their own wonder. The dropouts who'd been there since the early sixties, eyes permanently glazed in a mellow high; the Vietnam veterans and the baby boomers. Here at last was a place where everyone could meet on an equal footing, without the dictates of societal expectation, where colour, nationality and creed were rendered meaningless abstract concepts.

It was a Shangri-La, an Eden, a utopia. They embraced everything Kathmandu had to offer and decided they would never leave. They talked about starting a guesthouse or opening a bakery and selling magic brownies. The plans for her future that Evie had put on hold were quickly forgotten and she stopped calling home, occasionally remembering to send a postcard.

Then Ronda fell in love with an Aussie called Steve, who was twice her age and already had a family back in Adelaide.

By September she was pregnant, and they decided to go to Australia to continue the hippie dream somewhere with safe water and fewer road accidents.

Evie found herself alone with a still valid return ticket. The endless smoking and talking about setting the world to rights while doing nothing about it was beginning to grate, and a career in nursing didn't seem so meaningless after all. She called her parents and heard the relief in their voices when she said she was coming home.

On her last night she wandered away from Freak Street, letting her feet take her down narrow streets and through busy market squares until she was completely lost. She paid ten paisa to a woman rotating charred corn over a fire. The woman rubbed it in melted butter and salt before handing it to her in a piece of brown paper. It was the most delicious thing she'd ever eaten, and she felt an overwhelming grief for all the things she would never experience.

When the light was fading from the sky, she saw a tall Western woman in a vivid turquoise turban and stopped to ask her for directions back to Freak Street.

The woman regarded Evie.

'Do you really want to go back there?' She had an American accent.

Surprised, Evie nodded. 'I'm flying home tomorrow.'

The woman's eyes moved slowly across her face as if reading all the secrets written there.

'But why did you come to Nepal?'

Evie laughed awkwardly. 'Oh, you know. To expand my mind and find my people, I suppose.' She could already hear the cynicism in her voice, see a future where she spoke of her summer in Kathmandu with a hint of mockery directed at the young dreamer she used to be.

'Sure. That's what you tell everyone else but tell me the real reason. Why did you come here, Evie? What are you searching for?'

Evie stared at the woman, unsure of how to respond. She had no memory of their ever having met, but the woman knew her name.

'I don't know,' she said eventually. 'I guess I wanted to find a different way to live. One that was more accepting. More real.' She shrugged, unable to articulate what she meant.

But the woman seemed to understand. She nodded, still looking closely at Evie's face, and again Evie felt that she was being read, understood in a way that no one had understood her before.

'Come drink chai with me, Evie Sinclair.'

The woman smiled brightly, breaking the intensity of her gaze. And without quite knowing how, Evie found herself walking along beside her.

The woman was called Lorrie. She told Evie that she and her partner had found a deserted hunting lodge deep in a valley in the Himalayan foothills of northern India. That they had patched it up and started a community there. Not many people, just a few like-minded souls who wanted to be part of something different, something more.

'It's hard work,' she said, stirring her chai.

Outside, the streetlamps were on. They were still in a part of the city that Evie didn't recognise. She saw an occasional traveller in the stream of people walking past, but it was mainly locals.

'You'll need to pull your weight and you need to commit to spending a year with us, because once the snows set in that's it, you're stuck till spring.'

Evie shook her head. She had so many questions it seemed impossible to begin. In the end she settled for the most obvious.

'Why me?'

Lorrie gave her a frank look. 'You're a nurse. We need someone with medical knowledge. Like I said, it's remote. And you haven't been here long enough to have completely addled your brain with drugs.' She took a sip from her cup and placed it delicately back on the table, her eyes never leaving Evie's face.

She must have been asking around, Evie realised. That's how she'd known her name.

'And I'm a pretty good judge of character,' Lorrie continued, with a smile. 'I have a feeling about you.'

Evie was still confused; the woman spoke as if she was recruiting her.

'But *I* stopped *you* back there. I asked for directions.'

Lorrie reached a hand to the large moonstone pendant at her throat.

'Did you?' she said lightly.

They sat in silence while Evie contemplated the roads that lay before her: home and her parents' house, a job at the local hospital, fish and chips on a Friday night in front of *Dad's Army*; or setting off with this enigmatic woman into the unknown, blazing a new trail, building a new life for herself, part of something truly special.

She turned to Lorrie, who was still watching her, eyes focused and unblinking as a cat.

'When do we leave?'

IX

ESTHER

'Evie stayed at the Sunshine House for twenty-six years.'

Robert had made cheese on toast while she told him Evie's story. When Esther finished talking, he silently took their plates over to the sink and then turned back to look at her.

'Are you saying that Torran was there? At this hunting lodge in the Himalayas? When?'

She glanced down at her notes although she already knew.

'She says he turned up in the late summer of ninety-seven.'

'The year he disappeared.' Robert shook his head, started to speak, and then stopped. He ran his fingers through his hair and over his face and then looked around as if trying to place something he'd lost.

'How can she be sure it was him?'

'She seemed pretty certain. There are the photos in the article. She said he had a Scottish accent. Was the right age. But he didn't call himself Torran – he had some other name.' She consulted her notes again. 'Yatri.'

'Yatri,' Robert repeated. He walked over to the Aga and back to the sink, and then came to stand by his chair before walking back to the sink again. The wind whined down the chimney. It was pitch-black outside.

'What was he doing at this lodge? How did he get there? Did that woman pluck him off the streets too?'

'According to Evie, he was just wandering the mountains, ended up finding some sort of retreat hut they'd built and was living there. They didn't use it much and when they found him, he was in a bad way. Half starved and hallucinating. They took him to the Sunshine House and nursed him back to health.'

35

Robert was staring at her.

'He decided to stay.'

'And no one thought to notify the authorities? His parents?'

'Evie got a bit cagey when I brought that up. Apparently most of the people were living there illegally.'

'So that's it? They just kept him?'

'I don't think he was held there against his will.'

Robert made a strangled noise that was somewhere between a cry and a laugh. By the stove, Tessa sat up, round eyes following him as he paced the room.

'But what was it – this Sunshine House? Some sort of cult? What were they all doing there? Twenty-something years in the Himalayas? It doesn't seem feasible. And who is Evie Sinclair? Why now?' Robert turned to face Esther. 'Why come forwards now? What does she want? Money?'

'I don't think so. She said she only came across my article recently. She wanted to help. But she also said that time was running out – that's why I came when I couldn't get hold of you – something about the whole thing ending in a few weeks.'

'What thing? What are you talking about?' Robert's voice rose with the wind. Tessa looked at him and whined. Esther wanted to take his hand, to offer some sort of comfort.

'The Sunshine House. Evie says that the plan had always been to end the project this summer. The community or cult or whatever it is.'

Robert took the bottle of whisky and sat down again.

'End it how exactly?'

Esther looked back at her notes, but she'd already told him everything. 'Evie didn't say.'

'These things rarely end well, though, do they?'

After a moment's silence Robert poured himself another large glass of whisky, filling Esther's too, though she'd barely touched it.

'*Yatri*,' he said, shaking his head. He drank half the whisky in one gulp and then looked at Esther, his eyes not quite focused in the artificial light. 'But he's dead. All these years I thought he was dead.'

X

ROBERT

Robert sat up long after Esther had gone to bed. It was a comfort and a tension, having another person in the house after so long. The floorboards shifting, the taps, the pipes, the whisper of the door. As if Anne was home, as if Torran was home. As if nothing had changed when everything had. An illusion that made him want to weep. Made him ache in the space between his ribs and his heart where he missed his family the most.

He placed his empty whisky glass in the sink and turned out the kitchen lights. As he passed the phone in the hall, he thought about calling Anne. But it was early morning in India, too early; the sun not yet risen, the air damp and fragrant, the pre-dawn hush. The sense of it ran through him, and if he closed his eyes, he could almost be there.

And if he was, would he go? Should he go? Into the mountains in search of this Sunshine House. In search of the son he knew, deeply and unshakably, to be dead.

Outside, the wind was howling like a lost child. He switched off the hall light and climbed the stairs. His house was full of ghosts.

Upstairs, Robert sat in his study and listened to the dial-up as the internet connected. He opened his emails and tried to focus on writing to Anne. There was nothing from her, of course. Maybe he should go.

His eyes fell on the bronze statue of Kali, Hindu goddess of death and destruction, which he kept on his desk. She'd been his mother's, one of a vast collection of crystals and figurines of women from various spiritual traditions which had fascinated him as a child. Kali stood with one foot atop a prone male figure, four arms wielding a severed head, a bloodied sword, a trident and an upturned bowl. Red tongue, snake hair, skull necklace. Her expression dancing somewhere between rage and euphoria.

Robert could not have said what had first drawn him to this particular manifestation of the feminine, but years later, searching for his son in India, he'd felt a calming reassurance whenever he encountered Kali's image. Her presence drew an invisible thread between his present and his past, a comforting symmetry in the chaos. He'd tried to express this to Anne but she could not – would not – see it.

She hated Kali as she hated most of the Hindu deities. Baffled by the graphic and bizarre representations of so many gods, she turned towards the gentler Bodhisattvas of Buddhism: the serene face of Tara in meditation, Buddha imparting wisdom to his followers. Robert couldn't help but point out the less pacific depictions in the Buddhist temples, the devils and the many-headed dogs in the lower regions of the Wheel of Life; Yama, lord of the underworld, with his vampire teeth and skull headdress. But Anne would just shake her head and turn away.

You only see the parts you want to see, he'd tell her.

And she'd give him that look, the one that told him he'd failed to understand something fundamental. *The same could be said for you.*

Turning his attention back to the screen, Robert pictured his wife now. Alone. Waiting. And his son. Gone without trace, like words written on the sand at low tide. He had failed them both, he knew that – God, he knew that – but he didn't know how.

Torran had returned almost a year after his disappearance. A June night, unseasonably cold, Anne in bed and Robert by the fire with Tessa. The shadows brought to uncanny life by the flames.

A sudden noise in the hall and Tessa's ears had pricked. She glanced at him and they both looked towards the open door. The noise came again. The turn of the latch, the tender whine of the hinges, the unmistakable tread on the mat. Hairs lifted on the back of his neck as a blast of night air shot down the hall. Tessa sprang up and raced from the room, Robert hot on her heels.

The front door was open. As he knew it must be. The night a yawning void that could swallow them all. Tessa growled, low and urgent, and his hand found the soft hair at the nape of her neck. The lighthouse pulsed on the horizon.

'Torran?' He never knew if he'd spoken aloud, but at that moment something fell from the sideboard and he stared at it for a long time before picking it up.

The last postcard. The one from Mussoorie. The one that should be pinned to the board in the kitchen with the others. And that's when the realisation had shivered through him. But before he could articulate it, even to himself, Anne was behind him, at the turning of the stairs, hair loose and face full of sleep.

'What is it?' She'd looked to the open door and he'd hurried to close it, slipping the postcard in his pocket, trying to stop his hands from shaking. The door had been bolted, he was sure of it.

'Nothing, love. Go back to bed.'

'I thought I heard voices?'

They'd stared at each other then. 'Voices?'

She looked suddenly uncertain. 'Perhaps I was dreaming. I heard him calling me.'

Robert swallowed; the last ember of hope extinguished. His son was dead. Once the thought came there was nothing else. His boy was dead.

XI

ESTHER

Waking in her old room was disorientating. The storm had blown itself out and the silence lay heavy across her chest. Esther stared at the ceiling, tracing the cracks in the paint-work, wondering if they'd always been there. Torran had moved into the room after she'd moved out, and though most of his things were boxed up in a corner, others remained – a faded Nirvana poster above the bed, a few set texts on the shelf, Converse trainers in the gap beneath the wardrobe. An unsettling combination of absence and presence; not here but not entirely gone.

When she opened the curtains, sunlight tumbled impatiently into the room. Outside, the world had turned technicoloured and razor sharp. The neatly laid beds and bright flower bor-ders; the drystone walls; the pebble-dashed shore; the narrow island of Inch Kenneth, its trees and hillocks and crumbling ruins. And the sea, still as glass, shimmering to meet an endless horizon. And for just a second Esther was overwhelmed with the familiarity of it, with the sense of herself as a child, lost and lonely. Invisible, yet again, to those who should be taking care of her.

Downstairs, there was no sign of Robert and the dog's bed was empty. Esther made herself a cup of tea, finding everything where it had always been, and looked again at the photos on the wall, lingering over the one of Anne and Robert, his ease and her distraction. Both so young. They'd been older, of course, when she came to live with them. Anne already in her mid-twenties and finally pregnant. That longed-for event overshadowed by the arrival of Robert's nine-year-old niece. But still.

Through the kitchen window the sea looked closer, the beach hidden by a dip in the land. Esther scanned the garden and fields but they were empty; she had the house to herself. Without thinking too much about it, she slipped from the kitchen and made her way back up the stairs.

There's something about other people's homes when they're not there: their private spaces; the signs of intimacy and distance, measured in the objects left lying together and apart. She'd once briefly – disastrously – had a boyfriend living with her, and their two toothbrushes thrown together in a glass by the sink would fill her with a terrible longing. Like standing on a dark street looking in through lighted windows. It struck her now that she'd always felt like that in this house: on the outside looking in.

But it was a fractured kind of living, and five years is a long time. Always travelling back to Edinburgh to visit her dad, and, after she turned twelve, spending the weeks boarding with the other island children at the high school on the mainland. She'd avoided coming back, spending weekends with friends as much as she could. And she'd moved home to her dad's when she was fourteen, insisting that she was old enough to look after herself, to look after them both. She'd already been looking after herself for years anyway.

Upstairs, she went into Robert's study, feeling that illicit thrill of entering a room that has always been out of bounds. The walls were lined with books. There was a large desk facing the window, awash with papers and lidless pens. Her grandmother's old statue of Kali. Torran's school photos on a high shelf, arranged chronologically to show how the gap-toothed boy had passed through adolescence to become the man in that last known photo downstairs. Esther paused beneath the pictures: the familiar little boy, the older Torran who was practically a stranger, someone glimpsed at family weddings and funerals.

She was nine years older; he hadn't even started school when she left Taigh na Criege.

She rummaged through the drawers and papers but there was nothing about his disappearance. Only a postcard sent from Mussoorie, tucked between the pages of an old atlas. She didn't know what she'd been expecting to find. Letters from Anne, perhaps. But Evie's words were heavy on her mind, about how some stories needed to be told, and here she was again, in the middle of this one.

On the windowsill was a collection of shells and a black pocket diary. She opened it, looking for the day's date, but stopped when she noticed that every day had a short entry. The words 'call' or 'no call' written carefully under the date. Occasionally there was a question mark after the words. Frowning, she continued turning the pages, looking for more.

'What are you doing?'

Robert's voice made her jump. The diary slipped from her hands and fell to the floor. He was standing in the doorway, arms crossed, watching her.

Esther put a hand to her chest. 'God, you gave me a fright.'

Robert stared impassively at her. Tessa appeared beside him, panting and wagging her tale.

Esther tried to smile. 'I was looking for a pen.'

For a moment Robert didn't move and neither did she.

'I'll make coffee,' he said at last, turning abruptly and disappearing down the hall.

Robert brought a tray out to the bench beneath the kitchen window, handing Esther a cup as he sat down beside her. In the sky a pair of gulls threw their shapes against the blue. Tessa ambled round the corner of the house and flopped on Esther's socked feet. She scratched the dog's belly with her toes.

'I don't think I slept,' Robert said, his eyes on the gulls. 'I can't get hold of Anne. There must be a problem with the hotel's phone. It's monsoon season; everything is unreliable.'

Esther blew on her coffee and watched the ripples that ran across the black surface.

'I sent her an email,' he continued. 'Although I don't think she checks them regularly any more.'

'I'm sorry I was in your study,' she said, because he hadn't looked at her since he'd come out. Now he glanced over, before turning back to the sky.

'I take it you're still hoping to get a story out of us.'

Esther watched his profile, the tightness in his jaw, the shadows under his eyes. 'Why are you here when Anne is in India? Why has she been gone so long? I thought Anne hated India.'

Robert sighed and leant back against the wall. 'So did I. Look – I'm not doing this with you, Esther. I appreciate you coming here to tell me. And you know you'll always be family,' he paused. Following some thought to its conclusion. 'But what you wrote really hurt Anne. It hurt both of us.'

'I wasn't trying to hurt anyone – I was trying to write things as they were. To find the truth.'

Robert shook his head. 'You're a writer. You know there's always more than one version of the truth.'

'Is there?'

'You were a kid when you lived here, you had your own stuff going on. Things may not always be how you remember them.'

She scanned the sea for the lighthouse, but it was invisible, the line of the horizon hazier than it seemed.

'They may not be how you remember them either.'

They were both silent.

'I think you did mean to hurt her,' Robert said quietly, and Esther didn't know what to say to that.

'I wish I knew what Anne was doing over there,' he continued after a pause. 'She was searching, moving about, contacting people. It gave her a purpose. But over the past year she seems to have stopped.'

'And you? Why aren't you out there?'

Robert shifted, crossing one leg over the other.

'Do you think it's true? This story about the Sunshine House? It sounds like a fairy tale. Like one of my stories.' He ran a hand across his face, tugging his beard as he stifled a yawn. 'So many people have wasted our time with these stories.'

'I know. But there are places like that in India – ashrams, communities; travellers who've dropped out of society. I think it's worth following up.'

'Yes,' Robert said. 'Anne would never forgive me if we didn't.'

Esther thought of Anne the last time she'd seen her. She and Robert just back from India. The second time. They'd met at her grandmother's place in Edinburgh, the streets piled high with autumn leaves. Esther was heading to India the following week for her research trip, the article already half written. She'd been surprised by Anne's warmth, her willingness to talk. As if they'd once been close.

'I want to help,' Esther said.

Robert drained the last of his coffee. 'I think you've helped enough, don't you?' His words were pointed but there was no fight in them. He never was much good at holding on to grievances. 'You didn't write that book in the end.'

Far out to sea a fishing boat was slicing through the water.

'No,' she said. 'Not yet.'

He shook his head. 'I was angry for a long time. About that article. The things you said about Anne. She already blamed herself.' ·

Esther kept her eyes trained on the boat. 'It wasn't personal. It made a better story.'

'It was our lives. Of course it was personal. It wasn't your story to tell.'

At Esther's feet Tessa stirred, cocking her head to look from Esther to Robert and then back again. She twitched her nose as if sensing the tension.

'I've followed your career over the years. You really made a name for yourself with that article – for a year or two I couldn't open a Sunday magazine without seeing your by-line.'

He leant his head against the wall and turned to look at her. 'I thought things would get bigger for you after that. That you'd travel the world.'

'So did I.' She shrugged. 'It's hard, with Dad. To get away. The big stories don't tend to happen in Edinburgh. At least not the ones I'm interested in.'

She could feel Robert watching her. A breeze had sprung up, stretching gossamer clouds across the sky.

Robert cleared his throat, startling a chicken who was pecking the ground by his feet. 'I'm sorry I haven't been there for you. With your dad. Whatever else has happened, you're still Lucy's daughter. And I should have been there.'

Esther swallowed. She hadn't asked for this, and she forced a laugh to show it didn't matter. 'It's fine. You've had more than enough on your plate. I've been fine. I'm fine.'

There was an awkward pause as she cast around for something else to say.

'So when do you leave?'

Beyond the garden, a flock of geese took to the sky, squawking and beating their wings as one.

'I can't go.' He spoke so quietly Esther thought she must have misheard.

'What?'

'I can't go,' he repeated with more resolve, watching the departing geese.

'You can't just sit here and wait for Anne to call. What if he's actually there?'

Esther could feel the moment slipping away, when the real story, the truth of what had happened, was so tantalisingly close. When Torran was so close. Because whatever Robert thought, Esther believed Evie was telling the truth.

'I just don't think he's still alive.' She saw the tears that always seemed to linger at the corners of his eyes. 'And I can't go back there. After all this time. When I know he's dead. I know it.'

'But what if he's not? What if—'

45

'Then you go. You can tell Anne. You can go with her if she wants to search for this Sunshine House.'

She stared at him, taken aback. He spoke as if he'd already given it some thought, as if he'd already resolved to suggest it.

'I'm the last person Anne's going to want to see.'

He smiled at that. 'All the more reason to go.'

And Esther could picture it, the mountain road twisting through the clouds to Manali and beyond, deep into the Kullu Valley and across the Himalayas. The beauty and the mystery of it. But she saw her dad too, alone in his dark flat, damp climbing the walls.

'I don't know if I can get away.'

Robert looked at her, and there was kindness in his expression. 'Maybe your dad doesn't need you as much as you think.'

The geese were little more than dark scratches in the sky.

'But no more articles. No book. Not about Torran. I'll pay for your flights; I'll pay for it all. You'd be going as a favour to me. As my niece. As Torran's cousin.' He ran a hand through his curls, grey-black and stiff from the salt air. 'Can you do that?'

'Yes,' she said, gaze fixed on the sky where the geese had disappeared. Because given the circumstances, what else could she possibly say?

XII

ANNE

They sat together among the geraniums of the Hotel Broadway's sunroom. It was late afternoon and the shouts of children drifted in through the open window. Anne was reading, enjoying the novelty of not sitting alone.

'Was it this one?'

She looked up as Liam offered her the book he'd been flicking through and there, captured beneath his index finger, was a small, coloured illustration of the bird she'd encountered just before their walk to Jinsi falls. She smiled at the memory, seeing again the splash of twitching, watchful colour, the inquisitive black eyes. The enchantment of the moment.

'A purple sunbird,' she said, reading the text beneath the illustration. 'Yes. That was it.'

'I saw one from the balcony the other day,' Liam said. 'So tiny, so full of colour and life. They're quite something.'

Anne caught his eye and smiled. 'They really are.'

There was a pause as Liam held her gaze in that steady, half-amused way of his.

'Beautiful book,' she said, looking back to it and carefully turning the pages. It was hard-backed and sun-yellowed, *Birds of the Indian Himalayas* embossed in gold letters on the spine.

'Isn't it? There's a bit of story to it, actually.' He shifted, leaning out of the previous moment, and Anne nodded for him to continue. She liked listening to his stories. And with Liam, there was a story to everything. 'I swapped it for a Stephen King someone left in my hotel room. There was this old guy in Haridwar who'd built a house from books. I mean, it was a fortress really. I think he was trying to sell them, but

47

he'd put half the spines facing in, so it was impossible to read the titles. He said, no problem, that he was a book teller – you know, like a fortune teller? Before he chose the book for me, he didn't ask any questions, but he studied my fingers.' Liam reached over and took one of Anne's hands in his. 'Just like this – examined them really closely.' Liam peered myopically at Anne's fingers, and she laughed. 'And now I guess I'm interested in birds.'

Anne looked down at her own hand. 'I wonder what he would have given me.'

'Well, if you're ever in Haridwar . . . He was delighted with the King because it was thick enough to block up a draught.'

'What does he do when it rains?'

'I asked him that. But he said the book gods kept him dry.' Liam laughed, taking the book back and finding the picture of the sunbird again. He had a sketchbook on the chair next to him, the stub of a pencil in his hand. 'I did see a tarpaulin tucked away, though.'

'I wonder who got your King.'

'Oh, I don't think he was letting that one go. It was structural.'

Anne smiled, turning back to her novel, letting the words wash over her. Familiar but surprising, the way a good story should be, worthy of rereading.

Liam propped the bird book open on the coffee table between them and turned to a fresh sheet in the sketchbook. 'He did read me pretty well, though. I'm not a big fiction fan. I like to learn stuff. Identify things. I studied biology at uni.'

It was an invitation. Since they'd met neither had said much about their lives before India; Anne still hadn't mentioned Torran.

She watched as he examined the illustration of the sunbird.

'I studied English literature,' she said. 'When I was older. I did a correspondence course.'

Liam's eyes were on the book, but he inclined his head to show he was listening.

Anne looked through the window at a sky dimming to evening. 'But I was a musician – or almost. In another life.'

'Another life?'

She watched his hand as he drew the first line – the breast – strong and confident, his eyes darting between his work and the illustration.

She didn't know why she'd put it like that; it was the sort of thing other people said.

'It was a long time ago. Before I met my husband. I'd been accepted at the Royal Academy. My parents had great plans for me.'

She found that she thought about her parents more and more: the things they'd done for her, the sacrifices they'd made. But also the things they hadn't done, the ways in which they'd failed.

From downstairs came the sound of a group arriving, exclamations and rucksacks hitting the floor, chairs scraping back, the bell on the front desk. And meanwhile Liam's bird was growing wings, legs, feet, beady black eyes. Not an exact copy of the one in the book, she realised; this one was perched on the low branch of a tree looking directly out of the page at her. It was her sunbird. Just as she'd described it to him.

'I played the cello,' she said, to fill the silence.

'Were they disappointed?' He glanced up at her, hand still moving across the page, shading and defining. 'That you didn't become a musician.'

'I suppose they must have been.'

He returned his gaze to the paper. 'Did you never ask?'

'I never had the chance.'

He stopped then, put down the pencil and turned towards her, but whatever he was about to say was interrupted by footsteps on the stairs and loud American accents exclaiming over the view and the tiles and the geraniums.

'Hey man!' They both turned as a tanned college student stopped behind them, grinning broadly. 'No way – it *is* you!' He flopped down on the chair next to Liam.

49

Liam closed his sketchbook and nodded to the American. 'How's it going?'

'"How's it going?"' The young man laughed. 'Shit! We haven't seen you since Goa.' He turned to call to his friends and Liam shot Anne an apologetic look, but he had a bemused expression on his face.

'Hey guys, look who's here!'

Three blonde girls and a tall boy wearing a baseball cap turned from the hallway and broke into grins and calls of greeting at the sight of Liam, who now stood with a resigned air.

There were hugs and high fives and stories clamouring to be heard. And finding herself completely invisible, Anne slipped away.

Later, in her room, Anne sat on the end of her bed and watched the sun sink behind the mountains. The windows were open and a chill crept in, raising goosebumps on her bare arms. She could hear the Americans on the terrace, the smoke from their joints mingling with their laughter. Someone was strumming a guitar, 'Redemption Song' accompanying lazy chatter.

She wondered if Liam was still with them and she thought of those blonde girls, beautiful and young and unfettered by life and loss. Free in a way they would never truly understand until they were looking back after so much of life had already passed.

She remembered the confusion and doubt of her own youth. She knew it hadn't felt easy at the time, but even that knowledge didn't stop her seeing it now in its perfection. Although in the actual living of those moments, there had been no knowing how things would go. And when Torran had first disappeared, she could still believe in a future where she might be looking back on all this from a place of certainty. But Karl, and all the other Karls that followed, had stolen that from her. The solid ground glimpsed on the horizon was nothing but a mirage.

XIII

ESTHER

That afternoon, while Robert organised her flights, Esther walked down to the beach with Fiona, Torran's high-school girlfriend. She'd moved back to Mull after university and now taught at the local school. From the way she'd entered the house without knocking, helping herself to tea and refilling the biscuit tin with homemade flapjacks, it was clear she was a regular visitor, and Esther had felt a twinge of jealousy at the ease between her and Robert.

The tide was out, exposing a rocky shore strewn with black seaweed. Tessa ran ahead, barking at the crabs that scuttled into bright pools of water.

'Perhaps I should have talked to you at the time,' Fiona said, stooping to pick up a shell. She scraped off the sand with her thumb and put it in her pocket.

'Why didn't you?'

Fiona had never exactly turned down her requests for an interview. The messages Esther left with her parents had just gone unanswered.

'I don't know. I guess I still didn't really believe that Torran was missing. It'd only been five months. People go AWOL on their travels sometimes. Especially in places like India. We met a fair few, slumming it on the beaches, drifting from place to place. I didn't really believe that he was gone gone.'

'You didn't think he might have been in trouble?'

Fiona shrugged, her eyes following Tessa zigzagging across the sand. 'I never thought he was dead, if that's what you mean. I still don't. He was adventurous but he wasn't stupid. He knew how to look after himself. I know Rob thinks he's dead. But I'm

51

convinced he's sitting on a beach somewhere, getting stoned and talking to *sadhus*, or – yeah, why not in some hippie commune in the middle of the Himalayas? He was getting into that stuff before I left.'

'What stuff?'

'The hippie dream. Enlightenment. All that.' Fiona said it with a wry smile. 'He wanted to save the world. He always cared too much. But also not enough.'

Esther wondered what Robert and Anne would make of this assessment. Her impressions of the teenage Torran were fractured, cobbled together from different family members and friends, inevitably incompatible and contradictory, kaleidoscopic projections thrown upon a screen.

'Did he mention going north, before you left?'

'No, he was heading to Kerala. At least that was his plan. But he wanted to travel with the wind.' She rolled her eyes affectionately. 'He could have ended up anywhere, with anyone.'

They were approaching a rocky outcrop, algae and barnacles skirting the lower sides. The tide had left rings of colour, granite crystals sparkling. Fiona clambered up the highest boulder, its angles rubbed smooth. From the top her small figure cast a long shadow across the sand. She offered a hand.

'Want to sit?'

They stretched out their legs and stared over at Inch Kenneth. The ruined house gazed balefully back.

'That island always gave me the creeps.'

Fiona laughed. 'We used to swim out in the summer. Rob and Anne would take the boat and meet us in that cove on the north end, with all the seals. Didn't you ever go?'

Esther shook her head, trying not to dwell on the disparities between Fiona's memories of Taigh na Criege and her own.

'Torran was so little when I was here.'

Fiona gave her a sideways glance. 'I don't think I even realised you actually lived here until after he disappeared. Torran never mentioned it.'

'There's no reason why he would. I doubt he remembered much.'

'You were lucky to have Anne and Rob. I loved spending time with them. They seemed so sophisticated compared to my parents. So bohemian. And their story was terribly romantic, wasn't it?'

Esther didn't answer. She'd never considered Anne and Robert like that, never really thought about them as a couple at all – Robert was her well-meaning but largely absent uncle, and Anne was just always trying. Trying but never quite succeeding.

'And they treated us like adults,' Fiona continued. 'My parents still talk to me like I'm ten.'

'Torran got on well with them? As a teenager?'

Fiona glanced over, her eyes screwed up against the sun so it wasn't clear whether she was frowning. 'Is this an interview?'

Esther pushed the morning's conversation with Robert aside, something to worry about later. 'Well, I'm not taking notes. But I guess it is, unofficially. Do you mind?'

'Unofficial interviews get you into trouble, though, don't they?' Fiona said, but she was laughing. 'I guess I don't mind. I do want to help. It kills me, the not knowing.'

'I always wondered if you did know something. Especially when you didn't respond to my requests for an interview.'

Fiona's eyes were fixed on the island. 'I don't know where he is. Believe me.'

'He never contacted you?'

'We agreed on a clean break. At least while we were travelling. His idea. He was reading about Buddhism. You know, non-attachment and that. It felt like a phase, like all these ideas he needed to grow out of. Because they don't work in the real world, do they? Non-attachment doesn't seem very compatible with love and family.'

'Did you think he'd stop contacting his family?'

'No, he was close to his dad. He really hero-worshipped Rob. It's because of Rob we went to India. Rob was meant to be one of the original beatniks on the hippie trail. He was always talking about the trip that never happened. And Torran seemed to think it was down to him to do it. Anne wasn't happy about us going off to India, but Rob was thrilled.'

'And now Anne's there and Robert's here.'

Fiona nodded. Tessa was splashing in the shallows, tail sending droplets flying.

'You had a lot to say about Anne and her relationship with Torran in the article. But it wasn't as bad as you made out. Not when I knew him. They just weren't close. Anne can be hard to get close to. But I didn't recognise the family I knew in what you wrote. And I don't think it's why he disappeared.'

Esther shrugged the words away, running her fingers across the rough surface of the rock until they stung.

'It must be hard. To know that if he's alive, he's chosen not to contact you.'

Fiona laughed. 'You don't mince your words, do you? And here I was, thinking you were too nice to have written that article.'

She paused for Esther to respond, but Esther kept her eyes trained on a pink buoy bobbing in the water like a drowning child.

'Of course it's hard,' Fiona said, her voice quieter now. 'He was my first boyfriend; we'd been best friends since primary school. And yes, he could be selfish, self-centred, thoughtless – like he couldn't see the wider consequences. But what teenager isn't? And I really loved him. I still do. And I'm also angry with him. Every day I still think I'm going to look up and see him walking down the path to my front door. That big stupid grin on his face.' She took a breath and Esther glanced over, but Fiona's eyes were dry. 'You learn to live with these things. But you live in a different way. And I'm angry about the life I could have had.'

'If you were still together?'

'No. I'm with someone else now. We're happy. But I've never been able to completely close that chapter. A part of me will always be waiting.'

Esther thought of Evie, of the stories Torran's disappearance had started, the lives it had impacted. Ripple after ripple expanding out.

Fiona sighed, the wind catching her hair and teasing it across her face.

'When he left me – when I left him – at the airport, he called after me. I guess I thought he might've changed his mind. But he pulled me back and said, "You'll always be my first love." Something like that.' She paused and shook her head. 'No, exactly that – I've never forgotten because it was so disappointing. Like something he'd heard in a film. It wasn't real; it wasn't enough. And that was the thing with Torran: nothing was ever real; nothing was ever enough.'

XIV

BEFORE

Robert believes in happy endings. He writes children's stories that always end well, no matter how great the peril, how impossible the situation. And though Anne is concerned when they don't hear from him, it takes Robert a long time to admit that Torran may be missing.

It is over three weeks before they call the police in India. The hotel where Torran was staying in Manali have assured them it is not out of the ordinary for travellers to disappear for a week or two, only to turn up safe and well. He'd paid for his room a month in advance, and it is only after this time that the hotel would want to know whether they should clear out his things.

Anne talks to the police and books them on the next available flight to Delhi. She packs their bags and prepares the house for their departure. She calls a neighbour to take Tessa and feed the animals. As always, she does what she expects someone in her position would do. She makes lists and crosses things off. She makes lunch and forces them to eat. She makes light of the situation when she talks to people: they are almost certainly worrying over nothing. The police and her neighbours and the travel agent agree. He'll turn up. Probably before they even get there. Her laugh does not falter.

Robert sits at his desk and stares at the pile of paper that is his almost finished novel. The seventh in his latest series. He tells Anne he must write, as if he can write a happy ending for his son. For Anne. For all of them. In the morning they will drive to the airport and catch the plane and travel into the mountains and find Torran. There is no other way for their story to end.

*

56

In Manali they accompany Superintendent Kumar as he examines Torran's hotel room, the things he left behind in his red Osprey rucksack. Anne rubs a sun-faded strap between her fingers, reaching for her son in his belongings. The clothes Torran had taken from home – the hiking trousers and quick-dry base layers – are all there, as are his *Lonely Planet* and camera, his first aid kit, his watch. But not the copy of *Kidnapped* she'd given him as a leaving present, and for a brief moment she tries to find meaning in that. But he'd probably passed it on to another traveller or left it on the shelf of some backpackers' hostel.

Then she pulls his passport and traveller's cheques from the top pocket of his pack and the polite smile slips from Superintendent Kumar's face.

They liaise with the Foreign Office and the British Consulate in Delhi. They are advised to contact a private firm that specialises in missing foreign nationals in India; the police will do what they can, but they're overstretched and have nothing to go on.

So Robert creates an email account. They talk to travellers, put up posters, hand out flyers. Anne stays in Manali while Robert travels to some of the other tourist hotspots – Goa, Jaipur, Agra, Kerala – to widen the search and follow up leads.

Nothing comes of any of it, and when they return home, in late August, they are no closer to finding him.

The fuchsias hang brightly across the walls of Taigh na Criege in riotous welcome. The swifts have flown their nests. Torran's return flight wasn't until mid-September; they can only hope he will be on it.

An American psychic emails. She has seen their son in a vision. He is alive and by the sea. Living in a purple house.

Or ashram.

He is happy.

For a small fee plus expenses she can lead them to his door.

Anne and Robert are at his mother's in Edinburgh when the call comes: Torran has not made the flight.

Robert's mother Iris stands on the bottom step of the staircase staring accusingly at Anne as Robert puts the receiver down and reaches for Anne's hand.

'No,' he says. And the floor falls away beneath them.

So it begins. They fly back to India. They follow every lead. They hike into the mountains near McLeod Ganj and meet Karl. Karl after Karl after Karl. Every time is different and every time is the same. When they return to Edinburgh it is the week before Christmas and the festive lights across the city are almost too bright for Anne to bear.

And then the article comes out and Anne hardly leaves the house. Despite Robert's protests, she knows people are talking about her, looking at her differently, glancing at one another when she enters the shop. She has always been an outsider here, but now she is an outcast.

Fiona is home from Australia. She brings flapjacks in a tartan tin and drinks whisky with them at the kitchen table. She spreads out photos of her time with Torran in India. Anne and Robert pore over them, but there are no clues hidden in the young couple's smiling faces. Fiona cries and so does Robert; Anne knows that if she begins, she will never stop.

They return to India the following spring. When they leave Taigh na Criege, the daffodils are dancing in the garden. Delhi is hot and humid but in the mountains it is still pleasant and the evenings are cool.

They travel to Mussoorie and visit an Indian astrologer who sits in the dim light of his shop behind a desk covered in papers and charts. He maps out their lives on an A4 pad, scribbling the times and dates Anne gives him with a precise hand. His glasses are too large for his face; his eyes are full moons. He tells them there will be a long journey and a valley of sun and a resolution.

'So we'll find him?' Anne says, glancing at Robert. She doesn't believe in this stuff, but she knows he does. Or wants to.

The man moves his head non-committally. 'That I cannot say. But you' – he points almost accusingly at Anne – '*you* will find what you're looking for.'

The call in the night comes three years after Torran's disappearance. They are both awake instantly, eyes meeting in the pre-dawn light. Robert jumps out of bed and runs down the hall.

A body has been found, a European male in his early twenties. Washed up on the riverbank twenty miles south of Manali. Superintendent Kumar coughs and warns them that it has been in the water for some time. Within forty-eight hours they are on a plane to Delhi.

They take the night express to Manali, and it is only after they stagger off the bus to shake hands with Kumar that they understand the other white middle-aged couple on the bus is there for the same reason. They are Italian and their son has been missing for five months, last seen at a rave in a forest near Jari. They speak no English and have brought their younger son to translate. He is barely a teenager and he keeps his hands firmly clenched in his pockets.

Afterwards – in the jeep on the way back from the police station – Anne and Robert sit opposite this couple, knees bumping. The father stares out the window, his mouth a broken line. And the mother – the mother whose son was lying in that windowless room, body bloated almost beyond recognition – is not crying but keening like a wounded animal.

There are no thoughts in Anne's head as she listens to that unearthly sound, no thoughts at all.

XV

ANNE

Anne didn't join in the *bhajans*, but she liked to slip in at the back of the temple and listen as the women sang, sitting on the floor, their salwar kameez and saris falling in pools of colour.

A white-haired woman in orange robes led the chanting, swaying backwards and forwards, moved by the power of her words. Beside her a younger woman played the box harmonium, fingers dancing over the keys.

Anne loved the music, the harmony of the voices. Her presence had caused some excitement at first, when she'd eventually mustered the courage to follow the singing she heard every morning and push through the metal gate that separated the temple calm from the chaos of the street. The women had stared that first day, turning their heads with the unselfconscious curiosity she could never quite get used to, smiling behind their hands, glancing at each other. She'd almost left, unable to hold herself together under such scrutiny, but something in the singing had rooted her there and she'd gone back the following week, and the next. Always arriving after the *puja* had begun and slipping away before it finished. And the women soon stopped staring, accepting her presence with the ease of people who already share their country with so many.

But that morning she didn't leave early. She remained sitting as the orange-robed woman blessed the room and placed an offering before a bronze statue of Parvati, the mother goddess. The women began to murmur and soon the temple was filled with chatter and laughter. The young harmonium player produced a metal teapot, cups were passed from hand to hand

and packets of biscuits appeared from inside bags and under dupattas.

The scene made Anne smile. When she was a child her mother had insisted on church every Sunday but always hurried them out afterwards, staunchly avoiding the tea and gossip of the church wives.

She was about to leave when the harmonium player appeared in front of her with a cup.

'Chai, aunty?'

Anne hesitated, but the girl's expression was so hopeful that she accepted with a nod. The girl clapped her hands together before skipping back to the front of the room to distribute more. Anne held the cup awkwardly, feeling the eyes of the women upon her. A general hush seemed to have fallen in response to this new development and Anne forced herself to take a sip of chai, wincing at the heat of it.

A woman with the longest hair Anne had ever seen, braided and hanging over her shoulder, turned to offer Anne a biscuit, and, as if it were the most natural thing in the world, a space opened so that Anne was no longer sitting alone but with them.

And Anne wanted to stay, she did. To sit there and drink their chai and eat their biscuits and answer their questions about her good husband and how many children she had and why she was in India without them and whether she was the mother of the missing boy and how she kept her skin so soft – there were several hands touching her arms and fingers – but it was too much. It was all too much. And she forced down the scalding chai and got to her feet. Muttering apologies and pulling herself free, she stumbled into her sandals and out the gate, realising as she did that she would never go back.

XVI

ESTHER

Mussoorie was in clouds – a monsoon fog the early sun had been unable to burn off. The bus wound its way up the mountain, taking the hairpin bends at terrifying speed, the driver leaning on his horn, the road so narrow two vehicles could not pass without mounting the verge.

On one side was damp, moss-covered rock, sprouting green, glistening life; on the other, a drop so sudden Esther couldn't keep her eyes from it, seeing only the misjudged turn, the slipping wheel that would send them over, the screech of twisted metal, the endless fall. She gripped the broken plastic of the seat in front, the fabric grimy and bursting at the seams.

When they finally arrived at the Picture Palace stand, she stepped gratefully from the bus, breathing in the crisp air, so pure after the pollution of Delhi. It was cool too, compared to the stifling heat she had left behind, and she pulled her cardigan tighter as she waited for the man who'd appeared from nowhere and climbed to the roof of the bus to retrieve the luggage. Handing down her pack, he accepted the few rupees Esther offered before swinging back up for another bag, smiling serenely with the air of one perfectly content in life.

A crowd of porters and hotel touts had gathered around the bus and, as Esther made to leave, they began to push in on her, calling out offers and prices and hotel names. Hands tugged her pack and pulled her sleeves and she struggled to break free. The peace of the morning shattered. It wasn't that she'd forgotten exactly – the press of people, the clamouring and haggling, the constant attention – but perhaps, now seven years older, she'd assumed it would be less overwhelming.

She'd called ahead but there were no free rooms at the Hotel Broadway. She'd hesitated, about to ask the man to pass a message to Anne, who hadn't returned Robert's calls or responded to his emails – who, for all they knew, was unaware of the new information about Torran, or that Esther was coming. But the line went dead before she could get the words out and Esther wasn't sure if the man had hung up or the connection had been lost.

She checked in to Hotel Clarks, less than ten minutes' walk from the bus stand and close to Anne's hotel. The room was large with French doors that opened to a narrow balcony, the decor a bizarre mixture of Raj-era features and seventies patterns in orange and brown. Beyond the terrace the great sweep of the valley disappeared into low lingering clouds. A magpie sitting on the rail of a neighbouring balcony let out a sullen cry and took to the air, shooting up before gliding down towards the clouds, turning grey and almost translucent as it vanished beneath them.

After a solitary lunch in the hotel, Esther ventured out in search of the Hotel Broadway, and found it tucked down a side street opposite a school. It was breaktime and the kids were running in all directions, braids and footballs flying. They called to her as she passed, thrusting tiny hands towards her.

She was exhausted from the journey. The plane had landed at two in the morning and she'd barely had four hours' sleep in the noisy hotel next to New Delhi station before catching the Shatabdi Express north. Dozing in the icy air conditioning of the train, the dry plains and tumbledown villages had passed by in a dreamlike haze. She must have truly fallen asleep not far from Haridwar because when she awoke, with the jolt of the train pulling into the station, she'd been dreaming she was on a boat with Torran rowing out to Inch Kenneth, but the island kept retreating the further they got from shore. She turned to ask Torran what they should do and he was gone and Esther was alone, the flip-flop feeling of a fish in her belly.

*

Mr Mehra – proprietor of the Hotel Broadway – was solemn and softly spoken. He smiled under his thin moustache as he told her he could not give out the room numbers of guests, but he could certainly pass on a message. Mrs Carmichael wasn't on the premises at present. He reached under the desk for a pad of paper and pushed it towards Esther along with a pen. Thanking him, she took it, but then paused, unable to think of what to say.

It was a relief to know Anne was still there; Evie's ominous warning about time running out was never far from Esther's thoughts. But, after all this time, and especially without warning, Anne wasn't going to be happy to see her. And Esther couldn't say she blamed her.

'Perhaps just give her this,' Esther said, digging in her bag for the letter Robert had written. If she was going to get anywhere with Anne, she'd need Robert's help.

Mr Mehra tilted his chin towards her. 'As you wish. I will put it with the others.'

'Others?'

With an unreadable expression, he motioned to the pigeon-holes behind him, his eyes lingering on the one labelled *Room Five*, a pile of letters and handwritten notes sticking out. Esther could see British stamps on the envelopes, the hotel's header on the notes.

'She's not picking up her messages?'

Mr Mehra regarded Esther. 'For several weeks now. She has not been wanting to collect them. I have tried. But she asks me to leave them here.'

They looked at each other and Esther could feel him trying to impress some meaning into the silence, but whether it was a warning or a plea, she couldn't tell. After a moment he simply sighed.

'If you leave a name and your hotel, I can tell her when she returns.'

Esther scribbled a quick note and put it on top of Robert's letter.

'Perhaps you can hand them to her personally,' she said, as he went to place them in the pigeonhole. He stopped mid-turn and gave her another inscrutable look. 'It's urgent.'

He returned the letter and note to the desk and smiled mildly. 'As you wish.'

XVII

ANNE

Too restless to return to the hotel, Anne had spent the afternoon walking the streets. Letting her feet take her along well-known roads. Past the bus stand and the Hotel Clarks, she reached the Highview Cafe as evening set in. Little more than a shack with a large veranda on stilts, it looked out across the valley and offered some of the best views in Mussoorie.

She ordered a Coke and sat at a table in the far corner of the veranda. Dark clouds shrouded the mountains, obscuring the colours of the setting sun. Lights shone in the valley below; along the ridge the flicker of butter-lamps marked a shrine.

'Looks like there's a beautiful sunset somewhere.'

Anne started. Turning, she saw Liam standing in the door-way of the hut. As he stepped towards her the bare bulbs strung around the veranda came on. They both blinked, waiting for their eyes to adjust.

'Can you ask them to turn those lights out?' she said, by way of greeting.

Liam gave a mock bow and stuck his head back inside.

'And get them to turn off that music.' Anne cringed even as the words left her mouth: she sounded like a mother.

She took her pashmina out of her bag and wrapped it around her shoulders as the lights went out. The shadows of the trees below were pooling to form a black lake, lapping at the moun-tainside. On the far horizon, the clouds were breaking above three sharp peaks, revealing glimpses of a sky still luminous. The lights in the shrine pulsed against the black silhouette of the ridge. Anne thought of the lighthouse at Taigh na Criege; she should call Rob.

Liam returned with two plates and put one in front of her as he sat down.

'What's this?' She motioned towards the plate.

'Chow mein. Vegetable.'

'Yes, I can see that.'

'I thought you might be hungry.' He shrugged. 'I didn't want to eat alone.'

Without the lights it was impossible to see his expression. He handed her a fork and she realised she *was* hungry.

The music from the hut ended abruptly. For a beat everything was completely silent, and then the sounds of night rushed in.

'I haven't seen you for a few days.' Liam's tone was neutral.

'I thought you might want some space with your friends.' She didn't say that she had been intimidated by their youth and energy.

'They're just a bunch of kids I met in Goa. We were in the same beach huts for a few weeks.'

Anne made a noise that could have meant anything and kept eating. What was it to have this existence? To be young and free to spend weeks at a time in a hut on the beach. What did they do all day? Swim and eat and smoke ganja. Philosophise over the campfire. She'd seen so many of them, these gap-yearers, the way they took everything for granted. Their right to be here, their right to do nothing but observe and judge and let the country 'soak in'. She could have been one of them herself once. Torran certainly had been. And on the whole, they were harmless. They were killing time and gaining life experience before going back to the 'real world', as if everything they experienced in India was somehow removed from that place. There simply to amuse or educate or enlighten them.

But perhaps she was wrong to put herself in a different category to these other Westerners. Didn't everyone always believe themselves to be the exception? The real deal. Was her purpose here any more meaningful than anyone else's? Others wanted India to give them an experience, an awakening, a few lines on their CV. She wanted India to give her something it had taken from her. She wanted her son. She told herself she was giving something in return – her time, her teaching – and yet wasn't she also benefiting from that? It gave her something to get up for, structure to her days, a purpose. How could she really claim to be giving anything back?

She pushed the half-eaten plate of food away. She could feel Liam's eyes on her. Was she supposed to be speaking? Sometimes she forgot how to be around other people.

'Sorry, what were we talking about?' she said, when she couldn't stand the silence any longer.

Liam finished his food and wiped his mouth with a napkin.

'You're not here tonight, are you?' He sounded amused. But then he always sounded amused.

'No. I don't know. I was thinking.'

'Dangerous. What were you thinking about?'

The terrace was very dark now.

'I don't know,' she said again. 'How are your bird pictures coming along?'

'Good. Although I can't quite get the movement. Static is fine. But the beauty is in that thrumming life, isn't it? The restlessness, the electricity. What it is to never be still. It's hard to capture on the page, but without it, it's not right. Something is missing.'

'Maybe that's where music surpasses art. It can capture all that movement. Every quiver.'

'Do you miss playing?'

'Sometimes.'

'You talk about it like you do.'

'Do I?'

The light from the doorway was momentarily blocked as a small man came through with a tray and gathered their plates. They ordered chai and he disappeared back inside.

'I came looking for you a few times.' Liam's voice dropped, as if they might be overheard.

'I've been busy.'

'I went to the college; they said you weren't in this week. The girls are on holiday.'

Anne frowned, knowing he couldn't see her face. 'Why did you go there?'

'Shouldn't I have? I was just passing, thought I'd stop in. You're never in your room when I knock. Or at least you don't answer.'

She'd heard him a few times. Stood on the other side of the door and watched the light fill the space where his shadow had been. She didn't know whether to be flattered or annoyed by his attention.

'Anne, if you don't want to spend time together, you just need to tell me.' He spread his hands on the table.

'It's not that,' she said, thinking about all the things she could say. How good it felt to be brought a plate of food, to have someone look at her and see more than a mother whose son is missing. 'I've just been busy.'

'OK,' he said after a minute. 'OK.'

They walked back to the hotel along Camel's Back Road, the imposing spire of Christ Church looming over them as they turned off the Mall. The road was dark, their way occasionally illuminated by the lights of houses scattered along the ridge. But the clouds were departing, and somewhere above was a full moon.

Liam told her about his time in a Buddhist monastery in Ladakh, the five o'clock prayers, the butter tea that congealed to form a skin as it cooled, the Sunday morning football, monks young and old kicking about in socks and sandals.

Had he ever thought about giving it all up and becoming a monk?

He laughed but didn't answer immediately. Anne liked that about him; for all his friendly talkativeness, he was a thinker, like her.

There were times, he said, when he'd considered it – watching a lunar eclipse with the community, celebrating with fire and dancing, teaching English to the young monks, all the simplicity and lightness of their days. Something in him responded to the routine; the discipline, so exacting and predictable at first, became the thing he valued most. The new day held no surprises, and yet he found himself living more consciously; with no future or past, the present became the only place to be.

But then another couple of volunteers arrived – two guys from Devon – and they brought the old mindset back. He felt obliged to spend time with them. They wanted to know about him – his past, his future, his plans – and he felt the present drifting away. He left three days later.

'But I took something with me, you know?' Liam said, hunching his shoulders against the damp air. 'It's hard to explain. As if I had a glimpse of another way of being – not just of living but of *Being*. And I haven't lost that. I carry it with me here' – he pointed to his chest – 'a kernel of peace, of acceptance.' He paused, searching for the word. 'Contentment. I don't feel it all the time; I forget about it. But I can access it if I need to. I can bring myself back to it.' He glanced over at Anne. 'Sounds crazy, doesn't it?'

She looked up at the halo of light in the sky where a cloud still obscured the moon.

'No. I understand what you're saying. But I can't imagine ever really having that . . . that feeling.'

'What makes you so sure?'

Anne turned the question over in her mind, eyes still on the clouds. 'I don't know. But I've been alive for fifty years, and I've never felt able to let go of anything. I've always been stuck. Weighted.'

'But age is just a concept—'

'Age is not just a concept; it's a fact.'

'Is it? You know there's no scientific way to prove that time exists at all. Not as a linear process, anyway.'

She went to speak, but he continued talking. 'But if we leave that aside for now, the fact that you're fifty and don't think you've ever felt a particular way, doesn't mean you're not capable of it, that it won't happen. You're certainly in the right place for it.'

They turned a corner as the moon slipped from behind the clouds, a perfect circle, light glancing off the metal roof of the bandstand at the Hawa Mahal viewpoint up ahead.

'Don't do that,' she said.

'Do what?'

'Give me all that hippie India crap.'

He laughed again. 'Hey, I'm not giving you any hippie India crap.'

'But you are. What does every Westerner with a backpack and a two-week stay in an ashram think they can find in India that they can't find at home?'

Liam shrugged. 'I don't know, maybe they can find it at home – but, for me, it had a lot to do with *not* being home. Not having the distractions. The responsibilities, the attachments. It was the life of the monastery more than anything. Being a part of that rhythm. I don't know if I would have had an opportunity like that back home.'

Anne shook her head. She couldn't argue with what he was saying but, as always, she felt unable to articulate exactly what she meant. 'But we can't escape ourselves, can we? No matter where we go, how many ashrams or monasteries we visit. Maybe we do learn things along the way, but, ultimately, we're the same people. And that elusive "present", that feeling you're talking about, it comes from inside, right?'

Liam nodded but remained silent, the corners of his mouth twitching as if he were trying not to smile.

'Well, why couldn't you have found it sitting on a mountain in New Zealand? Or even sitting on your couch in front of the telly? What is it about being here?'

They had arrived at the viewpoint and, without discussing it, turned to walk across the concrete platform, under the

71

bandstand, to lean against the railings and look out on the valley's moonlit shadows.

'I never wanted to come here,' she said when he didn't answer, the metal cold on the palms of her hands. 'I only ever wanted one thing from India, and I still haven't found it.'

A transparent cloud drifted in front of the moon, mellowing its clear edges, all definitions seemingly impossible.

'Do you think you'll ever find him? Your son?'

How could she have imagined he didn't know? From somewhere deep in the valley came the mournful call of a bird. At home, Anne could recognise every species by its song; here, she was still learning their names.

'I don't know.' Her voice was little more than a sigh and he leant towards her so that their arms were touching. She didn't move away. 'I don't know what I'm doing here. If it's mad to think he could still turn up after seven years. And if he did, how we could ever go back. How he could ever come home as if nothing had happened. And would he want to? And would I? And maybe I'm also here because I don't know where else to be or how else to be if I'm not looking for him.'

Her words floated into the night. She imagined them falling softly on the trees below. She could feel Liam watching her, and when he spoke his voice was hushed too.

'Perhaps you're here for yourself as much as for him. And is that such a bad thing?'

Anne swallowed. 'I've forgotten who I was before I became a mother and now I don't know how to stop being one. I don't want to stop being one. And then – sometimes – I do. Sometimes I feel his presence so strongly that I know he must be dead. And there's a freedom in that.' She paused. 'That sounds dreadful, I don't mean—'

'I know what you mean.'

They were silent, leaving the night's whispers to fill the void. The thrumming vibrations and tropical buzz that Anne had been surprised to find this high in the mountains. So loud it had been hard to sleep at first. But it's funny, how the brain accepts and adapts until it becomes an effort to hear it at all.

They continued on, beneath towering Himalayan oaks and past the English graveyard, gothic headstones overrun with creepers and moss. Once again Liam talked and Anne listened, enjoying the sound of his voice and the ease that had returned to them.

He spoke of growing up by the sea and how he missed it now and wished to see it – as if it were a dear friend from whom he'd been parted too long. There was a beach south of Goa which was hard enough to get to that the usual tourists didn't make it, the sort of beach you could spend time on. He talked about the colour of the water and the vastness of the stars, the fineness of the sand and the freedom of endless days. He talked about it with such enthusiasm it was almost as if he were convincing her to go. And Anne briefly imagined how it would feel to be convinced.

When they reached the hotel Liam stopped, interlacing his fingers behind his neck. Light fell from the windows. Anne stopped too and looked at him, and neither spoke. And then they both started speaking at once and laughed.

'Aren't you coming in?'

Liam shifted. 'I have a call to make.' He smiled in a way which was new and which Anne couldn't interpret. His eyes were on the alley that led to the Lower Mall.

'I'll see you tomorrow, then.'

She started towards the hotel, but he took her hand.

'I *will* see you tomorrow, right?' His voice was casual but his eyes were searching.

She smiled uncertainly, allowing her hand to rest in his for a moment before pulling away.

XVIII

ESTHER

When Esther came down to breakfast the following morning, Anne was already there. The only customer sitting in the Hotel Clarks' restaurant, a cavernous room with elegantly laid tables and a picture window giving on to the valley. Esther watched her from the doorway, teacup cradled in her hands as she gazed out at the morning mist. Her dark hair pinned neatly back, her sea-green salwar kameez freshly pressed. But her expression was tired, and in that unguarded moment it seemed as if the past seven years of hope and defeat had settled into the grooves of Anne's face like dust.

Esther hesitated, ready to turn back to her room, to pack her things and jump on the next bus south – suddenly afraid of why she'd come and how Anne would react, of the book she was still hoping to write, of the promise she'd made to Robert that she couldn't keep. But even as she waivered Esther knew it was too late; she'd set the ball in motion, there was no going back.

Anne gave a tight nod of acknowledgement as Esther gave her order to the hovering waiter and sat down. He slipped silently away to the kitchen, leaving them completely alone.

'I always wondered when you'd turn up again.'

'Like a bad penny.' Esther was angling for a smile, but Anne didn't react. 'You got my note then – Robert's letter?'

Anne put her cup down and took a paper napkin from under her cutlery, dabbing it against her lips before returning it to the table.

'I'm here, aren't I?'

Esther had always found Anne awkward, even before the fallout from the article. She knew Anne had tried to be kind

74

to her when she was at Taigh na Criege, but there was always an intimation of the performative about it, and Esther could never tell if Anne was looking through her in search of something else or if she simply wasn't interesting enough to hold Anne's attention. The same feeling struck her now. She'd travelled halfway across the world to see her and Anne wouldn't even meet her eye.

'You were impossible to get hold of. Robert was worried.'

'If Rob was so worried, he should have come himself,' Anne said, looking down at the napkin as she folded it, slowly and precisely, so that the corners all met in the middle. 'I didn't think there was anything left to say. I assumed any news would come from here, would reach me first.'

'It must be a shock, after all this time.'

Anne kept her attention on the napkin, releasing it so that the corners began to unfurl.

'You were at Taigh na Criege?'

'Yes.'

She looked directly at Esther for the first time. 'How is Rob?'

The waiter returned with a tray, laying out the Nescafé and toast with sombre precision.

'You should call him,' Esther said.

Anne's gaze wandered back to the window. The mist was retreating, revealing the ghostly tops of buildings, the tangled wires of an electricity pole. Her calmness was unnerving. Esther thought of how Robert had paced the kitchen, unable to stay still.

'You do understand what this means? Robert told you about the Sunshine House in his letter – about Evie?'

Eyes still fixed on the window, Anne's face was carefully expressionless although she blinked several times before turning to meet Esther's gaze. Esther almost wished she'd get angry, that they could finally have it out. But that wasn't Anne's style.

'Of course I do.'

'We need to go and look for him.'

Anne shook her head, once, leaning away, and for a moment Esther saw it, as Anne's eyes darted around the room: the fear of a cornered animal. And just as quickly she regained composure, the veil of calm descended.

'How credible is this story? How can you be sure it's not another false lead?' There was something almost pleading in her voice, and if Esther didn't know better, she'd have thought Anne wanted her to cast doubt, to take it back, to never have come; that she was, yet again, an unwelcome intruder in Anne's life. 'Rob thought it was worth following up, did he?'

'Well yes, that's why I'm here—'

But Anne was shaking her head. 'That's what I don't understand. Why you – of all people – are here, and Rob is still at home. Why didn't he come?'

Outside a flight of swallows swooped in and out of the remaining mist, scattering and reforming to move as one.

'I don't know,' Esther said quietly.

'He thinks Torran's dead.' It was a flat statement of fact. 'He didn't come because he doesn't believe that we'll find him, even if this Sunshine House does exist.' Anne turned to Esther again, and for a moment her expression was almost kind. 'But he couldn't do nothing – just in case – so he sent you. Because he knew I'd never forgive him if he did nothing. And he probably thought this was a way for us to put the past behind us.'

The silence which followed felt strangely intimate. The green of Anne's eyes holding hers.

'I'd like that,' Esther said, emboldened by her unexpected candour. 'To put the past behind us.'

But she realised too late that Anne was looking through her again. She had a sudden memory of that photo of Anne and Robert and how Anne was looking through that moment too.

Anne gave a brittle laugh that told Esther they were as far as ever from moving on. 'I hope you didn't come all this way to ask for my forgiveness without so much as an apology.'

Esther tried to speak but Anne cut her off with a raised hand.

'No – now is not the time. This is not about you, Esther. I need as much information as you can give me and then I need to go. Rob said in his letter that the Sunshine House is cut off from late summer to spring.'

Esther leant forwards. 'So we're going to go?'

Anne almost scoffed. 'There is no "we". I'm not going anywhere with you. How can I when I don't trust you? I don't even know you any more.'

Anne stopped short of saying she didn't like her, but Esther could feel it emanating from her, and the feeling wasn't new.

'Why would you want to come anyway?' Anne continued, eyes narrowed. 'According to Rob, you've promised not to write about it.' Her tone made it very clear she had her doubts about this as well.

But Esther wasn't going to let her win. 'Robert made me promise I wouldn't let you go alone. And I agreed not to write about it if I went with you. If you leave me here – or if I go on my own, under my own steam – I guess the agreement doesn't stand.'

'That sounds an awful lot like a threat.'

It was Esther's turn to avoid Anne's gaze. She finished her toast as calmly as she could. The coffee had gone cold and she felt too wired to finish it.

A loud group of travellers entered the room, and Anne's eyes briefly scanned each face before returning to rest on Esther.

'I just want to help,' Esther said, trying to sound conciliatory. 'I gave Robert my word. I owe you both that.'

Anne regarded her a moment longer. Her expression gave little away and Esther never knew what made her change her mind; she never thought to ask.

'Fine,' Anne said at last. 'It'll take a day or so to organise the trip. We need to get up to Manali. We'll need a mountain guide. Meet me at the hotel this afternoon and we'll take it from there.'

She gathered her bag and dupatta and rose from the chair.

'No police,' Esther said, as Anne was about to leave.

She turned to give Esther a questioning look.

'I promised Evie we'd only involve them if we have to. There may be people there who don't want to be found.'

'The police usually turn a blind eye, given enough *baksheesh*.'

'I know. But still, I gave her my word.'

Anne looked as if she wanted to say something about the value of Esther's word.

'Fine. They lost interest a long time ago anyway. There's more than they can handle going on in those hills.'

Esther thought of the research she'd done on the Kullu and Parvati valleys and their surrounds, all those years ago: the missing travellers and the ones who turned up dead, the attacks and the violent drug cartels. Not to mention the inherent danger of venturing into such wild and remote places.

'Things haven't improved up there?' Esther tried to keep her voice light. But Anne wasn't fooled. A look of amusement tinged with something like pity crossed her face.

'No,' she said. 'If anything, they're a lot worse.'

XIX

LIAM

He saw them through the restaurant window, Anne and the red-haired woman, closer to his own age than Anne's. They were standing by the chai stand in front of the Punjab National Bank, not looking at each other but talking as they sipped from little clay cups. Anne was staring off down the street, a scowl on her face. She was tired, he could see that even from this distance, and the weight that had been lifting these past weeks seemed to be pressing down again, heavier than ever.

Something had happened. He shifted his gaze to the red-haired woman, gesticulating as she talked. There was something disjointed about the two of them, standing too far apart and avoiding each other's eyes. Liam hesitated, half out his chair, wondering if Anne would thank him for interrupting.

He felt irrationally protective of her, this woman who was almost twenty years his senior. Who kept herself tightly closed, except in those unguarded moments when he glimpsed another – freer, more beguiling – spirit underneath. Back home, the people in his life were all surface, sunshine reflecting off water, just going through the motions of life. And, to his great disappointment, the other travellers he'd met in India were much the same: so much talk and so little substance.

Liam glanced at the sketch he had been doing. It was another sunbird – a red one. He'd bought some watercolour pencils because the vibrant sunbirds appeared, disappointingly, like blackbirds with weird beaks when rendered in black and white. He enjoyed the challenge of trying to capture the myriad tones of their feathers, the unique light that danced off them.

He wasn't happy with any of his attempts so far, and now he closed the book and signalled for his bill. Looking out the window again to check they were still there, he paid quickly and headed for the door.

On the street, a seemingly endless swarm of uniformed children blocked his path, and when the last of the kids had passed he saw that Anne and her companion had vanished.

He was about to head across to the chai stand when a flash of red hair made him turn in the other direction. Sure enough, Anne's new friend was standing outside the Om Internet Cafe, fiddling with a long curly strand of hair that had come loose from the ponytail she wore.

Liam crossed the street and walked straight up to her.

'Hi,' he said, smiling and sticking out his hand. 'How's it going? I'm Liam.'

The woman gave him a bemused smile but shook his hand.

'Esther.'

He found himself nodding, as if he'd been expecting her to say this.

'It's a pleasure, Esther.'

Her smile deepened with amusement.

'Likewise.'

For a moment neither of them spoke and then Esther reached into the pocket of her mac and brought out a crumpled pack of Camels.

'Smoke?'

'Sure.'

He slid one from the pack and bent towards her so she could light it.

'Thanks,' he said, inhaling deeply. 'I haven't smoked in five years. Not tobacco anyway.'

'Oh god,' she said, lighting her own cigarette and shoving the lighter in her back pocket. 'Two minutes after meeting and I've already ruined you.'

He laughed.

'Don't worry about it. I've been meaning to start again.'

'Well, glad to be of assistance, then.'

Her words were followed by a clap of thunder. They both looked up at the sky, which was bright blue and incongruously cloudless.

'That'll be the rains coming.'

'It sounded so close.'

He nodded. 'The mountains are funny like that. They carry sound, like water.'

She turned to look at him, tilting her head to exhale sky-wards. 'Been here long?'

'If by "here" you mean India, then yes. Nine months. If you mean Mussoorie – I think it's been about three weeks? I lose track.'

'It's a hard life.'

'Someone's got to live it.'

The low rumble of thunder came again. Scattered clouds were beginning to appear in the sky.

'What about you?' Liam said.

'What about me?'

'How long have you been here?'

She studied the tip of her cigarette, flicking ash on the cracked concrete.

'Not long.'

'And how long are you planning on staying?'

She took a drag and exhaled slowly.

'Not long.'

A cloud covered the sun and they watched as the light slid from the afternoon, pulling the colours from the street.

'It's going to rain,' Esther said, just as a big drop of water fell between their feet, shattering on the concrete.

'And so it begins.' They contemplated the dark stain. 'And here we are, witness to the first drop.'

'Do you think they're like snowflakes?'

Liam stubbed his cigarette out.

'Unique? Perhaps.'

The sky darkened again, pushing the afternoon into a false dusk. Without the sun the temperature had already fallen several degrees. A few more drops fell to the ground. Liam felt them on his head and bare arms. Another crash of thunder. They both looked up again.

'Now might be a good time to seek shelter,' Esther said. But even as she spoke the sky cracked open and the rain began in earnest.

They stepped back automatically so they were pressed up against the window but protected, for the most part, by the narrow awning above.

The rain pounded the road, causing steam to rise from the sun-baked asphalt and scattering people like chickens as they ran to find shelter. Umbrellas blossomed, tourists pulled on plastic ponchos and a man rode past on a bicycle, blue flip-flops hanging off his feet, white vest already soaked through. He waved at them, shaking his head so that water flew from his hair. Three schoolgirls ran from doorway to doorway, clutching each other and laughing wildly. A large brown and white cow stood in the middle of the road, jaw working mechanically, seemingly oblivious to the rain and the commotion it was causing.

Puddles were quickly forming in the broken concrete, pooling in the potholes, while the two narrow channels on either side of the road had filled with fast-flowing water.

Behind them the door swung open, and they turned to see Anne emerge, eyes on the street.

She was tense, preoccupied. Liam wanted to put his arms around her.

'Hi,' he said instead, offering her a smile.

She stared at him blankly for a moment and then her pale cheeks coloured slightly.

'Liam.'

'Oh, you two know each other,' Esther cut in before Liam could say more.

Anne's eyes flicked from Liam to Esther and back to Liam. Whatever had opened momentarily in her face shut down.

'We're friends,' Liam said at the same time as Anne said, 'We're staying in the same hotel.'

Esther stubbed out her cigarette.

'Right,' she said, looking at them both curiously.

'Esther's a journalist,' Anne said quickly, as if pre-empting a question he hadn't thought to ask.

'Guilty,' Esther said, shooting Anne another look. There was a palpable tension in the air.

'You're getting wet,' Liam said, seeking to break it, and pulled Anne back so that she was next to him, pressed against the window. He felt the quickness of her pulse between his fingers.

'Any news?' Esther was talking across Liam, raising her voice above the rain.

'We'll talk later,' Anne replied, so quietly that only Liam heard her.

'What?' Esther leant forwards.

'Later,' Anne repeated, staring ahead.

Esther raised an eyebrow at Liam and rested her head back against the glass. He looked from one woman to the other, unable to work out their relationship.

'How long is this going to last?'

Liam shrugged. 'Impossible to say. Could be ten minutes. Could be hours.'

'Right.'

'Let's give it ten, then we make a run for it.'

They stood in silence watching the street, now almost deserted, aware of each other's closeness. Anne had her arms wrapped tightly around herself and Liam offered her the dry shirt from his bag, but she shook her head, avoiding his gaze.

XX

ESTHER

The rain stopped as suddenly as it had started. Anne cast a glance up the glistening street – water running down walls and dripping from rooftops – before turning to Esther.

'I have things to do,' she said, her eyes meeting Esther's briefly. 'I'll see you tomorrow.' She smiled tightly at Liam and walked off before either of them could say anything.

'Great. Bye then,' Esther called after her retreating figure.

'She doesn't like you much, does she?'

'Does she like anyone?' Esther drew the damp pack of Camels from her pocket and offered him another one.

Liam laughed. 'You know, I was actually beginning to think she liked me. A little.'

Esther sparked the lighter, leaning towards the flame. 'Lucky you.'

They walked in the direction of Kulri Bazaar, the sky slipping to evening as lights and music and people filled the streets.

'Fancy a drink?' Liam stopped beside a hotel, walls thick with grime. 'It doesn't look like much, but it's actually got a bar that serves alcohol. Pretty special in these parts.'

'And popular with tourists,' Esther observed, as they walked across the small foyer into a wood-panelled bar that must once have been quite swanky, with its intimate booths, elaborate velvet drapes and green library lamps. The air was choked with cigarette smoke, the floor sticky. Almost every table was occupied, but the only Indian in the room was the moustachioed man behind the bar.

Esther found a booth near the back while Liam bought two warm bottles of Kingfisher, nodding at several people as he made his way to the table. Dire Straits were promising 'Money for Nothing' over the laughter and chatter that filled the room. Esther sank back against a cushion, relaxing for the first time in what felt like days.

Liam took a swig of beer, his eyes roaming the room before returning to settle on her.

'So, Esther.'

'So, Liam.'

He leant forwards to rest his elbows on the table and cocked his head. 'Are you going to tell me what you're really doing here?'

She returned his smile. 'Are *you* going to tell me what's really going on with you and Anne?'

He laughed. 'We're friends. Your turn.'

Breaking eye contact, she looked at her bottle, tipping it slightly to read the label, tracing a finger across the logo.

'Perhaps you should ask Anne.'

'Is it about her son?'

'Oh, so you do know about that.'

He sat back and took another sip of beer. 'There are posters all over the place.'

'Has Anne talked to you about it?' Esther had her notebook in her bag, and she briefly considered pulling it out. She'd already composed a mental description of Liam – tall, muscled, surprisingly handsome when smiling – to transcribe later. She pictured his name in the middle of a page, the questions she'd scribble around it.

Liam ran a hand through his hair, which had dried flat against his head as if he'd been wearing a hat. Over at the bar a group of Australians were laughing too loudly. The music stopped mid-note and an old television crackled into life, a cricket match just discernible on the pixelated screen. There was a collective groan but the barman only smiled placidly.

'I read that article you wrote.' Liam was also watching the Australians.

'Oh yeah? Which one?'

He turned back to her. 'Do you have to ask?'

'What are you doing reading seven-year-old articles? Where did you even see it?'

'It's online. So it was you who wrote it?'

'You just said it was.'

Liam smiled. 'I couldn't remember. Lucky guess.' He lifted the bottle and drained his beer. 'Same again?' He stood and tilted the empty bottle towards her.

'I'll get it,' Esther said, rising too quickly and feeling the blood rush to her head.

When she returned Liam had a sketchbook out, but he flicked it shut before she could see what he was working on.

'So you and Anne,' Esther said after a moment's pause. Liam smiled, settling against the cushions, one arm slung over the back of the booth. 'You know, I went to see her husband before I came out here.'

He didn't blink. 'And why did you come out here? That's what I can't figure out.'

'You'd have to ask Anne that.'

Liam nodded. 'Glad to see you've finally learnt how to respect people's privacy, Esther. Shows real growth.'

She laughed into her beer but then put it down abruptly. The smile had gone from his lips but not his eyes. Esther began to speak, then realised she didn't know what she wanted to say. His tone was playful but edged with something else, like a cat toying with a mouse.

'I haven't spoken to Anne about it,' he continued. 'But I can't imagine her telling you all that stuff, knowing you'd print it. There's something else, isn't there?'

'You think you know her?'

He twitched a shoulder in a half shrug, his eyes fixed on Esther's. 'She's been through a lot. I don't like the idea of some-one hurting her. Exposing her in that way.'

The bottle, which for a slightly inflated price had come from the fridge, was slippery in Esther's hands. She wondered if

Anne had told Liam that they were leaving for Manali the next morning.

'What has Anne been doing here, these last months? Have you known her long?'

'I told you, I arrived a few weeks ago. She teaches in a girls' college near Sisters' Bazaar. And other than that she just seems to hang out.'

'With you?'

Liam shifted his gaze to the sketchbook. 'Sometimes.'

The conversation turned to other things as the empty bottles piled up and they both relaxed. Liam was a committed story-teller who used his hands to punctuate his conversation. And he laughed at his own jokes in such an unguarded way it was impossible not to laugh back. It had been a long time since Esther had sat for hours in a bar drinking and chatting and watching the person opposite grow more familiar as the hours passed. A rough sketch shaded in.

At ten the bar closed and back on the street they stopped at a food stall to buy plates piled high with *aloo chaat* and vegetable *pakora*. They wandered as they ate, watching the shops and restaurants shutting, blinds pulled down like closing eyes.

'You seem to really care. About Anne,' Esther said, throwing the remains of her pakora in a bin and linking an arm through Liam's, his solid presence reassuring in the shifting shadows. She realised she was drunker than she'd been in some time, although Liam seemed completely sober.

He didn't say anything for so long that her mind had wandered by the time he spoke, and it was an effort to remember what they were talking about.

'I do.' His voice was casual but she felt the muscles in his arm tense.

They stopped at a junction where their ways diverged. Two old men playing chess in a doorway waved cheerfully before

87

returning to their board. Further down the road, monkeys were quarrelling under a streetlight.

Esther turned towards Liam, ready to say goodnight, but he was looking at her with such a serious expression that she faltered.

'Was what you wrote in that article true, Esther? All of it?'

She hesitated, but something about the shadows and the lateness of the hour invited confession, and the beer had loosened her tongue. 'Essentially, yes. I suppose I may have used some artistic licence with the details, but the facts were true enough.'

He shook his head. 'I just can't picture Anne being so forthcoming, especially with a journalist she barely knew.'

Esther looked down at her boots, still faintly scuffed with the mud and sand of Taigh na Criege.

'But she does know me. And she didn't have to tell me because I was there.'

Liam dropped her arm and took a step back. 'What?'

'I'm Torran's cousin. I lived with them for a while when I was younger.'

'And you didn't think to mention this when I asked?'

'It's none of your business. Why are you so interested in all this anyway?'

Liam was shaking his head. 'So you were a journalist with a front-row seat to their lives.' He took another step away. 'And all that stuff in the article – postnatal depression and her leaving and the lake?'

'Loch,' Esther said automatically.

Liam held up his hands. 'Whatever. So that was true? Jesus. And you printed it? Isn't there some ethical code—'

'It was part of the story. People want to know why—'

But Liam was walking away, back past the men playing chess. When he reached the corner he stopped for a moment before turning on his heel and coming back to stand very close, face inches from hers. There was no sign of laughter in his eyes now.

'I don't give a shit why that boy disappeared,' he said, keeping his voice low so the men wouldn't hear. 'People do it all the time. Especially here. People get high and walk off a cliff or decide they're the next messiah and go meditate on a mountain, or join an ashram or a cult – there are plenty to choose from – or are just too off their heads to remember who they are and where they came from or – whatever. Welcome to India.

'But I'm pretty sure whatever you think Anne did or didn't do when Torran was a kid had very little impact on his disappearing. I don't know why you've turned up all of a sudden, but you need to back off. Anne is trying to move on, and you need to let her.' He glared at Esther for a moment more before stalking off.

'Why don't you ask her? Ask her why I'm here?'

Liam didn't stop. 'Go home, Esther.'

And before she could respond, he was gone. One of the chess players bobbed his head sympathetically and she managed a weak smile in reply. The air had turned thick and heavy again, low clouds trapping the persistent heat, and as Esther pushed through it towards her hotel she heard the distant rumble of thunder.

XXI

LIAM

Later that night, when he heard Anne crying, Liam rose without thinking and put his hand against the damp wallpaper. So thin and flimsy, he could have punched a hole right through it. She was crying like no one should cry. Great shuddering sobs that seemed to shake the hotel like the thunder that rattled the windows and doors.

Even after the earlier rains the air was charged, settling on his skin in beads of perspiration. He imagined electricity sparking from his fingertips, humming down the wires that hung haphazardly from the hotel roof past his bedroom window. Setting the valley on fire.

Turning from the wall he paced the room, following the crooked line of the floorboards, the dusty border of the rug. The table was strewn with papers covered in birds, half formed, deformed, coloured and black and white. Some still, some nesting, some in flight. Some labelled in scientific detail. Some merely lines hinting at the flutter of a feather.

He'd tried for days to draw her the purple sunbird. Now he saw that none of them would do. They would never do because he wanted to say something the bird could never say. The quiver of light on a purple breast, the blinking eye, the twitching head, impossible to recreate or capture or pin down.

In one impetuous movement he swept his arm across the table and let the papers flutter to the floor. One of the first sketches, one he had started as they sat together in the sunroom, landed on top of the pile. He looked at it critically for a moment and then stooped to pick it up. He couldn't hear Anne any more and the silence was suffocating.

Letting the paper drift back to the floor he turned to the balcony door, left open in the vain hope of catching a breeze, and went outside into the strange umbra of another brewing storm. The clouds were so close he could almost reach out and touch them.

He stood with his hands on the railing, leaning over as far as he dared, sensing Anne's presence the moment before turning.

She was sitting on her balcony, quite still, and in the darkness he couldn't see which way she was looking. He turned back towards the valley and the sky and thought about jumping, but only in that abstract way that everyone thinks about jumping.

Anne must have been looking after all because she said in a light enough tone that he could have been mistaken about the crying, 'Don't jump.'

He turned back towards her.

'I'm sorry about today,' he said. Because he was, or at least he felt he should be, but he wasn't sure why.

'There's no need to be sorry,' she said. Which wasn't the same as saying he had nothing to be sorry for.

He stood awkwardly by the railings, struggling to make her out.

'I never had much fun.' Her voice was light and apparently at odds with what she was saying.

He turned back towards the valley and wondered if she ever thought about jumping – if anyone else, in fact, ever did. Perhaps it was just him. He thought to ask her this but let the silence stretch on instead. They had been doing some intricate dance since that day at the waterfall, yet neither of them seemed to know the steps.

'Why can't you just be happy?' he said to the clouds. He said it quietly so that she may or may not have heard and when she didn't say anything he let the silence grow as big and heavy as the sky, charged and electric.

Somewhere not too far away there was a low growl of thunder. Perhaps she hadn't heard him after all.

'I think it's time for me to move on. But I don't want to leave you.' He spoke as a bolt of lightning pierced the sky and he knew she couldn't have heard.

He let his hands slip from the railing and felt the pressure break as a large drop of rain fell on his cheek. And then another. He put his hands up to catch them, like a child in snow. The next roll of thunder shook the hotel. Lightning lit the world and the sky opened. The rain had soaked him through before he had a chance to turn, before he saw that she was no longer there.

He was already shivering. He opened his mouth and tasted the water on his tongue.

As he turned back towards the room he saw her, standing in his balcony doorway, a dark outline against the light. He stopped, staring at her face as the shadows resolved themselves.

'I don't know if I can be happy,' she said. Or at least that's what he thought she said, but a roll of thunder crashed over her words.

'Why didn't you tell me about Esther? Why is she here?' He was almost shouting to be heard.

She folded her arms around herself. He stepped towards her and she took a step back into the room so that the light was no longer behind her.

'It's cold,' she said.

He followed her in and closed the balcony doors, hushing the relentless drumming of the rain. The ceiling fan cut through the air, humming as it rotated. Liam pulled off his T-shirt and threw on a dry one. Anne stood awkwardly, looking at the drawings on the floor. He switched off the fan, took the blanket from his bed to wrap around her shoulders. They stood very close, looking at each other.

Anne took a step back. 'I should go.'

There was another pause. He nodded. 'OK.'

She moved towards the door, the blanket still over her shoulders.

'I want you to come with me,' he said when her hand was on the door. She stopped but she didn't turn around.

'Where to?'

'I don't know. Anywhere. We could go south to the beaches or west to Rajasthan. East to Kathmandu. Wherever we wanted.'

Another crack of thunder sent the rain into overdrive, pounding against the roof, hurling itself at the windows. All the static and heat had gone from the room but the air was still charged.

'He's been gone for seven years, Anne. How long are you going to wait?'

She turned to look at him and for one reckless moment he thought she was going to say yes. Her eyes were wide; he thought he could read indecision on her face. But then she turned and opened the door and disappeared without a word.

He sat down heavily on the bed and stared at the floor as another bolt of lightning speared the sky. He nudged one of the drawings with his toe to see the painting he'd done that morning. Wondering again what Esther was up to, what news she'd brought Anne.

He was gathering the scattered papers when the power went out. The grumble of thunder that followed sounded further away, but the rain was falling as hard as ever. He stood in the dark with the pictures in his hand and waited for his eyes to make sense of the room, the blackness of night never as absolute as it seems.

He was still standing there when he heard the door open and Anne's footsteps cross the floor. She was a dark shape against a greater darkness. And then her hands found his and he let the sunbirds fall. A moment of hesitation, and her body pressed against his, her fingers on the back of his neck, in his hair. And her lips, so soft, murmuring 'I don't want to talk about this,' as she pushed him to the bed.

Liam watched the dust caught in the morning air as light streamed through the window. Contentment nestled warmly on his bare chest. He stretched his arms above his head, turned to lie on his side and thought about the days ahead. And the nights that would follow.

He smiled sleepily at the memory of Anne, her skin, her hair, her eyes. The way her body had responded to his, her breath on his face, her smell, the darkness wrapping them in its anonymous intimacy.

She'd refused to stay, slipping away as quickly and silently as she'd appeared. Impossible to read as always, but he knew he would try. They'd have breakfast together; it was Sunday. Maybe they'd walk to the waterfall again. He imagined holding her naked body in the water, sharp angles softened, droplets clinging to eyelashes. He wanted to explore every inch of her. To know every thought that flew through her mind. And maybe it was ridiculous, but he wanted to help her too. To show her how the world could be beautiful. She'd changed since he'd known her. Sometimes she looked at him and he couldn't see the sadness.

He would extend his trip. On the shelf at the top of the wardrobe, next to his passport and driving licence, was a return ticket to Auckland for the following month. Where, in another life, his three-bedroom suburban house was waiting: his landscaping business; his dog, Kit; his wife, Rachel. They were going to try for a baby when he got home. That was the plan. That had been the agreement. Their house was on the corner of a quiet street. At night the sound of sprinklers and the green smell of grass came floating in through the open windows.

XXII

BEFORE

The morning is still and bright, and Anne has been up baking bread. She has seen the sun rise, the sky turn from pink to blue, the clouds depart. By the time Robert enters the kitchen there is a fresh loaf on the table and coffee in the pot. She is at the sink, and he puts his arms around her and kisses her cheek.

She shrugs him off and he squeezes her waist before letting go. 'It's normal to feel sad.'

She nods, although it is not the word she would have used. Not exactly.

Robert pours himself a coffee and looks at the clock. 'Will you go wake him or should I?'

Anne is about to respond when they hear him on the stairs. Robert smiles. 'I guess he's old enough to wake himself now.'

They sit for breakfast and Anne can't eat. Robert is overcompensating, talking too much. Torran is distracted. He picks at his breakfast and nods vaguely at his father. Anne watches his face, trying to see the child he once was. He has changed so much these last months. The teenage awkwardness has given way to the man.

Torran catches her eye and she automatically smiles but he doesn't smile back, and she has no idea what he sees when he looks at her. They are strangers who have lived under the same roof for eighteen years. They are not close the way she once imagined they would be.

Fiona's parents are driving the pair to Edinburgh airport and all at once they're outside, loading Torran's rucksack into the Volvo, and everyone is hugging, and doors are slamming, and Torran and Fiona are waving through the back window as they are driven away.

The moment, anticipated for so long, is over before it has really begun. Anne stands beside Robert with her hand raised as Torran looks back at them. All the things she ever wanted to tell him press frantically against her chest.

He turns away just before the car rounds a hill.

He is gone. Her boy is gone.

Part Two

Part Two

XXIII

ANNE

Dawn broke through the trees in mist-lined light as the bus laboured around mountain after mountain, ever climbing. Occasionally the forest thinned to reveal a momentary glimpse of pine tops descending into cloud-filled valleys, giving Anne the feeling of being at the very top of the world, looking down.

It was four hours since the bus had stopped at a roadside restaurant somewhere in the vast darkness. They'd stumbled out to stretch their legs, taking turns to squat in the stinking toilets, faeces smeared across tiled walls. Then they'd sat for fifteen minutes under fluorescent strip lights drinking chai, sweetness humming in their gums.

Anne had spent the journey staring at the night. She'd seen the moon rise and fall, the futile twinkling of a few stars briefly claiming their presence.

Her back and neck were stiff. It wasn't cold but it wasn't quite warm enough either, and she kept tugging the blanket around her, tucking it in, knitting the end pieces together between her fingers. When she closed her eyes she saw the curve of Liam's smile, so she'd kept them open.

She studied her hands, which had always been so long and slender. Musician's hands, her mother had called them. And yet the other day she'd noticed how the skin was looser now, like a pair of overstretched gloves. Esther's hands had fallen open in her lap as she slept and Anne saw the lines that crossed her palms, a smudge of ink on her left index finger. She remembered Torran's baby fingers unconsciously clasping hers in sleep and she wondered, if she were to reach out then, whether Esther's would do the same.

*

With the sun streaming through the window and Esther now awake, they watched the steep slopes flatten to level ground and the trees draw back, leaving flowers of yellow and white in their wake. Long grass sang in the breeze. Birds swooped through the foliage, courting the morning air. The colours deepened as the sun climbed higher, light conjuring every hue.

Anne knew this road. She knew the tumbling waterfall around a future bend, knew how the trees pushed back until they were driving through a valley surrounded by altitudinous peaks, the endless sky where eagles flew. She knew the beauty and she knew the unease in the pit of her stomach. The fear coiled around stubborn hope as the road led them inextricably towards Manali. The town that had taken her son.

Every journey to Manali was that first journey. The jeep's shampooed upholstery and plastic flowers, the sympathetic eyes of their driver in the rear-view mirror. Rob's leg tap-tap-tapping. The younger hand she'd reached down to still it. And the smell – the one that obliterated all others – the deep, earthy headiness of marijuana plants, which started as a whisper but quickly became impossible to ignore. Even now, in the hermet-ically sealed bus, it was beginning to filter through. But that first time, in an open-windowed jeep, what started as a trickle was soon a deluge.

Rob had stared wide-eyed at the plants growing in incredible proliferation along the road and sighed for the days of his youth. But Anne had looked away, taking her hand from his knee.

'It's so beautiful,' Esther said, breaking into Anne's mem-ories. 'I forgot how beautiful it is.'

And Anne knew it was true. She knew it, but she couldn't feel it.

In Manali, Esther waited for their bags while Anne scanned the crowd for Dolma, the Tibetan woman who ran the Green Tara Guesthouse. A friend, she supposed, after all this time.

She soon caught sight of her, reading a book by the newspaper kiosk, thick black hair swept into a neat bun. She was tall and broad, almost matronly in her demeanour, but Anne had come to know her wicked laugh and generous heart, and she felt the tension in her chest ease as they approached.

'*Tashi delek*.' Dolma slipped the paperback into her pocket before pulling Anne into a tight embrace. Anne relaxed against her for a moment, feeling the strain of the material around Dolma's hips, the press of her breasts against her own, the steady rhythm of her breath. Dolma was close to her own age, but it was a mother's embrace and Anne allowed herself, for the briefest moment, to be a child. Then Dolma took her by the arms and pushed her gently back, looking long and hard into her face.

'You are too thin,' she said. 'But you look better than last time. It is good to see you, my friend.' She narrowed her eyes, a smile curling the corners of her mouth.

'It's good to see you too.'

Dolma broke into a full smile and let go of Anne's arms, turning now to Esther.

'You are the niece,' she said. 'The journalist.'

Esther smiled and offered her hand. 'Esther.'

Dolma returned her smile but didn't take her hand, and Esther let it drop, looking awkwardly away.

'I need to hear everything.' Dolma turned back to Anne. 'But first we must get you to the house.'

XXIV

ESTHER

They walked through the early morning streets as the town spluttered into life. It must have rained because murky puddles filled the holes in the road, rainbow films shining on their slick surfaces.

Dolma walked slightly ahead, the hem of her sky-blue *chupa* expertly tailored to almost touch the ground but not drag. She stepped over the puddles with effortless grace, her wooden clogs clipping smartly as she went. She was a striking woman, striding through the rubbish and detritus of the street as if she were a high-heeled CEO on a New York sidewalk, coffee and briefcase in hand. Esther wondered what life Dolma might have led had she been born somewhere else. And if it would have been better or worse, or just different.

Esther's memories of Manali were hazy and she was glad to be led through the maze of streets, past sleeping rickshaw drivers and just opening restaurants, bare-armed men in vests brushing their teeth in doorways or spitting out of windows. From behind thin glass and thinner walls came the sounds of morning: running water, metal plates, gas hobs, children.

The sun had not yet scaled the buildings and the narrow pavement was in shadows. Three goats tethered to a post bleated plaintively; one had an eye that was weepy and bloodshot and attracting flies. A boy filling a dirty bucket waved at them and when Esther raised a hand in return he shrieked with delight, splashing water over his bare feet.

They crossed a bridge and the road began to steepen, the houses growing bigger and less tightly packed. Some had balconies strewn with prayer flags; many bore signs for hotels and accommodation. They passed a school and a Hindu temple, shoes and flip-flops spilling from its open doors.

And still they walked, up and up, until there were terraced fields all around, donkeys and sheep, and small vegetable crops and houses that were very grand and set back from the road: farmhouses, guesthouses, retreats. Just as they were reaching a densely wooded area above the town, the paved road ended abruptly and they turned left along a well-trodden track, past a sign for the Green Tara.

The guesthouse was a large wooden building tucked into the side of the mountain, tall deodars rising up the slope behind, the Kullu Valley sweeping down in front. Dolma later told Esther that it was modelled on a traditional Tibetan monastery and, similar to a Moroccan *riad*, it had an open courtyard in the centre surrounded by four walls with rooms reached by a covered terrace, the wood dark and intricately carved.

After a quick wash and a change of clothes, Esther and Anne joined the other guests for breakfast in the courtyard, where sunlight flooded the flagstones. There were four long tables sheltered by suspended canopies to guard against the monsoon rain. An elaborate design of interconnecting circles and triangles resembling a Tibetan mandala was carved into the stone floor.

They filled their plates from the buffet table, which offered everything from banana porridge to dhal and rice, as well as fresh fruit and Indian and European breads, and joined a table of other travellers.

'So you're a journalist, Esther?'

Esther took a sip of chai and smiled politely at the woman who had spoken. Short spiky hair, snake tattoo that curled across her chest towards her neck, amber eyes fixed on Esther. 'What are you writing about?'

Esther glanced at Anne across the table, reluctant to be drawn, the conversation with Liam still fresh. Anne put her spoon down and touched a paper napkin to her lips.

'She's my husband's niece. She's here to help me find our son,' she said in that quiet, dignified way she had. The woman with the amber eyes turned her gaze to Anne.

'Where'd he go?'

Anne put her napkin down and blinked at the woman. 'If we knew that we wouldn't be looking for him.'

The woman laughed good-naturedly. 'Sure, stupid question.'

An older woman in a white tunic who was sitting beside Esther paused in peeling an orange. 'He's been missing some time, yes?'

'Seven years,' said Anne, frowning at the table. There was a collective intake of breath from the people sitting near enough to be following the conversation. 'He disappeared from Manali.'

A middle-aged man with dreadlocks running down his back and a Guns N' Roses T-shirt shook his head sadly.

'I met a couple from Dorset here a few years back who'd come to identify their daughter,' he said. 'She'd been at some midsummer festival in the hills. All illegal, of course. Drug overdose and exposure, they reckon. But she'd got lost in the forest and it was some weeks before they found her. Or what was left of her.' He took a bite of *chapati*, chewing thoughtfully before glancing up at the silence that greeted him.

Anne was folding her napkin into small squares. Her face, as always, gave nothing away.

'Jesus, Dave,' muttered a wiry bald man, shaking his head.

'I'm sure that's not what happened to your son,' the amber-eyed woman said softly, patting Anne's hand. 'I read about an Aussie girl who went missing back in the early nineties. Turned up three years later. Just strolled into the Australian embassy in Delhi. Without any shoes. She came all that way without shoes. No explanation where she'd been.'

'There are many people who go missing here,' said the woman in the white tunic. 'I've seen the posters around. Many Westerners, no?' She arched a thin eyebrow and turned to Esther. 'So that is what you're writing about?'

Esther shook her head, glancing at Anne again. But Anne didn't seem to be listening. She reached down under the table for her bag and produced one of the posters of Torran that she carried everywhere. She placed it on the table without speaking. Everyone leant in to peer at Torran's face.

'Handsome lad,' said Dave, smiling at Anne.

'Yes,' she said, eyes on the poster.

There was a short silence, filled with murmured conversations and the clinking of metal spoons. Anne stood and slipped gracefully from the bench, nodding a wordless goodbye before she disappeared up the stairs.

'Tragic,' the bald man said after a moment, motioning with his head to the poster. 'Is there any chance in hell he's still alive?'

Everyone looked at Esther.

'Truthfully? Who knows. There's a possibility he's living out in the mountains somewhere.'

Dave nodded. 'I've heard of people "dropping out" and disappearing to live in communes and ashrams, caves, even. Been happening since the sixties. But I thought that was more common round Goa and Rishikesh. It's all drugs and gangs up here, isn't it?'

'Perhaps both,' Esther said. 'When I interviewed the detective on Torran's case back in the nineties, he told me there were three main reasons Westerners were disappearing in Kullu: hiking accidents, attacks by gangs or bandits, and because they wanted to. The gangs are usually related to the drug scene, sometimes the travellers are too. There're rumours of a foreign mafia controlling large areas of the hash production.'

'Malana cream. Oh, man.' A lazy smile spread across Dave's face and he leant back on the bench, hands resting on his belly. 'Best. High. Ever.'

'That's why Dave makes the pilgrimage every year.' The bald man winked affectionately at Dave, who continued grinning as he nodded back.

'It's the crème de la crème.'

The amber-eyed woman smiled and leant across the table towards Dave. 'I've heard the best stuff is in Malana? I'm heading up in a couple of days.'

Dave nodded. 'They don't call it Malana cream for nothing. But seriously,' he leant forwards and the smile slid from his face. 'You don't want to be going up there alone, Bea. These disappearances, more often than not, are lone travellers getting set upon during a hike, or being drugged by dealers who sell them hash and then rob them and take the hash back when they're comatose – or worse. They're not exactly careful about the dosages.' He glanced at Esther. 'At least that's what I've heard.'

Bea turned to her as well. 'Do you think that's what happened to your cousin?'

'It's a possibility. But he left all his stuff in his hotel room. If he'd been heading to Malana – or somewhere else – to buy drugs, he'd have taken money with him. Or a T-shirt at the very least.'

'He left without a T-shirt?'

'He literally walked out in his fisherman trousers.'

'No shoes?'

'No shoes.'

'What is it with people leaving their shoes behind?' Bea's eyes twinkled.

'That is perhaps the greatest mystery of all.'

The older woman, who'd been listening while she ate her orange, put the last segment down and said, 'So we must conclude he was on a spiritual journey, yes?'

Esther thought about Evie and the Sunshine House and nodded. Around them, people were finishing their breakfast and drifting away. A young Tibetan boy darted from table to table, piling cups and plates into a plastic bucket that was almost as big as him.

The woman was still looking at Esther, the corners of her mouth pinched together. 'But this is not the proper way to go about it,' she said.

There was something combative in her tone, and Esther exchanged a glance with Dave, who rolled his eyes.

The woman carried on, undeterred. 'An ascetic, a renunciate, a spiritual seeker who sheds his old life in search of greater meaning, he must set his old life in order first. You cannot enter the spiritual life without first making peace with your family. If this boy was serious about what he was doing, he would have told his parents about it.'

'Did Siddhartha tell his old man he was leaving?' the bald man asked, taking a tobacco pouch from his pocket and laying it on the table in front of him.

'Or his wife?' Bea added. 'Didn't he just disappear in the night?'

The woman shook her head impatiently. 'Siddhartha made peace with his family, and they followed him. In the end.'

'In the end,' the bald man said. 'Well, maybe this Torran will come back and make peace with everyone once he's enlightened.'

Dave laughed. Reaching for the pouch and helping himself to some papers and tobacco, he pulled a small bag from his pocket and started rolling a joint. 'Picked this myself,' he said happily to no one in particular as he crumbled the dried marijuana leaves between his fingers.

'I think you're wasting your time,' the woman said abruptly, and Dave glanced up, but the woman's eyes were on Esther. 'The mother needs to know, of course. But you: there is so much else you could – *should* – be writing about here instead of wasting your time on one selfish foreigner.'

Esther could feel a pressure building behind her eyes. She opened her mouth to contradict the woman, to tell her she wasn't writing about any of it, but Bea spoke first.

'Funny how it's always men, isn't it? Women are usually too busy being responsible and caring for people to go off on spiritual journeys.'

'Women are the ones she should be writing about.' The woman turned her intense gaze on Bea. Dave lit his joint and leant back to observe them through the smoke. Esther started patting down her pockets and realised she'd left her cigarettes in the room. The bald man pushed his tobacco pouch across the table towards her.

'Female foeticide,' the woman continued, turning back to Esther with her hand raised to count the points as she made them on her fingers. 'Rising – yes, *rising* – dramatically, still, in the twenty-first century. Domestic violence and murder. Rape. Child marriage. *Sati* even.' She looked around the table incredulously.

Bea's eyes widened. 'Where the widow throws herself on her husband's funeral pyre?'

'I'm pretty sure that doesn't happen any more,' Dave said, draining the last of his chai.

'It's against the law, obviously. The last official case was about twenty years ago, but I've read that it still happens sometimes. It was considered a great honour for the woman to sacrifice herself to her husband – she became a sati mother: a pure mother.' She paused, a challenge in her eyes. 'And those are just some of the hazards of being a woman in India. Then there's the thousands of missing children. *Thousands* every year. So forgive me if I think that worrying about one spoilt Westerner who wandered off into the mountains – these notoriously dangerous mountains – is a waste of time.'

That afternoon, after a long nap, Esther went back to sit in the courtyard, where she could observe the Green Tara's residents while furtively scribbling some notes. Anne had disappeared to Dolma's private quarters, and though Esther had been hovering nearby, she hadn't been invited to join them. There was an ease between Anne and Dolma that surprised her; she'd always found Anne so distant, so determined not to let anyone in. But perhaps it was just her. She thought of Liam and the looks that had passed between him and Anne.

There seemed to be a lot of hanging around at the guesthouse. Travellers gathered on the couches of the common room and round the tables in the courtyard, swapping stories, leafing through guidebooks, playing cards, reading well-thumbed novels. Dave and his bald friend were at the same table they'd breakfasted on, smoking and shooting the breeze and for all the world looking like they hadn't moved since morning.

Esther was writing up their earlier conversation when she heard the main door open and saw a Tibetan man of around her own age walk into the courtyard. He had a broad, open face and dark hair that fell to his ears, lips that curled upwards and eyes that were already smiling as he walked towards her.

'Esther?'

She blinked at him in surprise. 'Yes?'

'Dawa Tsering.' He pointed to himself and then extended a hand. 'The guide.'

He spoke with the warmth of an old friend, and she had the disconcerting feeling of having met him before.

'How did you know who I was?'

His smile broadened as he sat down on the bench beside her. 'You look like a journalist.'

'I do?'

He nodded towards the pen and paper. 'Well, you're the only one writing.'

She glanced around. 'Quite the Sherlock Holmes.'

He laughed and his laugh made her want to laugh too. 'And I did look you up online. When Anne said you'd be coming.'

'Ah.' She waited for him to ask about the article, for his expression to harden, but he kept smiling, his gaze so frank and open that she felt awkward and had to look away.

'Is this your first time in India?'

She glanced back at him. 'No, I came when Torran first disappeared.'

'Of course – Anne mentioned that.' He gave her an appraising look, eyes lingering on her bare feet. 'Have you been hiking in the mountains before?'

'I did a Munro once.'

He frowned. 'A Munro?'

'Scotland's answer to the Himalayas.'

Dawa laughed again. 'Glad you came prepared.'

'Always.'

Esther closed her notebook. It had been Robert and Anne who'd dragged her up Ben More all those years ago. Torran must have been there too, though she had no memory of it. She turned back to Dawa.

'Have you known Anne and Robert a long time?'

'Since the first sighting. That was further west. But you'll know we've been searching in this area several times already.'

'Yes. It seems incredible that the Sunshine House could exist and no one know about it.' Esther looked at the ragged peak that towered above the guesthouse and felt a thrill of excitement edged with trepidation.

Dawa lifted his face towards the sun. 'Just wait till we get out there. This is one of the biggest mountain ranges in the world. You'll wonder how anyone who goes in ever comes out again.'

XXV
ANNE

Anne dreamt of Liam and woke with his hot breath in her ear. She turned over and watched the darkness retreat from the room. In her dream she'd been with Torran at Pattack falls, only they'd looked like the Jinsi waterfall in Happy Valley and she'd watched anxiously as Torran climbed higher and higher up the steep rock face.

'Come down!' she'd called. But he hadn't heard her above the water, which sounded more like rain on a hotel roof. 'Torran! Come down!'

She'd tried to run towards him but found she couldn't move. Or that she could but not well, as if her feet were stuck in deep mud. She'd looked up again and seen Torran was nearly at the top of the waterfall.

'Torran!' she'd called again and this time he'd turned and for a brief moment their eyes locked, and then he was climbing once more, higher and higher, and he should have been at the top but the rock face seemed to expand as he went. And when he cried out she thought he was falling but then she realised he'd seen something. Looking in the direction of his outstretched finger, she saw a flash of colour, purple and blue, and it was the sunbird swooping through the falls, and Torran was reaching and reaching to try and touch it, but it was already gone.

She'd watched as Torran lost his balance and fell, and she couldn't move at all, couldn't cry or scream but only watch as he tumbled down, limp body dashing against the rocks, crumpling as it hit the ground.

Suddenly released, she'd run to him, but when she turned the prone figure over it wasn't Torran at all. It was Liam. And he'd smiled, eyes heavy with desire, and reached up and pulled her to him.

Now fully awake, she sat up and flicked the switch on the wall beside her, letting the stark light wash away the feeling of Liam on her skin. She checked her watch. It was just after six. She could hear a murmur of voices from the neighbouring room: Esther and Dolma. She wondered if they were talking about her. She knew Dolma was worried about the turning season and the temperamental weather, about the dangers of such a long and gruelling trek. If the Sunshine House was where Dawa thought, it would take them at least three days to reach it. But Anne felt strangely calm about the journey ahead. Did she believe they would find the Sunshine House and that her son would be there? She honestly didn't know. She had to go, and time, it seemed, was against them, but she couldn't allow her thoughts to journey too far ahead.

She thought about the dream; now that it was at a safe distance, the feeling of it dissipated. It wasn't the dream itself that unsettled her – whatever a psychoanalyst might say. It was that for the first time in seven years, Torran had not been the person she most wanted to see when she opened her eyes.

XXVI

BEFORE

Confidence in motherhood never comes. Like so much else that she thought would get easier: marriage, Taigh na Criege, life. She keeps hoping that when the next hurdle is passed things will settle down and she will feel in control. But there is no comfort in a present too immense to tame. She knows she isn't a bad mother, but she isn't sure she is a good one either.

And still Torran thrives. The endless crying behind him, he is a mountain goat, scaling walls and clambering along the rocky coast. He teaches himself to swim in the sea while her back is turned. He climbs to the top of every peak within walking distance of Taigh na Criege and then he badgers Anne to drive him to the base of Ben More, Dùn da Ghaoithe, Beinn Fhada. By the time he starts secondary school he is already taking himself off on solo camping trips, although Anne never lets him go so far that she can't see the smoke from his campfire rising in the sky.

He worships his father and spends days following him around, suggesting ideas for the children's stories Robert is churning out with astonishing speed. Robert reads him books set in faraway places: the *Just So Stories*, *Arabian Nights*, *Aesop's Fables*. They construct Bedouin tents in the living room and drink sweetened tea from patterned glasses. Robert talks endlessly about his early travels in Turkey and Morocco, his plan to drive his old van all the way to India. *But then I met your mother and everything changed.* And he looks at Anne over their son's head and smiles and sometimes she smiles back, and sometimes she doesn't.

Torran brushes his teeth twice a day and she makes sure he eats his vegetables and wears clean socks. She hides her disappointment when he refuses to learn an instrument, drives him to football and drama club, to hang out with his mates, to see Fiona. She soaks his clothes overnight when he comes home covered in mud and sand; she mends the holes he's always getting in the elbows of his jumpers and the knees of his jeans. When he's sick or upset or over-tired, she sits by his bed and sings to him, her cool hand on his forehead, and she tries not to ask herself what it's all for.

XXVII

ESTHER

The driver left them in Jari, at the Malana taxi stand, and they stood in the early light, adjusting their packs and readying themselves for the hike.

It was another beautiful day. A clear sky and the sun's rays cutting through the heavy blue light which lingered over the trees and hills, the last whispers of night.

At the beginning of the path they encountered a small gathering of guides and porters, a handful of tethered ponies swishing flies with their tails. The men had been sitting on plastic chairs, smoking and muttering quietly, but they jumped to their feet when they saw the three hikers, calling out prices, routes and excursions, their words jarring in the hushed air. A three-legged dog with matted fur limped over to see what the fuss was about. The ponies stamped their feet on the loose earth, sending up clouds of dust.

Dawa approached the men with a placating gesture. He spoke in Hindi, but the gist of his words was clear from the annoyed and cajoling reactions of the would-be guides. Dawa continued to talk over their protests, the smile never leaving his face. The man with the ponies spat on the ground and went back to his chair. A gaunt man with a bushy moustache turned to Anne, offering her a better price than whatever she'd agreed with Dawa, offering to carry her bag. She shook her head firmly as he reached to offload her pack. Dawa said something sharply, and the men backed off muttering and casting dark looks over their shoulders.

They were a few minutes down the track when the thin man with the moustache caught up, calling to Anne.

'Lady, excuse me. Madam!' Anne kept walking but Esther glanced over, and he came up beside her, uncomfortably close. Dawa shouted something back at him, but the man dismissed it with a shake of his head. Esther quickened her steps, but so did he, his breath sour and intimate as he leant towards her.

'You must to be careful,' he said, keeping his voice low. 'Better you turn around. Or take proper guide. This is no good place.'

Esther glanced over again, despite knowing she should ignore him.

'Very danger,' he said, dark eyes fixing on hers. 'The hills here very danger. No place for women with one guide only who is not good local guide.' He reached long fingers to her elbow, gripping it painfully and forcing her to stop. They stood facing each other. 'What you know about this man?' He motioned to Dawa, who was pulling further ahead, Anne right behind him. Esther felt a flicker of panic; soon they'd be out of sight in the trees, and she supressed the urge to call out.

The man's fingers were digging into her arm. She pulled away from him and started walking after the others.

The man didn't move. 'You should listen to me.' There was something low and dangerous in his tone, and she stopped, half turning back to where he stood. 'There are people disappearing in these mountains. *Firangis*. Foreigns. Not everyone who goes in comes back out.'

Esther wavered, willing her legs to move again but somehow unable to turn away.

'You have heard the stories,' the man continued, something sly creeping into his voice. 'But you think won't happen to you. Everyone always think it will not be happening to them.'

He held her gaze and for the first time she felt genuinely afraid. She was about to ask him – what, she wasn't sure – when Dawa appeared at her side, his hand steady on her shoulder.

'Come on, Esther,' he said, voice kind but firm.

The man shrugged as Dawa guided her away, up the path towards Anne, but his smile was menacing. And when Esther glanced over her shoulder a few moments later, he was still standing there, staring after them.

They walked in single file, eyes on the trail. For the first hour they climbed steeply through dense forest, damp and fragrant with bark and earth. Roots twisted underfoot and branches snagged them as they passed, trying to hold them back. The earlier encounter had left Esther shaken, half afraid the man would follow them. But the further they went, the brighter the sun, the less credence she gave his words, and she pushed her unease aside.

They didn't talk much, but Dawa paused now and then, pointing to a quivering flash of colour where a hummingbird hovered, the faint tracks of a musk deer, the red and yellow smattering of mushrooms beneath a dead tree. He was knowledgeable and enthusiastic, and beside him it was easier for Esther to forget her fears. To forget, even, why they were there.

As they climbed, the trees thinned and after a while they were in the open, the path losing itself in knee-high grass, meandering round lone trees and piles of rock. From these open spaces they could see the mountain rising up ahead and the reach of the valley below, the Malana river curving in and out of sight in a rush of white and blue.

It was noon before they encountered anyone. Sitting under the shade of a cedar, eating the roti and dhal Dolma had packed for them, they heard the clink of bells before a shepherd and his goats appeared. Dressed in a long tunic with a grey blanket draped across his shoulders, he had the face of one who has spent a lifetime under the open sky. He raised a hand in acknowledgement as he approached.

Dawa called out to him in what Esther took to be Kullui, a local dialect of the region, and the man responded with a nod and a few words. Dawa got to his feet and went over, offering a roti from the food bag. The man accepted it wordlessly and together they sat on a boulder and began to talk. The goats fanned out to graze around them and the man's dog, a well-fed shaggy thing, watched closely from his master's feet, tongue out and panting.

Esther and Anne had finished their food and were standing in preparation to continue when Dawa returned, waving his farewell to the shepherd, who was already moving off down the slope with his herd.

'He doesn't take his animals that far north,' Dawa told them as they set out once more, slower now that the heat of the day was upon them. 'But he knows a nomadic tribe who have spoken of a house of foreigners before. A place known as the Sunshine Valley.'

Esther exchanged a glance with Anne.

'He can't tell me where exactly, but he agreed it's likely in the area we've been told. There are many valleys there, but with that name, the river, the vegetation – I think we have the right one.'

'That's good, then.' Anne spoke quietly, as if to herself, but Dawa answered.

'Yes, it is good. But he also told me there has been a lot going on in the region. A lot of change. A lot of tourists. There have been attacks.'

'But that's been going on for years.'

'It's getting worse.'

Anne didn't respond and they continued in silence, the sun beating down, the cry of a blue magpie piercing the sky.

They reached Malana by mid-afternoon, as their shadows were beginning to lengthen. The village was quiet. Its houses, with their ornately carved wrap-around verandas, were steeped in shadows. It was like entering a world time had forgotten. Tibetan prayer flags strung up around a small *stupa* cast their devotions to the wind.

Dawa led them through a narrow street, the houses clustered closely together as if leaning in to whispered conversations.

A black goat bleated loudly and came trotting over, pink tongue vibrating with every cry.

They paused in a small square, looking around at the buildings and the high mountains rising sharply behind. A voice called from the darkness of a doorway and an old man, bent under the weight of years, made his slow way towards them. He wore a colourful tunic and a flat hat over wispy white hair.

Dawa went to meet him and the two men stood and talked for several minutes, the elder gesticulating and laughing animatedly, but also pointing at Esther and Anne and shaking his head.

A few minutes later, as they followed Dawa out of the square, he told them that the man had given his permission for them to enter the village and stay the night, but had said that they must touch neither the local people nor their possessions.

'It's a big problem for them if you do,' Dawa said, smiling at Esther's expression. 'They believe it will make them impure and they'd have to sacrifice a goat to purify themselves again.'

They followed a twisting alley upwards to reach a bright guesthouse set slightly above the rest of the village. It was more modern than most of the houses, and although it had the ubiquitous balcony running its full length, it did not include the beautiful carvings that set the traditional buildings apart. It had recently been painted in bold rainbow stripes and a garish banner proclaiming *Hotel Cafe Shangri-Laa!* hung over the facade. A group of travellers were sitting on the balcony, the smell of joints floating down to greet them.

Inside, the cafe part of the hotel was dimly lit with Moroccan lamps and had a cushion-covered floor. Indian textiles decorated the walls and ceilings, blue and grey patterned elephants and camels printed in ever-decreasing circles. From hidden speakers, Bob Marley and the Wailers were remembering Trench Town. Two long-haired travellers lay in one corner smoking a chillum. A bespectacled young man, who would have been more at home in an Oxford cloister, sat as far away from the smoking bodies as he could, scribbling importantly in a notebook, stopping only to push up his glasses when they slipped forwards.

'If you've seen one hippie hangout in India, you've seen them all,' Esther murmured. Anne didn't respond but Dawa caught Esther's eye and smiled.

They stood awkwardly for a moment, waiting for someone to acknowledge their presence, and then a door behind them burst open and a surprisingly young, clean-shaven man bounced into the room, bringing a big smile and a lot of barely suppressed energy with him.

'Hello! Hello-hello!' He spoke so loudly that the bespectacled boy jumped. 'Good day. May I present myself? Taj. Your most gracious, ever-at-your-service host. I am ever so warmly welcoming you to Shangri-Laa!' And he spread his arms wide, as if beckoning them into the kingdom of heaven.

They agreed to meet back in the guesthouse restaurant for dinner before dispersing to their rooms on the first floor, which were accessed externally, via the balcony, oddly reminiscent of an American motel. Esther's room was at the far corner, with double-aspect windows looking down over the village and out across the mountains. A few of the distant peaks were already dusted in snow.

The room was simply furnished apart from a photo of Audrey Hepburn hanging above the bed, smiling coyly at the Dalai Lama, whose portrait was next to the door. Someone had carved their initials in the wood of the windowsill, and underneath someone else had written *The road to Shangri-La lies within.* Esther ran a finger along the wood, skin snagging on the grooves of the carved letters. There was another message on the side of the window frame in black biro: *Shangri-La is the journey not the destination.* Beside it someone had scrawled *Fuck off.*

She turned from the window and sat on the bed. It was almost five and she knew she should try to head out again before dinner. They'd be travelling on at first light, and she wanted to get a feel for the place, to talk to people and try to make some notes. Malana was a village of myths and legends, its people claiming to be descendants of Alexander the Great, their self-governing democracy believed to be one of the oldest in the world. She leant back against the damp pillow and closed her eyes, hearing again the guide's warnings, the woman at the Green Tara and her challenge to write about the things that really mattered. Esther was still trying to decide what those things might be, and whether she should be afraid of the journey ahead, when she fell into a dreamless sleep.

XXVIII

ANNE

Anne left the Shangri-Laa and made her way back towards the village. There were no cars, of course, the village being entirely cut off. The streets were narrow and largely made of compact earth and rocks with only occasional bits of paving. A deep trench ran down the middle, presumably to act as a run-off for monsoon rains and snowmelt. It was dry now but filled with litter, red packets of Lays crisps and the peel-like string of plastic confectionary wrappers, crumpled bottles, a broken flip-flop. The garish colours of the modern world were jarring among the dark beams and walls adorned with decorated yak horns, covered porches piled high with firewood. But even amid the prayer flags Anne saw the round moon of a satellite dish, pointing to the heavens.

She found a small rooftop restaurant just off the main square, plastic tables and chairs arranged on an open terrace. After ordering a chai, she sat at the only free table, enjoying the anonymity of being surrounded by strangers. In Mussoorie everyone had known who she was, sooner or later, even the visitors. But people's sympathy was comforting and suffocating in equal measure.

The sun hung low, burnishing the side of a far-off mountain, turning the sky purple and gold. She was already wearing a fleece over her hiking shirt, and she could feel the temperature was about to plummet with the setting sun. It would be good to feel really cold again. Woolly hat and extra blanket on the bed cold. Rob used to call her a salamander, not thinking how she might take being referred to as cold-blooded. He didn't always consider what he was saying; for a writer, he could be surprisingly careless with words.

A small bird with a long tail landed soundlessly on the terrace rail, cocking its head and peering at her with one black eye. She gazed back. The downy feathers rippled with every movement. It turned its head and regarded her with its other eye, hopped from foot to foot and dived down towards the street before rising sharply skywards, vanishing behind the smoke from a neighbouring chimney.

She thought of Liam, his hands when they sketched, movements quick and sure, the complete focus on his face while conjuring birds on the page. She would have told him about that bird; they'd have looked it up in his book, sitting side by side in the sunroom, heads bent together, arms and thighs touching.

She was walking back towards the guesthouse, the fading light infused with woodsmoke, when she passed three young travellers standing in front of a particularly grand-looking house. A thickset man stood in the doorway, shouting and waving his arms aggressively. The group were huddled together as if for protection, glancing at each other nervously.

Anne considered walking by, but they were so young. And they were frightened.

'Is everything OK?' she asked.

The younger girl turned teary eyes towards her.

'I don't know what he's saying,' she whispered while the man continued, his voice belligerent in the quiet street. His accent was thick and not everything he said was recognisable as English, although Anne caught the odd word – a tirade of anger and blame which was impossible to make sense of.

Anne steered the girl towards the shadows of the opposite house. The girl's arm trembled under her fingers like the bird on the railing.

'What happened?' She kept her voice low. Across from them, the boy in the group, tall with a shaved head and the broken skin of puberty still on his face, tried to speak, but this only incensed the man, who seemed to swell in size as his voice grew louder. Thinking of the rumours of magic and miracles in these hills, Anne imagined him bursting into flames or growing to the size of the house, like Alice in Wonderland.

When she got no response she left the girl and returned to where an older girl stood beside the boy. Pushing between them, she took an elbow each and quietly told them to apologise and walk away. Both began to protest but she was firm. No good could come of this. The girl relented and, muttering an apology, stalked off to join her friend on the other side of the road. Several people had stopped to watch; a skinny boy with big ears was leaning against the man's house and grinning.

'Come on,' Anne told the young man, who was stubbornly holding his ground. She put a hand on his chest to push him away and felt the tension in his body. He brushed her aside and went straight towards the man, as if to strike him.

'Listen, man,' he was shouting. 'We only asked for your help. We just need your help.'

The man shouted back, his words incomprehensible.

Anne grabbed the boy's shirt before he could climb the steps to the house and cause further trouble.

'No.' Something in her voice made him pause, and that was all she needed to stop his forward momentum and drag him away.

'They're sorry,' she said over her shoulder to the man, raising a placatory hand. 'They're young. They didn't mean to cause offence.'

The man shouted something in response, spittle flying as he turned back to his house and slammed the door.

Standing in the gloaming, the two girls both crying and the boy breathing heavily beside her, Anne looked from face to face.

'What was that about?'

'My brother,' the younger girl said, her American accent taking Anne by surprise – the other two sounded German. 'He's missing. He went trekking with his girlfriend and they haven't come back. It's been five days—'

'We were just trying to get someone to help us,' the other girl cut in.

'Dickhead,' the boy added, glaring at the closed door. But Anne could see the fight dissipating in his sloping shoulders.

'OK,' she said, putting an arm around the younger girl. 'It's OK. We'll get help. Everything will be all right.' And she sounded so confident that she almost believed it herself.

Dawa and Esther were waiting in the dining room, seated at a table by the window. It was dark outside now, the room's cheerful reflection superimposed over the lights of the village below. Anne ushered the young travellers over and Dawa jumped up to find them extra chairs. Esther shot a questioning look at Anne before smiling at the new arrivals.

It took a while for the full story to emerge. Lara – the American – kept bursting into tears and the narrative had to be picked up by her companions, a couple from Munich who kept lapsing into German, arguing over details. As they talked, Anne noticed Esther slip a notebook from her bag and quietly begin to take notes.

Five days earlier, Lara's brother and his girlfriend had set out on an overnight hike to a lake further up the Parvati Valley; they still hadn't returned. They'd gone alone, hiring a tent and camping gear, with enough food to last two days, three at a stretch.

'But not five,' the boy said flatly. 'And we hiked there yesterday – there are no villages or supply shacks en route. There is nothing.' He shook his head.

Lara closed her eyes, tears sliding down her cheeks. 'I just want to go home,' she said, and the German girl put an arm around her. 'I hate it here. I wish we'd never come.'

'We don't know what to do.' The German girl looked at Anne. 'We don't know if it's better to wait or go back to Manali and get help. There are no phones here. We went to ask that man for help – he's a town elder – but you saw how that went.'

'What are you writing?' The boy was looking at Esther, a finger worrying an old acne scar on his cheek.

'I'm a journalist,' Esther said, glancing up. 'The more information we get now, the quicker the police will be able to respond when you get to them.'

'You're coming with us?'

Esther glanced at Anne. 'I'll write it up for you tonight and you can take it with you tomorrow.'

'Where are we going tomorrow?' Lara's voice was very small and Anne could see her retreating into herself.

Around them, the dining room was filling up. There was a communality among the travellers in this last outpost; strangers greeted each other warmly as they sat down. The thin boy with spectacles from earlier sat in a corner on his own, placing a book on the table in front of him, like a shield. The ever-smiling Taj was dashing in and out of the kitchen, delivering trays of bottled Cola and Thums Up, taking food orders and chatting ceaselessly. Anne watched him unload a tray piled high with bowls of rice and vegetable curry and remembered she hadn't eaten since Dolma's dhal and rotis all those hours before. She wished she could slip away, with some food, and be alone.

'At least one of you needs to get back down to the nearest police checkpoint first thing tomorrow.' Esther was writing out a check-list as she spoke. 'Someone needs to stay put in case they turn up or there's any news. You should get flyers printed. The police will arrange a proper search once you've notified them. You need to call your parents. And the American consulate in Delhi.'

Anne watched the panic in Lara's eyes turn to numb disbelief. She knew too well the seasickness of a world once taken for granted spinning out of control. The paralysis of so much to do with no guarantee that anything would help.

Anne and Esther stood together on the balcony, pausing on the way to bed. The sky was black with only a smattering of stars, the faint glow of the village reflected on low-lying cloud. The air was sharp, burning their lungs with a hint of snow at the brink of each breath.

Esther turned to Anne. 'Perhaps we should delay our trip a few days. See if we can help?'

Lara and her companions had been persuaded to go to bed; there was nothing more they could do until first light. And people had rallied – as they always did – with such willing kindness it made Anne want to weep. Taj would accompany the girls down the mountain while the German boy stayed behind and organised another search. Even the bespectacled young man had offered to handwrite posters until some could be printed in Manali. It was still early enough for people to believe in a positive outcome and the mood when they left the dining room had been relatively upbeat.

Anne didn't say anything, and Esther lit a cigarette, leaning over the railing to blow smoke into the night. Her pose – almost as if she were contemplating leaping off – reminded Anne of Liam the night of the storm, and she realised she missed him. It was a strange feeling, to have a space inside that unfolded and made room for something which wasn't sorrow or fear or Torran. But it was fragile, this longing, the ache and pleasure of it, the way it quivered in her chest like a sparrow.

'I'm not suggesting we don't go,' Esther continued. 'I just wonder if we could be more use here. For now.'

Anne closed her eyes briefly. 'You're free to do what you want, Esther – it wouldn't be the first time. But I can't afford to delay this. Not now.' The tiredness she'd felt earlier was throbbing in her temples. Why had she allowed Esther to come? She still didn't know.

Esther shifted to look at her, but Anne couldn't read her expression. The dim light from the bedroom windows only deepened the shadows. Taking a long inhale, Esther blew the smoke upwards so that it drifted away like a rising spirit.

'I'm not suggesting delaying for long,' she said at last, and Anne could hear frustration in her voice. 'I want to find Torran too. But if this Sunshine House does exist – and if he's actually there – a day or two won't make a difference.'

After all Esther's insistence that they had no time to lose, that Evie had told her repeatedly how time was critical and they must hurry. Anne tried to see the mountains' outline, thinking of the snow that already lingered on their peaks and how the weather could turn in the blink of an eye.

'It could make all the difference,' she said.

'Fine.' Esther moved so that she was no longer in the shadows. 'We can leave in the morning. Let the kids fend for themselves.'

'They're not fending for themselves. You've given them a twenty-point plan. We've organised search parties. They'll reach the police tomorrow.' Anne could hear her voice rising and she turned away from Esther to look back down at the lights of the village, her grip tight on the rail. 'And we need to get to the valley before the snow.'

'You sound like you think we're going to find something,' Esther said, after a pause.

Did she? Anne would have said she'd grown too cynical for that, and yet here she still was. 'I don't know what to think. But if we don't go now, we miss our chance to find out. It's as simple as that.'

Esther finished her cigarette and leant back against the rail. 'It just seems a bit cruel to desert them. When you've been through the same thing. I wonder what Robert would do if he were here.'

'Don't start, Esther.'

'Start what?' she said, and for a moment Anne was back at Taigh na Criege, a teenage Esther pushing her to see where she might break. When she didn't respond, Esther sighed. 'I'm just saying, Lara's young, they all are, and these days are crucial to finding them. We could really help.' She paused, casting a sideways glance at Anne. 'And you don't seem to care.'

'No.' Anne knew she was being baited but she couldn't stop the anger from shaking her voice. 'No. Not this time.' Esther took a step back, her eyes reflecting light. She put up a placatory hand, but Anne kept talking. 'You sit there and you write us all out like we're some characters in your story.'

Esther's eyes widened. 'I'm not even—'

But Anne carried on over her. 'And when you're not actually writing I see you doing it in your head. I see you watching and judging and trying to figure people out, being so friendly and sharing things so they'll share things with you. But it's not a fair exchange because you're stealing from us. You're taking our thoughts and experiences and keeping them to use later. To use against us. You've always judged me, Esther. Even as a little girl. I'm done with it. And I'm leaving in the morning. With or without you.'

Back in her room, heart still beating in her ears, Anne put her hands next to the electric heater and let the hot air ease the stiffness in her joints. She was trembling, from the cold or adrenaline, she couldn't tell. Seeing again Esther's face, the shock at Anne's outburst and yes, the hurt as well. But that was the problem with Esther. Despite what Anne had said, despite the apparent calculation with which Esther acted and spoke, the tough exterior, Anne recognised a fellow performer stumbling through a part that ought to come naturally, terrified the audience will see right through it.

She sat on the bed and changed her socks, rubbing the heat back into her toes. Leaning against the pillow, she opened her book but found herself staring at the words without taking them in, her mind turning instead to the beaming faces of the missing hikers in the last picture Lara had of them. Wondering if that would be the photo which would come to haunt their parents' waking dreams. And she thought of those parents, going about their lives with no notion of the calamity already hanging over their heads. They would never be the same again, however this ended. They would never sleep with quite the same ease, or wave goodbye without hesitation. Today's worries would be insignificant tomorrow. Because things were probably OK now, but they would never be OK again.

Still, she envied them their ignorance. Those last precious hours where the ringing phone and the ticking clock remained as innocuous as the first ray of sun stealing over the horizon.

XXIX

BEFORE

He cries all the time. He has colic and won't keep milk down. Anne has no one to call and ask what she should do. He won't sleep unless he is strapped to her chest or in his car seat in the back of the car, driving around. He needs to be in constant motion. And his need for her is insatiable.

She follows the island's single-track roads, playing an old tape of Elgar's cello concertos until his wail turns to a whimper and he falls quiet. If Anne tries to park the car too soon, he wakes and starts screaming. Sometimes she doesn't have the energy to risk it and drives for hours, glazed eyes watching the road unfurl like a ribbon. There is no separation; she doesn't know where he ends and she begins.

Robert fades in and out like the turning tide. He is writing his second novel and has a deadline and often she wakes to feed Torran and finds they are alone, the light from Rob's study throwing shadows down the hall. His world is expanding as hers is shrinking. And in the background, she is aware of Esther's shadow, slipping unnoticed from room to room. Yet when she tries to focus on the young girl, her mind goes blank.

But there are moments of wonder too. The surprise of laughter; the first stumbling steps. She plays the cello and for once Torran doesn't cry or try to crawl away. He sits and watches her and claps clumsy hands when she's done. They collect seashells and marble-flecked pebbles. They pick blackberries from the garden wall and watch the chickens peck at the dark earth.

*

And one day in autumn, when he is two years old, she drives through the rain to the grassy area above Loch na Keal and parks facing the water. She watches the clouds push the rain into its opaque surface. Torran is wailing, his small hands clenched in impotent rage. She turns up the music until it drowns the endless rain and Torran's cries. She closes her eyes and she is on stage again, her cello in her arms, and the music is all there is. When she starts the car her hand pauses over the gearstick; her foot hesitates on the brake. And the rain falls on the water. Falls and falls and falls.

It is nothing and it is everything. Anne waits until Torran is asleep in the middle of their double bed. A full moon peeps through the space between the curtains, tracing a silver path across the room. He had been crying for three hours while she tried everything to soothe him. Now he smiles in his sleep, tiny hands clasped together, as she pulls on a jumper and picks up the bag she has hidden on the shelf in the wardrobe. She is shaking with adrenaline and exhaustion. She leaves the door open so Robert will hear Torran if he wakes.

At the top of the stairs she hesitates, her eyes on the light that spills across the floor from the open door of Rob's study. She can hear the stop and start of the typewriter, as familiar to her days as the waves breaking on the rocks. The door to Esther's room is closed and she briefly considers checking on her, but the hinges squeak and she doesn't want to wake her, or rouse Robert.

It is a cold November night, lit in eerie shadows. Anne starts the car, winces as the engine splutters. In the rear-view mirror she watches the light from Rob's study grow smaller and smaller as she drives away.

XXX

ANNE

When Anne went downstairs the next morning, Esther and Dawa were already waiting, sharing a cigarette on the guesthouse steps, watching as the early morning mist dissipated to reveal a still sleeping village. Somewhere unseen a cockerel was crowing.

Dawa stood when he caught sight of Anne, passing the cigarette back to Esther, and Anne wondered what they'd been talking about. She and Rob had hired Dawa on numerous occasions over the years, and though she was very fond of him, though she'd come to rely on his quiet efficiency and impressive knowledge of the region, she couldn't remember ever having had a real conversation with him. One that didn't revolve around the route or the weather or some other practicality. But that was Esther for you, ever the journalist, charming people until they opened up. Still, Anne envied the ease with which Esther found common ground when she herself seemed to struggle with even the most superficial of conversations.

Esther stubbed out the cigarette on the stone step and stood up as well, tying her wild hair in a knot at the top of her head, a few loose curls tumbling out. She turned a tight smile towards Anne, the evening's exchange clearly not forgotten.

Dawa hoisted on his pack. He was carrying at least twice as much as them but had refused to distribute the provisions more evenly. 'Ready?'

Anne nodded, adjusting the straps on her rucksack and taking her hiking poles from where she'd left them by the door.

'Ready.'

*

They didn't see a soul as they walked through the narrow streets, crossing the main square to join a trail that climbed steeply out of the village.

In less than an hour they were looking back at the tiled roofs, small and vulnerable now, far below them, white smoke rising from chimney stacks and prayer flags fluttering. Dawa handed round rolled chapatis spread thickly with jam and they shared a thermos of coffee. Anne curled her fingers around the heat of the plastic cup and breathed it in.

A stray dog had followed them out of the village and now she flopped in the dirt at Dawa's feet. He prodded her gently with his toe and said something in Tibetan. The dog cocked an ear but didn't move, saliva dripping from her open mouth. A tan-coloured mongrel of some sort, she was one of those dogs that was always smiling. Tessa was like that too.

'Do you think she'll follow us all the way?' Esther said, leaning over to scratch the dog behind her ears.

Dawa shook his head. 'We don't have enough food to share. She'll go back when she gets hungry.'

'Shame.' Esther stroked her under the chin and the dog gazed up at her with adoring eyes. 'I'll share my food with you, you beautiful creature.'

Dawa laughed. 'You British and your dogs. You treat them like gods.'

Malana had been out of sight for several hours when they reached the chai shack, perched precariously on a steep ledge yet sheltered by the cliff face above. A wooden hut which looked completely run-down from the outside, a patchwork of wood and corrugated iron, but inside was clean and surprisingly spacious, with a wood burner and several sheepskin-covered chairs, a few small tables, some benches. There was a rudimentary kitchen, metal cups and plates stacked neatly on a shelf, and a wonky ladder that led to a mezzanine platform, presumably where someone slept.

A sign above the door read: *Be Ever Welcome to the Last Chance Saloon.*

The place was dark when they entered, the only light coming from the open doorway and several gaps in the shutters. There was no one there. Dawa walked back outside and called for the others to join him, indicating a piece of paper nailed to the door frame.

Gone out. Back in ten minutes. Pleased to be making yourself at home. Thank you.

Esther laughed. 'Where on earth do you go for ten minutes out here?'

Dawa went back inside to see if he could find something cold to drink and Anne and Esther sank gratefully on to a low bench. The sun blazed high in a cloudless sky and the shade of the hut's roof offered welcome relief. Esther fussed with her laces, eventually easing off her boots while Anne watched a pair of buzzards dive and swoop in the valley far below.

'You should take yours off too,' Esther said, speaking directly to Anne for the first time that day. 'Let them breathe a bit. Dawa says it helps with blisters.' She looked at Anne expectantly, and when she didn't reply, Esther sighed. 'Look, I'm sorry about last night.'

Anne was careful not to show her surprise. The sun had brought the freckles out across Esther's nose, softening her sharp features. She was only nine years older than Torran; young enough to be Anne's daughter.

'Just last night?' she said, turning back to the valley.

Esther reached into her pack for her cigarettes. 'I was never going to let you go alone. I promised Robert I'd look after you. And that's what I'm trying to do.' She took a cigarette from the pack but didn't light it, rolling it instead across her fingers, back and forth. There was a tremor in her voice and Anne turned to her, sensing she wanted to say more, but before Esther could continue Dawa emerged from inside the hut, triumphantly brandishing three bottles of Fanta.

Dawa left ten rupees in the kitchen, and they were just preparing to leave when a man appeared further up the path,
making his way towards them. The dog barked and bounded
over to meet him. He was small and wiry with a big smile, hair
smoothed back with oil, a red thread looped through a gold
band hanging loosely round his neck, an abundance of energy
manifested in quick birdlike movements. He was already talking when he reached them: expressing his delight that they had
come; that they had found something cold to drink on this hot
hot day; most insistent that they drink more, eat something,
stay the night. His smile didn't waver as they apologised, they
were sorry but they couldn't, they had to keep going.

'But you must have something.'

'Really, we can't.' Anne's eyes were already on the mountains
ahead.

'But I absolutely insist.'

Dawa gestured towards the path. 'We have far to go today.
But we can stop on the way back.'

The man sighed, as if it were quite the imposition to have
to wait.

'There *is* something you could do for us,' Anne said, turning
her attention back to him. She rummaged in the side pocket
of her pack and drew out a crumpled poster. 'We're looking
for this man. He went missing seven years ago, so he probably
looks very different now. Perhaps you've seen him before,' she
added, watching the man's face closely as he took the poster
from her and studied it.

'Yes, this is ringing my bell. But . . . no. Maybe just from the
posters. There are posters in Malana, yes?'

'Yes.' Anne forced herself to smile. 'Yes, of course. You
would have seen them around.'

The man nodded apologetically. 'I can put this with the others?'

'The others?'

'Yes, the others. My friends.' He turned towards his shack. 'We
keep each other company here.' He closed the door, revealing

at least seven missing person posters in various states of decay. The most recent appeared to be a Dutch national who had disappeared while camping on the Chandrakhani Pass the previous summer. Anne stepped forwards for a closer look. All the names were familiar to her and she presumed they were to Esther as well.

'This boy is your son?' He held the poster with the utmost care, for which Anne found herself irrationally grateful. She nodded and the man nodded back. 'I will put him with the others. And when you come back, I will make you food. You are all most welcome here at the Last Chance Saloon.'

As they turned to go the man called after them, rocking on the balls of his feet, one hand in the air. 'What are your good names if you please?'

And as they introduced themselves, he shook each of their hands in turn, repeating their names under his breath. 'I am Danny,' he said finally, with an elaborate bow.

'Danny?'

'Yes. Danny the Champion of the World.' He grinned, and his face was eclipsed by his smile. 'My father was number one big fan of your Mr Roald Dahl.'

XXXI

ESTHER

They reached camp by late afternoon, eyes narrowed against a pale sun sinking towards the horizon. Dawa was happy with the weather and happy with their progress; he'd turned back to them frequently during the long day to smile his encouragement.

The camp was on the far side of a broad plateau, sheltered beneath a sharp rise that they would climb the following morning. A glacial stream bordered the site, providing water and a welcome break from the monotonous silence of the plain.

The dog was still with them, and she watched as they set up camp, lying by an old firepit with her head between her paws. Dawa filled their water bottles from the stream and then, with a sideways glance at Esther and Anne, poured some into a metal food bowl and placed it in front of the dog, scratching her ears and muttering something to her under his breath.

There were no trees around the camp, save for a few scrubby alders growing sideways against the rocks. But Dawa knew the site well, and once they'd pitched the tents he jumped the stream and disappeared around a pile of boulders, which had long ago tumbled down the escarpment, in search of firewood. They had a gas stove, but Dawa wanted to save the fuel; soon they'd be too high in the tundra for trees to grow.

Anne disappeared into the tent, and Esther sat with the dog on a flat rock by the stream, looking out at the empty plain and the path they'd followed, cutting through the grass like a snake. Behind her, to the north, were the mountains still to climb, and back across the plain, to the south, were the mountains they'd climbed that day. Small and inconsequential seeming now, though they'd been hard won. Every muscle in her body ached and the tobacco from her cigarette thrummed pleasantly through her blood. She stroked the dog, glancing over her shoulder towards the place where Dawa had disappeared.

They'd met no one all day, aside from Danny at the Last Chance Saloon, but more than once she'd sensed movement on the periphery of her vision, had turned just in time to imagine she'd seen a head disappearing beneath a rise or ducking behind a rock. And several times the dog had stopped dead, nose in the air, and barked, eyes fixed on something she couldn't see. Even now, looking out at so much empty space, Esther had the uneasy feeling of being watched.

'It's the mountains,' Dawa said later, as they sat around the fire, faces ghostly in the flickering light.

Esther glanced at Anne, huddled in her blanket, staring intently at the flames. Dawa poked the fire with a stick, shifting in his seat. He had his hat pulled low over his brow, collar turned up so all Esther could see of him were his eyes and high cheekbones.

'The locals believe they are full of spirits – of gods and ghosts.'

'Are they different things?' Anne asked.

'Perhaps not.'

Esther turned to Anne, surprised. 'Do you believe in ghosts? In gods and spirits?'

She didn't reply and Esther looked to Dawa, who tilted his head and narrowed his eyes, as if listening to another voice around the fire, one that she couldn't hear. She glanced behind her into the blackness.

'Maybe they are all the same. Just different ways to talk about the same thing.'

'Rob thought he saw Torran once,' Anne said. 'He didn't tell me at the time. He thought it was Torran's spirit returning home, like people used to see the ghosts of loved ones return during the war. That's why he's so convinced Torran is dead. He gave up. Sometimes I think it was just an excuse to give up.'

'He saw what he wanted to see,' Esther said.

Anne looked at her sharply. 'Why would he want to see his son's ghost?'

'There are many legends of the gods who inhabit these regions,' Dawa cut in before Esther could respond, breaking the tension. 'And the ghosts, the monsters. The Yeti is the favourite of foreign mountaineers. But it's not uncommon for villagers who stray too far to be possessed by ghosts, or to anger the gods who live in the high places. Every community here has their own legends, their own rituals for appeasing the spirits.'

'Trying to control the uncontrollable.'

Dawa's smile was non-committal. 'Mountains are wild places and they must be respected. Even feared. But people are practical. For all the blessings and rituals to keep the ghosts from their door, they have guard dogs too, to frighten away the snow leopards and bears.' He looked at their own self-appointed guard dog, flopped on her side, head resting on his boot, nose twitching when the fire spat.

'What do you think happened to those kids?' Anne was fiddling with the edges of her blanket, braiding and unbraiding the tassels. She had her eyes down, her face in shadows.

'There have been attacks on lone hikers this summer. A few have returned with reports of being robbed in the night. One man was attacked during the day and only survived because a group of hikers passed him soon afterwards. It's a hard life for some people here; tourists are seen as easy targets.'

'It makes you wonder why people keep wandering off into the mountains.' Esther tried to keep her voice light, but the darkness beyond their small camp seemed to creep closer.

Dawa held her gaze, the firelight animating his face. 'Perhaps, like us, they come here looking for something: adventure, escape, freedom, God.' His gaze shifted to Anne. 'A missing son.'

'Is it possible they ended up at the Sunshine House as well?' Anne said. 'That some of the other people who've disappeared have found their way there? Have even been recruited – like Evie?'

'It's possible,' Dawa said slowly, leaning forwards to throw another branch on the fire. 'And the Sunshine House will not be the only community hidden in these mountains.'

'But you don't think it's likely.'

Dawa returned his gaze to Esther. 'No, I don't. The majority of missing tourists have turned up dead. We know there are attacks. There's involvement in the drug trade. And hiking accidents. If you fall into a ravine or a river or are swept away in an avalanche, it's very easy to disappear and never be found. Or found years later. Some hikers recently came across the body of a woman who'd disappeared in the eighties—' He stopped speaking as Anne stood. She moved towards the fire, the blanket trailing from her shoulders like a cloak.

'I'm going to bed,' she said. Dawa stood too, waking the dog, who leapt up and then immediately sat back down.

'But there are those who travel to the high places to be closer to God, to find a different life there. In some Buddhist traditions there is a belief that hidden valleys – *beyuls* – exist in these mountains. Places where the physical and spiritual worlds collide. A paradise on earth. Perhaps the Sunshine Valley is such a place.'

Anne stood motionless, staring at the flames. 'And what if it isn't? What if it was something else altogether? Something more sinister? I keep thinking of Evie saying we had to get there quickly. Why? What if we're already too late? Or what if we're walking into a trap?'

A heavy silence fell around the fire as they contemplated her words, and then, with a small shake of her head, Anne bade them goodnight.

'I was meant to write a book about it,' Esther said when Anne had gone. They sat closer together now, their voices low. The dog was curled in a protective ball between them and Dawa stroked her head as he stared into the fire.

'About Torran?'

'Yes. But also more generally about the disappearances. The Kullu Valley – India's Bermuda Triangle.'

Dawa nodded. 'I've heard it called that. What happened to your book?'

'There wasn't enough of a story because there isn't just one thing. One reason why so many travellers have disappeared. Too many possibilities and no coherent narrative.'

'Like life.' Dawa tipped his head to the side, considering her words. 'But isn't that your job? To make sense of the mess. To find a narrative where none exists.'

'Yes. But I needed more.'

'And now you have the Sunshine House.'

'But that's not where everyone ends up, is it?'

The fire hissed as it consumed a damp log and they watched the flames turn green.

'So you're here to find the story you need for your book?'

Esther gave him a sideways glance. 'I'm here to find Torran. I promised Robert I wouldn't write about it.'

A light frown creased his forehead but he didn't respond, and after a moment's hesitation she continued. 'There was a woman at the Green Tara who thought I should be writing about other things – inequality, poverty, women – the "real" issues in India.'

Dawa leant forwards to adjust the burning logs, the flames briefly illuminating his face.

'All those things deserve attention.'

'I know. But—'

'You're still chasing this story.' There was no judgement in his voice.

'It's not just Torran or the other missing people. It's the after-shocks. All the lives that get nudged off course. Or shaken. Or briefly touched.'

'Like yours.'

Esther looked at him. 'And yours.'

He held her eye for a moment before smiling. The dog twitched and sighed and the fire burnt low. Dawa's pile of wood had dwindled to the few sticks he would use for boiling water in the morning. The smoke was shooting straight for the sky in the still air. There were stars up there, hovering on the edge of her vision, but when Esther tried to focus on them, they disappeared.

XXXII

ANNE

Another day of walking, watching the sun arc across the vast canvas of sky, their shadows shortening and disappearing before lengthening once more. The path they followed was less established than that of the day before, and several times Dawa stopped and took out his map to trace its contours before continuing. They didn't talk much, each locked in their own thoughts. The dog had been gone when they awoke, and Anne found herself missing the reassuring presence.

Around them the landscape was in constant motion, rocky rises giving way to high plateaus covered in long grass, shivering patterns in the wind. They climbed wooded slopes, fallen leaves crackling underfoot, releasing their scent into the air. But as the day wore on they passed the treeline and the land grew barren, the vegetation low and scrubby save for the odd profusion of purple flowers patterning the rocks.

In the late afternoon they crested a rise and saw the lucent waters of a high mountain lake, surrounded by craggy peaks. They stopped to have a drink after the steep climb, shading the slanting sun from their eyes with raised hands. No one spoke, but the silence was companionable. A playful breeze waltzed across the water. The path ahead wound down to the lake's edge and then alongside it, before rising once more and disappearing over yet another pass. Anne found the immensity of the landscape liberating; the path demanded only to be followed. And that, at last, was something she could do.

As evening fell they set up camp among the boulders on the far side of the lake but away from the water, which Dawa said would turn the ground icy overnight. Even so, when they awoke the condensation from their breath had frozen, forming icicles on the inside of their tents.

They climbed the final pass in the late morning. Anne had spent the last hours staring at the path ahead, all effort focused on breathing in the thin air and not stumbling on the loose stones. Dawa was in front, his pace measured. He turned often to give her a reassuring smile, which she struggled to return against the hammering of her heart, the effort to snatch a lungful of air.

On they went, following switchbacks up and up across ground that was stony and cracked. It would soon be covered in snow, impassable until spring. She thought of the people who lived in the Sunshine House, cut off from the world for almost half the year: how did they survive the brutal winters when ice and snow covered everything?

Above her, Dawa had reached what seemed to be the summit. She saw him pull an apple from his bag and sit down, surveying the valley she could not yet see. The Sunshine Valley. At last.

She glanced back; Esther had fallen behind and Anne wondered if she should wait for her, but Esther raised a weary hand, summoning a smile to show she was all right. Anne tried to smile back, but the effort of it defeated her.

The ground beneath Anne grew steeper as she reached the last few switchbacks, short and tight, as if the giant hand which had drawn them had grown tired and scribbled slightly before lifting the pen. Her legs resisted the increase, the muscles in her calves screamed. Her breathing was shallow, a fish out of water. The pack on her back, so light when they left Malana three days earlier, was made of lead. She was struggling against a surging tide that wanted to sweep her away, back down the mountain and to oblivion.

And then she was there, standing beside Dawa on the narrow ledge at the top of the pass, loosening the straps on her rucksack so it fell to the ground, sinking on to a boulder. She briefly rested her head between her knees, waiting for her heart to calm, the gasping breaths to even. Her lungs were on fire. A wave of dizziness and then her head cleared.

She sat up, opened her eyes and stared down at the Sunshine Valley.

Shockingly green and lush after the barren landscape they'd journeyed through, it was alive with colour, with trees and wildflowers, with birds and the blue river that wove in and out of sight. There was no sign of a house from where they sat, but it wasn't hard to imagine one existed, at the top of the meadow, perhaps, or tucked into the woods.

With a rush of understanding Anne imagined Torran sitting here, on this very stone, looking down at the Sunshine Valley for the first time.

Dawa handed her an apple and she took it with a grateful smile, drinking deeply from her water bottle before biting into the sweet fruit. It tasted incredible. The juice ran down her chin and she wiped it with the back of her hand, smelt it on her skin. She had made it; she was alive. And she felt a profound gratitude for the valley and the expanse of mountains, the wideness of the sky, the blood singing in her veins. And Torran – who had led her here.

She turned to Dawa, a huge grin on her face, and he smiled back, eyes almost disappearing behind the laughter lines.

If it were now to die. The words appeared in her mind as if someone had placed them there. *If it were now to die, 'twere now to be most happy.*

Ludicrous, yet true.

'And now we really are at the end of the world,' Dawa said.

'The end of the world?' Anne looked back as Esther appeared behind them, dropping her pack and collapsing beside it. Dawa handed her a water bottle.

'That's where the name Kullu comes from. *Kulant Peeth*: "the end of the habitable world".'

'So not quite the end of the world, then,' Esther said, sitting up and catching the apple Dawa threw to her.

Dawa smiled again. 'No,' he said. 'Not quite.'

XXXIII

ESTHER

The path they were following did not lead directly to the Sunshine House. It ran along the opposite side of the river, eventually reaching a natural crossing point over large boulders much further down, and continuing on to the bottom of the valley where the nomad caravans set up camp in summer. There should have been a tree trunk across the river higher up, which – according to Evie Sinclair – met a path used by the inhabitants of the house. But it had either been moved or washed away when the river was in flood, and they didn't find it.

Dawa continued to lead them downstream, looking for a safe place to cross. The water was high and running fast, swollen by monsoon rains, a constant thundering and relentless rush of white noise rendering conversation almost impossible. Not that they felt much like talking; the afternoon was wearing thin.

Just as it seemed they'd never find a place to cross before reaching the bottom of the valley, Dawa stopped and pointed to a fat log wedged between several boulders to create a bridge. Esther and Anne stopped beside him, and they all watched the water running over the log, making the wood slick and dangerous.

Anne turned to Dawa, a question on her face.

'It's either here or the crossing at the bottom of the valley,' he said. 'That's another mile at least. Then we'd have to set up camp – it'd be too dark to make it back up to the house tonight.'

Anne nodded, eyes darting from the fast-flowing water to the sky overhead. The sun was still high but deep valleys lose light early, quickly flooding with shadows and the chill of night; according to Dawa, they had roughly two hours of daylight left.

'I think we should try, don't you?' Anne turned to Esther as she spoke, but she'd already made up her mind.

Esther nodded, attempting to look unperturbed, but her heart was racing. The water was wild, churning and frothing and throwing itself against the rocks. One misplaced step and it would sweep you away.

Dawa dropped his pack and removed his shoes and socks. From the back of his rucksack he drew a length of rope, and Esther and Anne watched as he tied one end to a nearby tree, pulling it with the weight of his body to test the knot. Satisfied, he threaded his arm through the remaining coil, picked up his poles and jumped on to the first rock. It was large enough to be dry on top, and he stood there for a moment, judging his next steps, then flashed a confident smile and stepped nimbly to the next boulder. This one was submerged and the water came up to his ankles, hitting him with such force his whole body wobbled against the current. He stretched his arms out like a tightrope walker, poles in the air, found his balance and took another cautious step.

He made slow but steady progress, stopping to unwind the rope as he went. Around halfway, when he stepped on to the log, he made such a theatrical lunge that Esther thought he'd go in, but he managed to right himself and continued edging forwards.

Once across, Dawa jumped to the bank with ease and secured the remainder of the rope around the trunk of a sturdy oak, again testing the knot and the tension of the safety line he had created. He turned back and gave a double thumbs up. With the rope to hold, it took him less than a minute to recross the river.

He took their packs next, one by one, crossing more quickly each time as he learnt the best footholds. Then he returned and stood on that first boulder, offering a hand towards the women.

'Who's going first?'

Esther and Anne looked at each other.

'You go,' Anne said. She was still unlacing her boots, sitting on a rock, the sunlight through the trees making patterns on her legs. Esther's shoes were already tied together by the laces and slung over her shoulder. Dawa took her hand and pulled her up on the boulder beside him.

They stood close together, the water even louder now that it surrounded them. He took both of Esther's hands and put them on the safety rope.

'Don't let go,' he said, eyes meeting hers. 'I will lead. Watch where I step. Just put your feet where I have put mine.'

Esther nodded, hoping she looked more confident than she felt. The water seemed faster from where they stood; the force of it made her knees weak.

'OK?' Dawa was looking anxiously into her face.

She nodded again. 'Let's go.'

In the end it was easy. She did as Dawa had instructed and looked only at the place where he had put his feet, landing hers into the space as soon as he vacated it, so focused that she didn't realise they'd reached the other side until her feet hit the grassy bank.

She grinned at Dawa and turned to wave at Anne, the adrenaline kicking in now that she was safe. From the other side, it didn't seem that far at all.

Sitting to put her socks and shoes on, she watched Dawa go back over and pull Anne on to the boulder. They paused and Esther knew he was telling Anne the same thing he'd told her. Anne nodded and he took the first few steps across the rocks, Anne following behind.

Esther pulled a dry leaf from her sock and as she glanced up saw Anne look over, her attention caught by something in the trees behind Esther. She was about to turn to see what it was when Anne slipped.

It happened so fast. Anne was standing on the rock and then she was falling, hands grasping for the rope she was no longer holding, the water already rushing away with her, pulling her under.

But Dawa got there first. Wedging himself between the rocks, he plunged his arms in to grab her flailing hands just as she was disappearing. For an endless moment nothing happened. He kept hold of her but couldn't fight the current to pull her out of the river. Esther saw the tension in his body, the sheer physical effort of not letting go, and realised the river was going to take Anne – now, after everything, when they were so close to finding Torran. And Esther was already on the rocks, grabbing the rope in one hand as she jumped across. She couldn't let it happen. Not here, not now.

'Esther! Don't move!' Dawa shouted, without turning, and Esther froze. The memory of a neighbour who drowned trying to rescue a dog from a river flashed through her mind. And – irrationally – that buoy she'd seen at Taigh na Criege, bobbing like a drowning child.

Dawa braced himself harder against the rocks and pulled Anne up beside him. She'd been under for less than ten seconds.

They all stared wide-eyed at each other, Anne blinking as water ran down her face, Dawa panting, Esther still frozen on a rock near the bank while the river rushed on.

'That was close!' Esther shouted at last, over the pounding of the water.

Anne and Dawa stared at her for another moment and then they both started laughing.

The sunlight retreated from the valley as they walked through the trees along the path to the house. With the evening shadows came the cold, biting at their fingertips. Esther's feet grew heavier as they got closer but Dawa walked quickly, head bent, determined to get them there before night claimed the valley and forced them into their tents.

Anne had been strangely unfazed by her narrow escape from the river, her main concern being the wet clothes, which she'd tied to the back of her pack in the hope they'd dry before dark. There was a certain recklessness about her sometimes, seemingly at odds with her usual cautious and reserved demeanour.

And now she walked behind Esther for the first time, as if to prolong the uncertainty she'd been trying to overcome for so long. She needed to know; she couldn't bear to know.

Because what if it had all been for nothing? This one last search. And if he wasn't here, where was he and how could she ever stop searching? Esther thought of Robert, alone with the sea and the sky. All that emptiness and no one to keep him company. How could she go back and tell him they had failed?

The trees thinned; the shadows stretched. The darkness crept around them. And just when Esther thought Dawa was going to call it a day and insist they set up camp, the path emerged from the woods and there, right in front of them, was a gate, hanging off its hinges, attached to a low, roughly made stone wall. A garden.

Dawa slowed and turned to them, eyes wide. Esther smiled uncertainly, her heart in her mouth. Behind her, she heard Anne murmur something under her breath.

The way the gate was hanging, supported only by half a broken hinge, made Esther nervous. Dawa pushed it cautiously and it came away completely, a crack of metal and wood, falling heavily to the ground.

'This doesn't look good,' Esther said.

They followed Dawa through the gate and into a garden overrun with plants gone to seed. Paths hard to pick out in the gloaming. A rustling in the undergrowth. An abandoned wheelbarrow. A peace pole surrounded by overgrown rosemary and lavender bushes. And just beyond, looming darkly, the Sunshine House.

For a moment no one moved, the shock of it rendering them mute. Where there should have been light and movement and life was a dark, burnt-out husk. Doors and windows empty, shutters gone or hanging loosely. Part of the roof above what looked to be a kitchen had collapsed, fallen bricks and wooden beams scattered across the ground.

Dawa was first to rouse himself, flicking on his torch and scanning its light across the facade. It was larger than Esther had imagined, more substantial, made of bricks and two storeys high. As the light passed over the open door of the kitchen, she caught a glimpse of a massive table collapsed like a lame horse.

There was only the faintest hint of burning in the night air; this was not a recent event. The Sunshine House, so alive and full of activity in Esther's mind, had been silently decaying for some time. First by fire and now by the elements as nature reclaimed her.

With a backwards glance, Dawa made his way carefully across the debris and stood in the doorway, peering in.

'It's not safe,' he said softly, almost reverently. 'We should come back in daylight.'

Esther turned to Anne, eerily pale in the darkness, but before she could say anything Anne pushed past her.

She moved quickly, sidestepping Dawa and disappearing into the house before they could stop her.

Esther cursed under her breath, fumbling with her torch.

Dawa called after Anne as Esther joined him at the door. Their eyes met in the glare of their torchlights and they hesitated.

'Torran?' Anne's call came from deep within the house, raising the hairs on Esther's arms. 'Torran. Torran. Torran!'

And for a heartbeat she was at Taigh na Criege and Anne was calling him in for supper, down for breakfast, out of the sea, into the car, from whatever hiding place he had found – and Esther strained her ears to hear his reply, his running feet, Anne's gentle scolding. The resolution.

But her call remained unanswered.

Again and again. The sound seeming to shake the building to its core.

And then a panicked cry.

Dawa's eyes widened, and Esther saw her fears reflected in them. Wordlessly they followed, tripping in their haste to reach her.

Anne stood at the bottom of a grand staircase that swept up in a graceful curve. She was staring white-faced through an open door. Esther and Dawa turned as one to see what she was looking at and Esther felt the ground tilt beneath her.

Bodies.

The room was full of bodies. Esther made to move but Dawa put a hand on her arm. With the tiniest shake of his head he stepped forwards just as Anne spoke.

'It's nothing,' she said, and the words seemed to break her and she dropped to the ground so quickly Esther thought she must have fainted. But she was still upright, sitting on the bottom step of the stairs.

'It's nothing,' she said again.

Dawa moved to the doorway and swept the beam of his torch around the room, and Esther saw that it was empty. What she had taken for bodies were shapeless piles of cushions thrown haphazardly upon the floor.

'The house is empty,' Anne said.

'Have you been upstairs?' Dawa came back and crouched before Anne, taking her hands. She was trembling.

Esther knew she should go to her, offer words of comfort, but she was unable to move. Her heart still pounding.

Anne nodded. 'I nearly fell through the floor.' She stifled a laugh that may also have been a sob. 'He's not here. No one is here. We're too late. They've all gone.'

XXXIV

ANNE

Esther's sleeping bag was empty when Anne awoke and she sat up quickly, reaching for her gloves and another pair of socks. She had slept in most of her clothes.

Unzipping the tent, she saw the valley was shrouded in a mist so dense it quickly surrounded her, engulfing her in a blankness like the unloving embrace of the sea. Her joints were stiff as she stood and stretched, squinting to see Dawa's tent through the whiteness. The flap was open, but when she stepped closer she saw that the tent was empty and for a moment imagined being completely alone, lost forever in a world turned silent and white. She didn't feel afraid; if anything, there was relief in the spectre of oblivion.

And then she heard the clang of metal on metal and Dawa appeared out of the mist, carrying two bottles and a pan filled with water.

'Have you seen Esther?' Anne asked, as he set to work reviving the fire, blowing on the faintly glowing embers. He turned to squint up at Anne, wiping his hands on his legs.

'I think she was going towards the house.'

Anne walked in the direction she judged the house to be in, although it didn't appear through the mist until she was almost at the stone steps leading to the main entrance. The door was large and wooden and surprisingly untouched by fire. It was also ajar, and Anne slipped through the gap like a shadow.

She could now see its origins as a British hunting lodge in the high ceilings, the sweeping staircase. The light inside was muted, creeping in through windows and the holes left by the fire, but it was enough to see all the details she'd missed the night before. There was an oriental rug under her feet, covered in ash and debris; she bent down and scraped it with a finger, the colours revealing themselves like a secret language. It made her think of the magic colouring books Torran had had when he was younger, how the colours appeared when brushed with water. He was never that interested, but she'd loved the way a hidden world revealed itself, a black-and-white Dorothy stepping into a technicoloured Oz.

She stood quite still, looking around at the open doors. The silence in the house was different from that of the mist-filled valley: outside it had been heavy and full; here it was a void, the house holding its breath, waiting for a sound.

'Esther?' Her voice was as hollow as the house, an echo of itself. She thought of how she'd cried Torran's name the previous night, stumbling through the darkness. It already felt like a hundred years ago. She could hardly believe she'd actually expected to find him.

There was no reply and she crossed the hall to the door on the opposite side to the kitchen, pushing it fully open to step into a room that must have been some sort of lounge or library, for there were armchairs and couches and walls lined with bookshelves. It was smoke-damaged and damp but otherwise intact, protected from the elements by wooden shutters that covered the glass doors leading to the veranda. Anne walked across the room to pull them open, the swollen wood protesting loudly but yielding. The valley's strange white light filled the room.

She looked around, taking in the colourful mandalas, the Tibetan *thangka* painting of Buddha and another of the Wheel of Life, framed in orange and yellow silks. The furniture was extraordinary, antique wooden frames re-upholstered in vibrant fabrics, a mixture of traditional Indian and Tibetan textiles. The colours were dulled with neglect, but still Anne had the feeling of walking into a room just vacated. Sad to think of it abandoned here, at the end of everything.

And what had she expected to find? The question curled itself around her. She wasn't sure she had truly believed in this place, let alone that Torran would be here waiting to be found. But now that she was here and standing in this room, she realised that she had, on another level, perhaps unconsciously, known that they would find something. That they were on the right track at last.

From somewhere above she heard timber falling and a voice cursing. And even though she knew it must be Esther, something clutched at her heart.

Because why couldn't it be him? Upstairs and sitting on his bed with his legs not yet reaching the ground, nervously waiting to be driven to school for the first time, to a swimming competition, to the airport. She shook her head; grief was a tethered animal, only ever allowed to stray so far before being yanked back.

Upstairs was lighter, a large part of the roof having collapsed, and the mist hovered above, peeking in.

'Esther?'

'In here.' Her voice was coming from the end of the corridor and Anne followed it, stepping cautiously over pieces of rafter and around collapsed boards, bracing herself lest the floor give way beneath her. There were doors on either side, all open, and she glimpsed the abandoned bedrooms within.

She found Esther in a large corner room with cracked windows on two sides. There were yoga mats and cushions arranged in a circle, and in the corner a neat pile of blankets.

Against the back wall a long narrow sideboard appeared to contain some kind of shrine. It was covered in statues and figures of various gods from both Hindu and Buddhist traditions, as well as a Celtic marble cross, a silver menorah and a blue hand with the eye of Fatima staring out at them. There was a metal bowl full of sand, half-burnt incense sticks protruding like the spikes on a porcupine. It seemed impossible that this had all been left here.

'It looks like a meditation room,' Esther said. She was standing behind what was left of the door, the wood badly burnt, the hinges buckled.

'This place—' Anne said, and then stopped. Behind the incense bowl, covered in dust and ash and almost unnoticeable amongst the clutter, was a picture frame, a garland of fabric flowers draped over one corner, a string of prayer beads on the other. She picked it up, letting the beads and flowers fall to the floor and brushing the glass with her sleeve. Unable to see clearly in the dull light, she moved closer to the window. Esther came and stood beside her and they both looked down at the photograph.

A group of maybe twenty people, gathered on the steps of the house, some sitting, some standing, all smiling. Arms around each other's shoulders, hair long and unkempt. Their clothes colourful, bell-bottoms and loose shirts, bold prints and long braided hair. Anne thought it must be a picture from the seventies.

And then she saw him.

XXXV

BEFORE

Somewhere in the night a child is born. Slick with sweat and weak with exhaustion, Anne looks down at the perfect being that has been wrapped in a blanket and put in her arms and knows she will never be the mother he needs. Love is not the only thing wringing her heart. She feels fear's trapped wings beating against the bars her body has made for her.

Tiny fingers grasp the air like panicked lungs, like someone falling into the abyss. She wants to offer him something to hold on to, but she is unable to move. The impossibility of allowing those flailing fingers to wrap snugly around her own. His eyes turn towards her in surprise. She tries to smile but is engulfed by his howl of rage at waking to a world of oxygen and light.

XXXVI

ANNE

They went through the rest of the house methodically, searching each room from top to bottom. But they found nothing
more, no other sign of Torran's presence. Anne carried the
photo with her, stopping often to look again at her son's face,
trying to reconcile herself to this new image, this new reality where he hadn't fallen into a river or been kidnapped or
murdered or eaten by wild animals, but had lived here, in this
house, with these strange smiling people. Where his hair had
grown long and sun-bleached and he'd laughed and thrown
his arms spontaneously around others' shoulders. Where he'd
chosen to stay. For it was hard to believe, looking at his happy,
open face, that he'd been here under duress. That they'd pre-
vented him from leaving.

When there was nowhere else to search, she and Esther left
through the front door and sat together on the top step. The
mist had lifted and the valley unrolled before them in shades of
green and blue, tall trees and jagged rocks, statuesque peaks.
Layer upon layer of mountains kissing the sky.

'How did they survive the winters?' Anne said. 'They must
have been snowed in for almost half the year.'

'A lot of provisions? A lot of board games?' Esther shook her
head. 'It must have been tough though.'

'It's quite remarkable, really. All this.'

'It's beautiful,' Esther said. 'It really is a paradise.'

'But it can't have been easy. Especially in the beginning. And
being so remote. I used to think Taigh na Criege was at the
end of the world. But this—' Anne stopped, lost in her own
rememberings.

On the lawn below, Dawa had finished packing the tents, all trace of their little camp almost gone. Only the fire still smoked under the water pot, filling the air with the same acrid smell that clung to the house, that would stay on their clothes and hair for days.

Anne thought of the long journey back to Manali. And then what? She looked down again at the photograph. God, she was tired.

'I thought this might have been it. I really did.'

Esther followed her gaze. 'I know. But it's not nothing. It's a breakthrough. We know he was here.' Her voice was gentle. Kind. Like Anne was the child and Esther the mother. 'We know he's alive.'

'What if he died in the fire?' Anne's voice was very small, and Esther shuffled closer.

'He didn't die in the fire,' she said, so firmly that Anne wanted to cry.

'Evie said they'd still be here?'

Esther nodded. 'She said we'd have till the end of summer.'

'But how did she know? Didn't she leave years ago?'

Esther rubbed her eyes, running her hands down her cheeks in a gesture that reminded Anne of the girl she'd once known.

'She left three years ago,' Esther said. 'But apparently there was already a plan for the community to come to an end this year. Although she didn't say exactly what that meant.'

Anne let out her breath slowly. 'I just don't know where we can go from here. I keep telling myself it should feel better. Knowing he was here. But it doesn't. In some ways it feels worse. Because he was here, and he chose to be here, and he didn't tell us.' She pressed her knuckles to her forehead to stop them shaking.

Esther put a tentative hand on her arm. 'Can I look at the photo?'

Anne passed it over; she'd already studied it so closely she could see it when she closed her eyes.

'Evie's here,' Esther said. 'See.'

Anne looked at the woman Esther was pointing to in the front row: white-blonde hair braided, a round, open face.

'So it was taken at least three years ago,' Esther continued, her eyes scanning the other faces. 'That must be Lorrie, one of the leaders.' She pointed to a tall woman wearing a turban. 'And look, that girl beside Torran—' She stopped abruptly, glancing sideways at Anne.

'What?' Anne took the photo back to study the young woman beside her son. She was short and blonde and pretty, a little like Fiona.

But it wasn't the girl herself that had caught Esther's attention; it was the child she carried on her hip, small body and curly head almost obscured by the people in front. And yet now so obvious Anne wondered how she hadn't seen it before.

XXXVII

ESTHER

That first night after leaving the Sunshine Valley was colder than any so far. The sky awash with stars so bright the sweep and fall of the landscape was aglow in a shimmering half-light. Esther crept from the tent when she thought Anne was asleep and wandered along the path until the lantern Dawa had left burning was no longer visible, the whole camp hidden by one of the immense clusters of rock that littered the sloping plateau.

She was wearing every item of clothing she had, the condensation from her breath beading on the fleece of her scarf, its warmth quickly cooling. And though the air froze her lungs, it was impossible not to stare in awe at the sky, the endless expanse, the silence that was absolute. She could hear her pulse in her ears, as if her body felt obliged to fill in the aching silence. And she tried to feel the beauty of it, but the stars seemed to mock her with their indifference, feigning friendship with familiar constellations that only exist because someone long ago looked up and joined the dots. The timeless need for order and meaning in an orderless, meaningless universe.

'Incredible, isn't it?'

She turned to see Anne standing behind her.

'What are you doing out here?' Esther asked, surprised she hadn't heard Anne's approach. 'I thought you were asleep.'

Anne sighed. 'I don't know if I'll ever sleep again,' she said, and then laughed at her own hyperbole. 'It's been quite a day.'

'It's been quite a seven years,' Esther said, looking at her and seeing, for a moment, the woman she'd been when Esther first went to live with them. Only twenty-five. Ten years younger than Esther now was.

'It's been quite a life,' Anne said, as if reading her thoughts, and something in the way she said it made Esther wait, to see if she'd say more. But Anne remained silent, and they both looked up at the stars again.

'Beautiful,' Anne said at last, the word reaching Esther on a cloud of condensation. 'It's just . . . breathtaking.'

'Don't you find it a bit intimidating?' Esther glanced again at her face.

Anne frowned, considering. 'No, actually.' She sounded surprised, and vaguely pleased, as if it had been a test and she'd passed.

'It makes me feel lonely,' Esther said, trying and failing not to fall back on cliché. 'Insignificant. Don't you feel that out here? The mountains' indifference.'

Anne was looking at her again, really looking, and Esther had the not unwelcome feeling of being seen by her, like being bathed in sunlight. Starlight. And she reached again for the differences between them.

As if sensing her retreat, Anne reached a hand towards her. Her gloved fingers hovered by Esther's arm for a moment before she withdrew them.

'The mountains are only themselves,' she said. 'Ancient, true, without story. Without artifice. There's something comforting in that . . . It's humbling. It's awe-inspiring. It gives me hope.'

Esther could feel her searching for the words to explain something that was beyond explanation.

'Sometimes I think—' Anne paused, looking at her again in that direct way Esther was not accustomed to.

'What?' She held her breath, afraid to dispel the moment. But Anne only smiled.

'Nothing. It's been a long day. We should sleep.'

She hesitated and Esther willed her to continue, but after a moment Anne just sighed and turned back towards the camp.

'Don't stay out here all night, Esther. It's freezing.'

And she walked away, leaving Esther feeling vaguely like a child who has been admonished but doesn't know what they've done.

They broke camp early. The morning had dawned clear and dry, the sky serene, and Dawa was hopeful they'd reach Malana by late afternoon. But less than two hours later a shroud of darkness fell, as swiftly as someone pulling a blind across a window. Looking upwards, they saw clouds as the first clap of thunder echoed against the rocks.

They took shelter when the rain began, crouching low under a pile of boulders, thunder shaking the earth, lightning cracking the sky.

Esther hugged her knees to her chest, transfixed at a world turned hostile and wild. The great immovable mountains seeming to shudder and shift, swept up in the storm's fury. Tempestuous as the sea. She thought of the storm on the first night of her visit to Taigh na Criege. Less than four weeks ago. The waves pitching themselves against the rocky shore, rain lashing the windows, wind howling down the chimneys. Lying sleepless and cold in her old room. Robert pacing the hall. From where they crouched on that isolated mountainside in the middle of a lightning storm, how tame and domestic that wild sea seemed, how warm and safe that chilly bed.

The temperature dropped as the thunder retreated, the lightning no longer upon them. Esther turned to Dawa, crouching close to the entrance of the natural shelter, and something about the look on his face made her afraid.

People die in the mountains. All the time.

'What's wrong?' Anne was watching Dawa too, and when he didn't immediately answer she shot Esther a worried glance.

'The snow is coming.' Dawa held a gloveless hand to the sky, still dark though the rain had turned to a light drizzle. He brought his fingers together as if plucking something from the air, then looked at Esther and Anne, a serious expression in his eyes. 'We need to go. Now.'

He was already standing, heaving on his pack, tightening straps and pulling his hood closer around his face, as if battening down the hatches at sea.

Neither woman moved, his urgency somehow rendering them immobile.

'Now.' His voice was calm but brokered no argument, and as one they sprang to action, hoisting packs as they stumbled out of the rocks' shelter.

Dawa was already walking back towards the trail. 'We must move quickly. When the snow comes it will cover everything. We will not be able to find our way out, and we do not have supplies to be stuck here for long.' He flung the words back over his shoulder as they hurried to keep up.

Anne reached for his arm. 'How far do we have to go?'

Dawa paused, looking around, reading the landscape and comparing it to the map in his head. 'Malana is too far. But the Last Chance Saloon is—' He paused again, looking this time to the sky as the drizzle began to take on the colour and form of sleet. 'Five hours from here. Four if we go very quickly.'

Anne nodded, eyes falling on the unmistakable flakes of snow now landing softly on their jackets. 'Let's go,' she whispered. And they went.

XXXVIII

DANNY

Danny was sitting with his feet before the fire, listening to the storm and stroking the ears of the dog that had wandered back down the path alone a few days earlier. She'd been with the two Western women and their guide, but had either been sent back or had sensed the weather changing and made a wise decision. Animals were more in tune with the world than their human counterparts. They could smell rain a mile away. He imagined the rumbling of the storm vibrating in the earth long before it hit, so subtle that only those with four legs could feel it.

The shutters were closed, the hut dimly lit by the glow of the fire and a storm lantern he refilled every morning, taking it apart and cleaning it once a week, as his father had shown him. He had never seen the sea but his father had, and he had told him about the lighthouses placed on deadly rocks to prevent boats from being wrecked on them in rough weather. All electric now, of course, but in the old days there were men living there, on those barren rocks in the middle of the angry sea, feeding the light.

Sometimes Danny fancied himself a lighthouse keeper too. But his house was in the mountains, not the sea, and his light was there to signal safety rather than warn of danger. A beacon in the wilderness, a shelter in the storm.

The wind whipped itself around the hut, shaking the wooden structure and pounding at the door. Indra, king of gods, in a fury. But Danny knew the hut was sturdier than it looked – he had built it himself. Everything might shake and creak, but it stayed put. It was built on solid foundations and nestled snugly against the rocks. Yet sometimes he still dreamt that a mighty wind would come and carry the whole place away with him inside, to be deposited in another land, like in *James and the Giant Peach* – one of his children's favourite stories. Once upon a time.

The fire crackled and the dog pricked up her ears. Danny had a book open in front of him, but he didn't think he would read any more. His eyes began to close as he imagined the feeling of flight, surfing the wind like the vultures who haunt the high places.

XXXIX

ESTHER

The snow was light at first. Falling silently around them, melting instantly on the wet ground as they raced down the track, fear nipping at their heels.

The path took them through another valley where nothing grew and the ground was the colour of rock, debris from centuries-old glacial movements strewn around, boulders piled into weird formations and incongruous logs crystallising into the earth. As they reached the end of the level ground, a steep descent of switchbacks dropped them into a lower valley, narrower and more sheltered than the last, where stunted trees and brittle bushes clung and an occasional scuttling creature disappeared into its burrow.

The wind dropped, the high valley walls protecting them from its northerly blast, leaving them feeling strangely lighter, no longer having to battle against it. The unexpected hush was disorientating, the snow now falling harder and beginning to sit on the path, patchy at first but spreading steadily.

Up ahead, Dawa kept glancing back to make sure they were keeping pace. Anne stayed close behind him and Esther tried to keep within touching distance of her. Whenever she felt her body protest after five days of hiking and the sudden increase in effort, she pushed back harder, forcing her legs onwards, using the fear to keep her moving.

Of all the many things she was afraid of, dying in the mountains had never been one. Naive, she realised now, because these enormous temples of stone and ice were far more dangerous and uncaring than so many of the things she feared on a daily basis. Just like the stars, the mountains cared not for their fate.

What would it be like to freeze to death? How long would the mind and body fight? At what point would they simply give up?

At least she wouldn't be alone.

But what if they were never found? Just three more souls lost to these mountains. And what about Robert? Esther began to apologise to him in her head and only after the conversation turned to the techniques of rural farming did she realise she'd fallen into a waking dream.

Panic.

She stopped in her tracks. The snow was now so thick it was getting hard to see ahead and in less than a minute Anne's blue jacket had disappeared. Esther tried to call out, but her mouth seemed to fill with snow and her body wouldn't respond to the commands being fired by her frantic brain. She wanted to lift her arm to wipe the snow from her face, but everything was too heavy.

In another part of her brain a calm voice was telling her that she couldn't have deteriorated so rapidly, to pull herself together. To walk, and walk quickly because every second she was standing there the others were getting further ahead and the track was getting harder to see. But her legs were beginning to shake and fear was shrieking through her.

This is it. This is it. This is how I die. She looked at the thought, frozen in the air before her.

Head unbearably heavy, she decided to rest for just a moment. The snow looked soft. Didn't people build shelters out of snow? She would start digging just as soon as she'd lain down for a time. Balance gone, she began to pitch forwards, and as she did so two figures materialised, her fall halted by strong arms and human voices.

'Esther.'

'Esther.'

This is where I wake up, she thought. But the snow kept swirling and the wind that had found them out was whistling in her head.

'Esther!'

Anne's face, inches from hers. Anne's green eyes bright as emeralds. She had her scarf over her mouth and her hood low across her brow. But Esther could see her eyes, long lashes catching snow. 'Esther. We've got to keep going.'

Pressure on her hands as Anne squeezed them.

'It's not far now.' Dawa's reassuring face appeared beside her.

She had a choice, she realised. She was standing on the precipice. And something deep inside her longed to fall. But Anne's eyes held hers.

'You're OK.' She must have shouted the words to get them past the howl of the wind but they reached Esther like a whisper, like a thought sent to seed itself in her mind. And somehow it took root. Her legs began to move, the world refocused.

Anne held her hand as they struggled through the confusion of snow and rock, almost flying in their haste. Esther could no longer see the path but still Dawa managed to guide them. Down through another valley, up and over several rocky passes and down once more. Trees grew taller, straighter, sometimes close enough to provide shelter, keeping out the worst of the wind and snow. The path re-emerged, ground muddy and wet but not snow-covered. Ferns and grass. And all at once they were hurtling down a narrow twisting path and Dawa was pointing towards something below them and they strained to see and there – not more than two hundred metres away – was the Last Chance Saloon.

XL

DANNY

The dog was already on her feet when Danny heard the noise. His eyes snapped open, and he turned to look as the dog ran over to sniff and paw at the door.

Someone was outside.

He jumped up to undo the rudimentary bolt, there mainly to stop the door blowing open on nights like this. The wind was still driving snow against the hut and it almost ripped the door from his grasp, slapping him with an icy blast.

He stepped back quickly to let in the three hikers, and then heaved the door closed again, sliding the bolt across with a reassuring click.

Danny surveyed the bedraggled group for a moment before springing into action, helping them with their packs and hanging their wet things on the rail above the fire. He pushed a few more chairs towards the stove and once they were all sitting, huddled around the heat, he put a pan of milk and spices on the hotplate and lit another lamp in the kitchen so he could prepare food.

He chatted to them as he chopped carrots and onions, heated oil and began frying. His visitors were silent, staring into the flames with the shaken expressions of those who have felt the ground at the edge of the cliff crumble.

Leaving the vegetables to soften, he poured out the chai, seeing how Esther's hands shook as she accepted the cup. She looked into his eyes, her face confused, as if she were waking from a dream. The whites of her eyes were red.

Back in the kitchen, he added noodles and eggs to the pan, along with dried cumin, fresh coriander and sweet chilli sauce, then dished it all up.

While they ate, Danny sat on a stool beside them. He wanted to know where they'd been and why they were still on the mountainside in this weather. He would have thought Dawa, who seemed competent, would have set up camp as soon as the weather began to turn, but he kept his counsel.

There was no question of them travelling on that night. While they finished eating, Danny climbed the ladder to the mezzanine and laid extra blankets on the mattresses. He took one back down for himself; he would sleep on a chair by the fire.

After supper, Dawa and Esther went straight to bed, but Anne stayed where she was, the dog curled at her feet. Danny offered her the blanket and opened the stove to throw in another log. The scrape of metal made the dog twitch in her sleep. He wiped the soot from his hands and sat down on the other side of the fire. Anne wrapped the blanket around her shoulders, pulling it tightly across her chest.

'We found the house,' she said at last, still staring at the stove.

Danny had the feeling she was talking to herself.

'They called it the Sunshine House. Hidden in a valley full of trees and meadows and flowers. Birds, too. Such beautiful colours.'

Danny made a non-committal sound to show he was listening and reached over to refill her cup and pour one for himself.

'It just seems incredible that all these foreigners could live there for so long, without being detected.' She turned her gaze to Danny, who returned it for as long as he could.

'People are good at keeping secrets in these mountains,' he said. 'There are many people here who don't want to be found. The mountain people have their own laws, their own reasons to stay silent.'

Anne sipped her chai. The logs in the stove shifted as they burnt.

'I wonder where they all went. When they left. You must have seen them. Some of them, at least. This is the most direct route back to civilisation.'

171

When Danny didn't respond, she put her cup down and went over to rummage in the dry bags they'd removed from their soaking packs, eventually pulling out a photo frame. She offered it to Danny, and he took it, leaning towards the lamp to look at a group of hippies on the steps of a large house.

Anne pointed at a tall man standing at the back, his arms around the people beside him.

'That is my son,' she said.

Danny looked closely at the smiling young man, the long hair, the broad shoulders. The face tanned and open, matured and different – very different – from the photo on the poster. A flicker of recognition.

He handed the photograph back to Anne, and she took it with her to the chair, wrapping the blanket about her.

The silence settled between them. The dog snorted. Danny's eyes grew heavy. The wind still whistled, but it sounded less frantic to gain admission, its attention called elsewhere. The fire crackled and the top of the stove hissed as their wet things dripped.

The storm would pass by morning and the women and their guide would be able to reach Malana by lunchtime. Danny doubted he would see them again. He looked over at the boy's mother. Her mouth a line, her eyes narrowed, facing down some thought he couldn't see.

His own son had died, along with his wife and daughter, in an earthquake in Kathmandu twenty years ago. Their house had been a good one, made of stone, two levels. They'd had a comfortable life. He was a civil servant; his wife was studying biology. She wanted to be a doctor. At night the sound of traffic was muted by the thick glass windows in their bedroom. The children slept on the same mattress as them, the little sighs of their breathing sweet and warm.

He'd heard the dog before it happened and got up to check there wasn't an intruder.

Animals know.

Tarka was barking madly at the front door and when he'd opened it the dog had raced out to the street. Danny followed and was in the middle of the road when the earthquake hit. Just a trembling at first. He'd turned back in time to see the full impact of the quake as it shook the street to its foundations.

He would never understand how it was possible to stand one minute in the balmy night, the crickets singing, the houses solid around him, for it all to collapse the next. Like a house of cards. But with a noise so loud it would echo through the rest of his life.

Everything a confusion, everything in motion. When the ground stopped shaking he looked to where the house containing his sleeping family should have been and saw the blank yawn of the night sky. That was when the world had ended.

He turned his attention back to Anne. She looked dog-tired. He recognised the exhaustion of one who has lost something more precious than sleep. Only her loss was not a single event but an infinitely repeating thing.

There is a time to keep silence, and a time to speak.

'I have seen your son.'

Anne turned her eyes to him.

'He has been here, several times, over the years. Coming and going from the Sunshine House. I wasn't sure from the first picture. But I looked again after you left. And now – this picture – I can say that is definitely the young man I met.'

'Torran was here?' Anne looked around, as if seeing the place for the first time.

Danny nodded. 'Yatri, he called himself.'

'Yatri,' she said. 'Yes.'

'He was a very good boy. Friendly and polite.'

'Was?'

Danny saw the shadow cross her face.

'Only that I haven't seen him in some time. One – maybe two years – since he was here.' He saw her disappointment and wished he could assuage it.

'It means pilgrim, traveller, wanderer,' he said instead. An offering.

'Yatri?'

'Yes.'

Anne exhaled slowly.

'I just want to know why,' she said. 'Why couldn't he tell us something? Anything. Just let us know he was all right. What happened? What did we do to make him hate us so much?'

Danny was surprised. 'What did you do? It was most likely nothing to do with you at all.'

'Then why didn't he tell us he was leaving? It feels like he was punishing us. There must have been something we did wrong.'

He shook his head. 'Sometimes there is no reason. No logic. No answers.'

He waited for her to speak, to ask more about her son. But when she didn't, Danny felt the promise of sleep creep over him, and it wasn't long before he found himself falling.

XLI

ESTHER

She woke to silence, the smell of wool and timber, the strangest feeling she was back in Taigh na Criege. The same absolute stillness after a storm. She'd lain awake the previous night shivering, adrenaline flooding her body with life and fear now the danger had passed. In the nest of blankets and sheepskins, Dawa had reached for her hand and held it, his skin rough and vital, until she stopped shaking and fell asleep.

There was no sign of either Dawa or Danny downstairs, but Anne was asleep by the fire, her breath so quiet Esther stood above her for a moment to check she was breathing. She looked peaceful, vulnerable in a way she never did when she was awake. Esther could see the woman she once was, or perhaps the woman she could have been. She wondered if Anne ever saw that woman, glimpsed in the reflection of a darkened window. All the selves we are not but carry about us somehow, hidden shadows of another life. And the girl in the photograph in Taigh na Criege, where was she now? And where were all those things she'd given up to find herself here, at the end of the world, chasing the memory of her son?

Outside a bird was singing, long notes vibrating in the stillness. The storm had left the air so clear that even the furthest peaks were sharp, revealing their ridges and crevices, a fastidious study in depth and shadow. Snow coated the higher slopes and Esther shivered to think of the previous day, of the endless white and how her knees had buckled. She'd never thought she'd be the one who needed coaxing off a mountain.

*

175

She must have drifted back to sleep in a chair by the fire because the next thing she knew Danny was standing in the kitchen, cracking eggs over a hot pan. Dawa was behind them, packing their kit. He caught Esther's eye and smiled.

Anne was awake too. She got stiffly out of the chair, stretching her arms above her head, looking down with an openness Esther hadn't seen before.

'How are you? That was quite intense yesterday.'

Esther nodded, the sympathy taking her by surprise. Anne pressed a cool hand to her forehead, like a mother with a sick child, and Esther had to turn away quickly so as not to cry.

They ate omelette and toast on the bench outside. It was almost noon, and the sun was high. Two eagles glided on an airstream above the valley, magnificent wings spread wide. The dog sat at Esther's feet and accepted the scraps she threw with unsuppressed delight.

Danny and Dawa had been down to Malana to buy the eggs, milk and bread. It was a six-hour round trip and they'd left at dawn, the ground still frozen and sparkling in the last of the moonlight. Esther and Anne couldn't stop thanking them, but the words slid from their backs like water.

Anne asked about the missing Americans and the two men exchanged a look.

'There are posters everywhere,' Danny said. 'Police and army too. They are still searching. I've seen a helicopter three times in the last two days.'

'What about the parents?'

'I haven't seen them. The children were not hiking in this direction; I don't think it is a possibility they would be this far north.'

His use of the word 'children' made Esther pause. Because they were, after all, only nineteen. As Torran had been. That age when you feel fully formed and invincible.

Dawa cleared his throat. He was sitting on the ground, leaning against the shack. He put his empty plate down and the dog sidled over to lick the grease from it.

'We were talking,' Dawa said, looking pointedly at Danny.

Danny hesitated and then nodded, resolving some internal conflict.

'I have to tell you,' he said, angling his body towards Anne but looking at his hands. 'I have not seen Yatri for a while. But perhaps it was more recently than I remembered.'

Anne stopped tapping her foot on the ground as Esther turned to her in surprise, but Anne was looking at Danny.

He raised his eyes to meet hers. 'He was here perhaps a year ago, perhaps less, with some others from the Sunshine House – Jana and Ace, their daughter Maeve – they have been in these mountains longer than me. They are good people. For many years they have been building a house – I believe they call it Shambala. For their retirement, Ace used to say. They moved there. And Yatri went with them.'

No one said anything. The dog looked around, beating her tail softly on the compact dirt. A tiny bird landed close to Danny's foot and began pecking at the ground.

'Where is this house, Danny?'

Danny took Anne's hands in his. 'I will draw it on the map for you. I haven't been there, but I know the village. Less than five hours' walk. You will be there by nightfall.'

Anne nodded, taking it in. She turned to Dawa.

'We're ready to go,' he said.

She turned back to Danny, who was watching her anxiously.

'They are good people,' he said again. 'But they could get in difficulty if too many people know they are here. The police. They deserve to be left in peace. I have made promises to protect those who seek refuge in the mountains. That is why I did not speak sooner.'

'It's OK.' Anne's hands were still in his. 'I understand. Thank you for telling me.'

She continued to look at him, their eyes locked in their own private conversation.

'You've lost a child,' she said at last.

'Two,' Danny said. 'And my wife. The very loves of my life. If you can find your son, I want to help.'

'And you have. Thank you.'

Danny grinned, a cheeky smile that softened the sorrow in his eyes and transformed him into a much younger man. He let go of her hands and stood.

'Danny the Champion of the World!' he said, with an elaborate bow. 'Always at your service.'

Part Three

XLII

ESTHER

The sun was setting in an explosion of crimson and gold as they approached the unobtrusive village of Ramini. The path, which had zigzagged steeply down the mountainside, now became level, weaving in and out of deodars and oaks growing ever more densely on the high slope. The freshness of leaves filled Esther's lungs, the air sweeter and thicker at this lower altitude, and she felt half drunk on it.

They came to a dilapidated house with a mule tied to the gate. Dawa knocked on the door while the animal stared suspiciously at them.

A squat woman in a dirty apron appeared, hands covered in flour. She replied to Dawa's questions with sharp words and a deep frown, her voice rising in the still air. She motioned back the way they had come and then closed the door before Dawa could say more.

He turned with a shake of his head, and they continued walking, passing a few more houses before Esther spotted the entrance to Shambala, which, it turned out, was impossible to miss.

The wooden gate was exquisitely carved, twisting and turning in Celtic knots, varnished so that it shone. In the centre was a large sign with the house's name in beautiful script below the outline of a Buddhist temple. After the broken gate that had greeted them at the Sunshine House, Esther was relieved; this was no abandoned dwelling.

She couldn't see the house itself, only a wide path lined with rhododendrons, which grew to form a natural arch. There was a deep hush. Not a bird sang nor a breath of wind disturbed the leaves as she followed Anne and Dawa through the gate.

Before long the house appeared, rising over several storeys and extending down with the slope of the hill, its wrap-around balconies reminiscent of those ancient houses in Malana: the carefully crafted workmanship, the intricately carved wood. But this house looked fresh and alive with its hanging baskets of trailing flowers, window boxes of geraniums and honeyed sweep of jasmine framing the door.

It was the stuff of fairy tales, the enchanted cottage in the woods. It was, Esther realised, exactly how she'd imagined the Sunshine House would be.

As they approached, a woman rose from the shadows of the lower veranda. She had a strong build and fair complexion, greying hair braided and wrapped around her head. She wore a simple tunic over dark trousers patched at the knee. A smudge of dirt on her nose, nails edged with soil.

Esther and Dawa instinctively hung back as Anne continued walking. She stopped when she reached the steps and looked up at the woman. The movement of their arrival resettled around them but nobody spoke.

The woman was looking at Anne, searching her face the way Anne was searching hers.

'You've come,' she said at last, the hint of an accent in her vowels. She didn't seem surprised. She glanced over at Esther and Dawa and then back at Anne. 'I always wondered if you would.'

'You know who I am.'

The woman nodded. 'I'd know those eyes anywhere.'

There was another silence, something unspoken passing between them.

And then Anne's shoulders dropped, as if all the strength had gone.

'He's not here, is he?'

They followed Jana inside, along a dim corridor and up several flights of stairs to the top floor, which opened on to a huge round room with floor-to-ceiling windows thrown wide. There were oriental rugs and armchairs covered in Indian textiles, floor cushions of Tibetan cloth, a coffee table inlaid with a mother-of-pearl mosaic. In the centre of the room stood a wood burner with a narrow chimney which went straight up and out through the ceiling, logs piled high on either side. There were plants everywhere, hanging from baskets, growing tall in ceramic pots, by the windows and on the decking.

Against the back wall hung a huge patchwork quilt in myriad fabrics depicting a tree, wide branches reflecting the four seasons. Behind the tree were snow-covered peaks and a setting sun; a fiery phoenix dominated the sky.

Jana led them on to the veranda where the tops of trees murmured and birds chattered through their branches. They sat around a table with an enormous wax candle in the centre, which Jana busied herself lighting.

She paused, watching the flame take and grow, seeming to steel herself, before pulling out a chair and sitting beside Anne.

'I am sorry that you have not found him here,' she said slowly, eyes running over Anne's face. 'He was here – on and off – for some time. And he was happy and well when he left.'

'When did he leave?' Anne's voice sounded far away, dredged up from the depths of herself.

Jana glanced at the sky. 'Nine months ago. More or less.'

Esther looked at Dawa, sitting with his chair pushed back, distancing himself in a small way, giving Anne this moment. She wanted to say something, but what was there to say?

The air was cooling rapidly, sweetly fragranced and vibrating with the singing of the cicadas. Anne turned slowly from Jana and put her head in her hands.

'We're always one step behind,' Anne said as they changed out of their hiking clothes. Jana had shown them to a small guest room, a single bed against each wall and a window looking out on the garden, now cloaked in night. She'd left them with a solar-powered lantern that cast a fractured orange light across the room.

'I know,' Esther said, pulling a long-sleeved top over her vest. It had been at the bottom of her pack, and although she'd worn it several times it smelt wonderfully clean compared to the clothes she'd been wearing over the past days of hiking.

'But I'm optimistic,' Anne continued, a brightness in her voice that didn't seem quite natural. 'For the first time in a long time. I feel like we'll actually find him. That if I stretch my hand out just a little further, I'll have him.'

Esther sat on the bed and ran her fingers through her hair, looking at Anne through curly tangles. She was buttoning a thick cardigan that Jana had lent her after whisking away most of their clothes to be washed. Perhaps feeling Esther's eyes upon her, Anne glanced up and smiled brightly. Esther returned her smile but she wasn't convinced. They seemed further away than ever. Chasing rumours across the mountains like shadows chasing the sun.

In the kitchen, Jana introduced them to Ace, a big man with a huge beard and a laugh that came straight from his belly. He gave them each a rib-crunching hug; his woollen jumper smelt of woodsmoke and sawdust and reminded Esther of Robert.

They sat around the kitchen table with mugs of tea as Jana stirred soup and sliced bread. Ace laid the table, pouring water from a big ceramic jug. Dawa was beside Esther. He'd changed into jeans and a loose tie-dyed T-shirt embellished with the ubiquitous traveller quote: *Same same, but different*. The clothes were too small for Ace, and Esther realised they had probably been left by Torran. Dawa's hair was still wet from the bucket of hot water Jana had given each of them to wash with, combed back from his forehead. He caught Esther's eye and gave her a bemused smile, as if in acknowledgement of the unexpected turn their journey had taken.

Anne was studying her mug, its abstract colours conjuring brooding skies and wild seas.

'Funny,' she said, when she noticed Esther watching her. 'We have some just like it at home.'

And it wasn't just the mug, Esther thought, looking around the warm, brightly lit room, that was oddly reminiscent of Taigh na Criege. This kitchen was more rustic, perhaps, but it had the similar feel of being handcrafted with an eye for detail – from the carved Tibetan wheels on the wooden island to the hooks and shelves ingeniously incorporated into every available space. It felt strange and yet right, to find this place here, in the mountains of India. *Same same, but different.*

'Are we waiting for Maeve?' Ace sat down beside Anne, looking over at his wife.

'She should be back soon. Maeve is our daughter,' Jana added, smiling.

'Maeve's the reason Yatri stayed so long,' Ace said, helping himself to a slice of bread and spreading golden butter across it.

'They were very close.' Jana spoke to Anne. 'She still misses him terribly. But it was his time to move on.'

'Always on the move, that boy.' Ace chuckled. 'He'd only arrive to leave again. You never knew when he'd be gone. Or when he'd be back. "Trying to catch the horizon," that's what he used to say. Like the sun.'

'That's why he chose that name.' Jana passed the bread-board to Dawa.

'From *Yatree* – Hindi for "pilgrim", "wanderer",' Dawa said, handing Esther a hunk of bread and reaching for the butter.

'Yes. He never told us what his name was before.'

'Torran,' Anne said. 'His name is Torran.'

Ace nodded kindly. 'That's right – we did see it on the posters.'

There was an abrupt pause as his words sank in. Esther started to say something, but Anne shot her a look and she bit her tongue. It was hard not to challenge them, though, despite their friendliness and hospitality. They were parents themselves, and they'd seen those posters Anne and Robert had put up all over the region, and they'd known, and they'd said nothing.

'I don't know what's keeping them.' Jana stood and bustled over to the stove. 'Let's have the soup. They can eat when they come in.' She began ladling it into deep clay bowls.

'They?' Anne said, when Jana rejoined the table.

'Maeve has a daughter. Maya. Our granddaughter.'

Another loaded silence. Esther hadn't forgotten the child in the photo, and she could tell from Anne's face that she hadn't either. Jana and Ace exchanged a look and Anne's eyes widened.

'Just how close were they? Torran and your daughter?'

Jana looked at her husband for a moment longer before turning to Anne.

'They were the only young ones in the valley,' she began, with another glance towards Ace. 'They were very close. Maeve was very much in love with him. And I think he loved her too. In his way.'

'And the child?'

Jana was about to speak but the sound of the front door made them all look up. A clatter of footsteps sounded down the hall and the kitchen door flew open. A young girl with blonde braids and a dishevelled school uniform ran in and then stopped to stare at the three strangers sitting around the table. She considered them for a moment before smiling shyly, shuffling over to Ace's elbow, looping her skinny arms in his. She was no older than seven. She didn't look much like Torran, but then she didn't not look like him either.

Esther turned to Anne and that's when she saw it: a hope and a longing that was too strong to contain, blossoming like a lotus in Anne's eyes.

And Esther saw the shadow on Jana's face before she could hide it.

'Go wash your hands, *Schatz*,' Jana murmured, and the girl skipped out of the room. They heard her calling to her mother down the hall.

'Is she—?' Anne began. Her voice cracked, and Esther bent over her soup.

Jana leant towards Anne. 'Maeve left the valley when she was seventeen. She wanted to explore the world. When she came back, she was pregnant.' She broke off as the girl returned, her mother close behind. Maeve had Jana's fair complexion, a smattering of freckles across her nose: a pretty, delicate face. Older, but still recognisable as the girl from the photo.

Her daughter turned to her. 'Who are these people, Mama?' she said, as if they were alone.

Maeve looked over her head at Anne.

'This is Yatri's mother and her friends,' Jana said, reaching a hand towards Maeve. 'They've come looking for him.'

XLIII

MAEVE

Maeve remembered seeing the Sunshine House for the first time in over a year, its hot roof shining in the afternoon sun. She had done the three-day trek alone: there was no way to contact anyone to tell them she was coming. But she was a child of the mountains, and it hadn't concerned her. At night she sat beneath the blanket of stars and felt the baby move, imagined one of those lights had fallen to earth and found its way into her belly. More poetic, at least, than the fumbling moments in damp sand that had left her sore and feeling foolish.

Making her way down to the Sunshine Valley, she felt the weight of the trapped bird she'd carried in her chest since leaving gradually lift. Life away from the valley had been breathing without air. The ease and confidence of her nature drained away until she hardly knew who she was. People, she decided, should not stray too far. Like the bar-headed geese who flew over the valley every spring to nest in the high plateaux of the Himalayas, it was in their nature to return home.

Lorrie was sitting on the other side of the river under an ancient deodar, cross-legged like the Buddha. Her eyes were closed and she couldn't have heard Maeve's approach over the rushing water, but she smiled before she opened her eyes and looked directly at Maeve. She brought her palms together in greeting and stood, brushing down her blue kaftan. As always, her long hair was wrapped in a turban. This one was deepest emerald. Blue and green for mother earth.

They met in the middle of the fallen tree Ace had cut to form a bridge. Lorrie encircled Maeve in her arms for a long time.

'I've been waiting for your return,' she murmured into the girl's hair.

At the house there was great excitement. Ace's face cracked with emotion when he saw his daughter; Jana could not stop kissing her. Nobody asked about her swelling belly, but hopeful smiles passed from face to face. It had been a long time since there was a child at the Sunshine House.

It wasn't until that evening that she met Yatri. He'd been at the bottom of the valley with the goats, lying on the hillside listening to the melody of their bells. Evie told her how they'd found him, delusional with fever and emaciated from hunger in the meditation hut on the southern pass. It was used for retreats and solitary meditation, but not often, and it was lucky Evie and Crystal had passed by when they had.

'How did he get there?' Maeve asked. The hut was high up on a ridge, far from the usual hiking routes and well hidden among the rocks.

Evie looked at the sky, a secret smile spreading across her face. 'His angels must have been looking out for him.' Evie was always saying things like that.

They were still sitting on the veranda outside the library when he returned, walking along the path which led up the grassy slope they called the lawn, a dozen black and white goats fat from a summer's grazing following behind. He led the herd into the small pasture by the barn and shut the gate, swinging on it like Maeve had done as a girl.

She felt nervous as he approached. His hair blond in the sun, shoulders broad and strong under his shirt, face open. She put her hands over her stomach, feeling the baby kick, and thought briefly of the man on Palolem beach who had disappeared the next morning without even telling her his name. Who would return to his country and live his life and never know about the baby he'd left behind. Torran's smile broadened as he reached the steps and Maeve wondered if the universe had provided a father for her child after all.

*

Yatri never talked about his life before he came to India, and Maeve never thought to try to place his accent or find out where he was from. Everyone at the Sunshine House belonged there; nothing else mattered.

She'd wanted to explain this to people she met while travelling, but they wouldn't have understood. Everyone was obsessed with where you were from, what you did, where you were going. She couldn't tell them anyway – the Sunshine House was a closely guarded secret.

But sometimes Yatri talked about his year of travelling in India. Getting stoned on the beach and joining the local fishermen to bring in the daily catch, crewing on a houseboat in Kerala, sleeping on a rooftop in Hampi. New Year at Kanyakumari – the southernmost tip of the country – looking out across three different seas. And once he mentioned a woman who had changed his life, although he wouldn't say how and he never spoke of her again.

He talked about the time his train broke down in the vast flatlands of the Tamilnad plains, how he played football with children from the local village, their mothers bringing food which they ate together under the shade of a banyan tree. He'd spent time in a spiritual community in the south, but he hadn't found his place there and he'd travelled on. He'd bathed in the Ganges at Rishikesh and met a sadhu who promised to teach him the ways of the yogi, but when Yatri returned the next morning with food and provisions the man was dead in his tarpaulin tent, milky eyes open and attracting flies.

He talked about this last event with the same equanimity with which he told all his stories, like they had happened to someone else and he was simply recounting them. It was only when he talked about the sea – and he talked about it often – that a light would appear in his eyes and Maeve would sense something more beneath the shiny surface of his words. Another life hidden within.

*

For Maeve and Yatri it seemed inevitable. They were the only adults under forty; they were best friends.

He'd been gone for several weeks. He did that. You'd wake up one morning and go down to breakfast and someone, usually Noula, would sound the gong and everyone would assemble and then someone would notice that Yatri wasn't there.

'Born to run, that kid,' Ace would say, giving his daughter a gentle squeeze.

Everyone was a little more attentive to Maeve when Yatri was gone. Crystal would invite her to the kitchen to make cookies; Evie would take Maya so that she could spend some time on her own. Maeve would catch Jana watching her a little more closely.

And he always came back.

'Like a boomerang,' Fred would say, pretending to throw something and waiting a few beats before raising his arm as if to catch it again. Fred always laughed at his own jokes. He was tall and thin and had a smile as wide as the sky.

And the strange thing was, Maeve would always know when Yatri was on his way home. She'd wake up with butterflies in her stomach and the certainty that he would be there before sundown. Lorrie said it was because they were connected on a soul level, that an invisible thread stretched between them like an umbilical cord, so they were never truly apart.

'I knew when you were coming home, didn't I?' she'd say, smiling her mysterious smile.

Jana would laugh when Maeve talked about soulmates and invisible threads.

'He comes home when he runs out of food, water or luck. It's as simple as that.'

But Maeve knew that he came back because he felt like she did: that the valley was home and the people who lived there were family.

The night before he returned that time, she had a dream he entered the valley riding an elephant, and when she went out to meet him she sprouted wings and flew up to sit beside him. He held her so close she could feel his heart.

In the morning she walked to the big deodar tree by the river crossing and sat beneath it, as Lorrie had done almost two years before. The water was high and rushed by in its own pounding symphony. She watched the sunlight play on its surface, dappled by the branches of the trees. A Himalayan flameback flew from the shadows and alighted on a boulder in the middle of the river, cocking its head one way and then the other, eyeing the water. Something upstream caught its attention and it was off in a bolt of red and gold.

Maeve sat by the river all day. When the sun was at its highest she ate a piece of bread and an apple. She stood and stretched her legs and sat down again. She closed her eyes and waited.

Yatri appeared late in the afternoon, whistling softly, making his way down the path towards the river in his familiar bouncing stride. She sensed the movement before she caught a glimpse of his face through the trees. And then he was there, standing on the other side of the log, grinning at her.

They met in the middle, just as she and Lorrie had done. And he pulled her close, like in her dream, so that her head was pressed against his chest and she could hear his beating heart in her ear, louder, even, than the river beneath them.

That night she slipped from the room she shared with Maya and her parents and walked down the dark hallway to the little room where Torran slept. The light of the moon cast shadows through the open doorway.

When she stood in front of the mattress, blocking the moonlight from the window, he lifted the sheet so she could get in beside him. He wasn't surprised to see her. She thought of the sacred thread between them pulling tight.

XLIV

ANNE

After dinner they returned to the round room at the top of the house. Ace had lit the wood burner and drawn the curtains against the night. The room was alight with flickering candles, the colourful tapestry illuminated so that the phoenix seemed to dance.

Anne sat on a cushion near the fire, briefly remembering the abandoned rooms of the Sunshine House, how the cushions had loomed like bodies in the darkness.

Jana's words from earlier repeated themselves like a mantra in her mind.

Like a father to her. Like a father to her. He was like a father to her. And Maeve had bit her lip and looked at the floor and the implications had swirled around the room so that Anne found she couldn't eat. Like a father and yet he wasn't here. Like a father, and yet still he'd left. Like a father, but the leaving kind.

And what had she hoped for? The idea of a grandchild? Of finding some vital part of herself, of her son, in this little girl of the mountains? The longing, the possibility of it, had winded her.

Maya sat on one of the couches with her mother, Maeve's voice gently lilting as she read her a story. Ace was on the floor, leaning against the chair where his wife sat. He was strumming a guitar, absently picking out the odd riff that Anne recognised: The Stones, Bob Marley, James Taylor, Cat Stevens. Music from another time, another place. Jana had produced a bottle of whisky, a single malt from an island not too far from home, and Anne found herself comforted by its familiar peaty notes.

Esther and Dawa sat together on the other couch and Anne could see some of the exhaustion she felt on their faces. She saw also how they leaned in to one another, and she realised they'd become close. They all had, she supposed. Esther caught Anne's eye and a look of understanding passed between them. A look of having survived something together that made Anne smile despite herself.

'Torran is an unusual name,' Jana said, breaking into Anne's thoughts. 'Where does it come from?'

'It's Gaelic,' Anne said. 'The Torran Rocks are a reef of small islands and underwater rocks off the Ross of Mull – the island in the Hebrides where we lived. They're notoriously dangerous. The name means "from the craggy rocks".' She paused, looking down into her glass. 'Rob's choice. He thought it sounded like a Viking god.'

'Yeah, I get that,' said Ace, pausing in his playing to tighten a string. 'It's a fine name.'

'It's also literary. The Torran Rocks cause the shipwreck in the novel *Kidnapped*. They change the hero's fate forever. I think Rob liked the connection. He's a writer . . .' She trailed off, unsure why she was saying so much.

But something had caught Jana's attention and she stood abruptly and left the room, returning a minute later with a small pile of battered paperbacks.

'I knew that name was familiar. Look.' She handed Anne the books. 'These were Yatri's – Torran's – he brought them with him to the Sunshine House and he took them when we left. He always seemed to be rereading them.'

Anne looked at the three slim paperbacks. *Siddhartha, The Prophet*. And the novel she'd slipped into Torran's backpack the morning he left for India, the book that had been missing when they'd searched his belongings with Superintendent Kumar. Robert Louis Stevenson's *Kidnapped*.

'I gave this to him,' she said at last, eyes fixed on the cover, fingers caressing the broken spine. 'I assumed he'd given it away.'

She flicked through the pages, but though worn and stained, there was nothing scribbled between the lines, no note slipped in and forgotten. She searched for the title page, where she knew she'd written something, some farewell note – she couldn't for the life of her remember what, but it suddenly seemed incredibly important. She missed it and went back through the first pages, once, twice. She opened the book wide and saw the serrated edges of a torn page. Gone. He'd ripped it out.

She put the books down. She could feel the rest of the room watching her and she didn't know what to say.

Esther broke the silence.

'Are you going to tell us what happened?' She was speaking to Jana and Ace, and Anne found herself pathetically grateful to have the spotlight taken away from her. 'The fire? At the Sunshine House.'

Ace stopped playing the guitar and glanced at Jana. She returned her husband's look and nodded.

'The Sunshine House was always a temporary place,' she began, with the air of one resigned to telling a story. Ace started strumming the guitar again, a soft accompaniment to his wife's words.

Maeve had finished reading and she put the book aside. Maya wriggled off the couch and crept over to Anne. She rested her arm on Anne's legs with the trusting intimacy of the young, then, after a moment, crawled sleepily into her lap, her head against Anne's chest. Anne gazed down at her as Jana spoke.

'Lorrie and Noula – they were the ones who stumbled upon the hunting lodge during a trek – they always said that no utopia could last. They'd been in some sort of cult back in the States and things hadn't ended well. There was a lot of that sort of thing back then. People looking for nirvana and discovering humans just don't live that well together. Lorrie used to say there is no place for humanity in heaven.

'But they wanted to try to live off-grid, to create a place for the freaks and hippies who truly wished to drop out. They thought that if they set a limit on the time the community was there, it would keep it more focused, truer to the original ideal. It was a strange theory, but in many ways it worked. We agreed that in thirty-three years everyone would leave.'

'Why thirty-three?'

Jana looked over at Esther.

'It's the number of years Christ was alive. Not that they were Christians, their beliefs were more pan-religious. But it was an auspicious number. And they both wanted to return home while they were still able.'

'They were sisters?'

'Partners. Met at eighteen and never looked back. True soul-mates. Even those who disparaged the notion had to agree there was something special about them.

'They spent a few summers setting the place up. They had a whole group of people by then. Dropouts they'd met in Nepal and Rishikesh and Goa. They were careful about who they invited to join. Very careful. They knew the dynamics of the group would dictate how successful the community was.

'We met them in Pushkar, in the deserts of Rajasthan. They'd come down for the winter – the house wasn't yet sustainable for the colder months. Ace got talking to Lorrie one morning while Noula and I were doing yoga on the hotel roof. He'd signed us up for the Sunshine House before breakfast.'

'But I thought you said they vetted people carefully,' Esther cut in. 'How could they, if you were invited so quickly?'

'Lorrie was perceptive; she saw people for what they were. Some would call her a psychic, although she'd never say that of herself. But she had a sense about things. About people. And she always followed her feelings. It worked out – most of the time.'

'So you all lived there for over thirty years, completely cut off from the world – no income, no valid documents – and then, after all that, everyone was happy just to leave?'

'Yes,' Jana said, as if it really could be that simple. 'And no. We had a lot of time to prepare for leaving, obviously. Ace and

I started scoping out the surrounding valleys and villages for land to build on over ten years ago. We had savings when we went to the valley, which we kept. Things are cheap here. The cottage industries in the valley – honey, jams, woodwork, candles – they managed to keep us all fed and the house in good repair. We bartered with local communities. And, of course, the sort of Westerners who can afford to be slumming it in India usually have money in the bank to back it up.'

'And Noula had family money,' Ace interrupted. 'A lot of it. Came from a family of bankers – at least that's what we gathered, we didn't talk much about our past lives. More in the early days, before people started forgetting. Detaching from the old existence. She was an only child and had inherited a fortune. And she was in India legally, the whole time, so she had access to things in a way a lot of us didn't. Don't ask me how. Although in India enough money can get you anything. Passports included.'

'Are they still here? In India?'

'Noula and Lorrie? No, they went back to the States. At least that's what they planned; it's hard to imagine them there. But they were getting on. We all were. It wasn't sustainable to be getting old and living three days' hike from civilisation.'

'Still,' Esther said. 'It must have been hard to leave.'

Jana nodded, the firelight dancing in her eyes.

'We had this house all but ready by the time of the fire. We were willing to go. To start the next chapter. But it was difficult, in those last months. Endings are always hard. No matter how non-attached you try to be.'

'But why the fire?' Anne asked. 'Why not just shut the place up?'

'You're assuming it was started on purpose,' Esther said.

There was a pause. Outside, the wind hummed. The logs in the fire spat, a cascade of red-hot embers falling on the hearth. Ace brushed them back towards the fire with his foot and nudged the stove door shut.

'It was,' Jana said quietly. 'We couldn't leave it to be ransacked by dope farmers, or by the bandits who hide out in the mountains. It had been our home – our everything – for so long.'

'And it was a purification,' Ace added. 'A fire ritual. Fire was the way we blessed and welcomed new people and it was the way we said goodbye.'

'But it's still standing,' Anne said. 'There's still so much of it left.'

Jana sighed. 'We left it burning. When we walked out of the valley it was still smouldering, but it was clear the whole thing wasn't going to go. Perhaps the house had ideas of its own. It had survived over fifty years before we got there. I like to think it might rise again, like a phoenix. Offer itself to some other people, some other time.'

She fell silent, the spectre of the Sunshine House rising before them. Looking into the fire Anne saw again the burnt-out rooms, the ash-covered furniture, the kitchen ceiling open to the sky.

'But what about Evie?' Esther looked from Jana to Ace.

'She left long before the fire.' Jana leant forwards to retrieve the whisky and poured herself another measure before handing the bottle to Ace. 'Well, she left twice. After Isaac died. He was her partner; they'd been together so long. It was very hard for her. She came back after a few months, stayed.' She looked to her husband. 'Another three, four years? But it was never the same for her without Isaac.'

'But she must have known about the end date – the thirty-three years?'

'Of course.'

'So why did she tell us to go now? When she'd have known you'd all be gone?'

Anne stiffened as she realised what Esther was getting at. Why *had* Evie sent them now? But Jana was shaking her head.

'No. She knew, of course, but thirty-three years would have been this year. Next month, in fact. We brought the date forwards. Things happened: Crystal had a stroke, we had a few accidents, a mountain leopard started taking out the animals. Everything just seemed to be telling us our time was up.'

'Otherwise, we'd still be there now,' Ace said.

'And we'd have found Torran there with you.' Anne felt another wave crashing over her.

Ace glanced at his daughter, curled on the couch, eyes fixed on the fire.

'Quite possibly.'

'Did everyone else go back to their countries?' Esther asked, shooting a worried look at Anne.

'No,' Jana said. 'Most stayed. There are a few we see from time to time, living in the next valley over. Some went to Nepal. Others went south. Occasionally we get an old Sunbird turning up at the door.'

'A *sunbird*?' Anne said, a little sharply, but it was disorientating to hear that word here. It inevitably brought Liam to mind. And where was he now, with his sketchbook and his easy smile? Perhaps home already, back in the real world.

'We called ourselves Sunbirds,' Jana said, smiling at Ace. 'It was a bit of a joke at first, but it stuck. It seemed fitting.'

'But it's more than that,' Ace said. 'It's an identity. A way of living, in harmony with each other and the earth, born in the Sunshine House. The valley is full of sunbirds in mating season; they nest in the trees around the house. And the more flowers we grew, the more they came.'

Anne thought of the sunbird she'd encountered the day she and Liam went to Jinsi falls, the flash of colour she thought she saw before falling into the river in the Sunshine Valley, and now this. But Rob was the one who saw meaning and symmetry in the world, not her.

Behind the fire, the colours of the tapestry glimmered in the candlelight.

'Of course the phoenix is a sunbird too,' Ace continued, following Anne's gaze. 'Symbol of renewal, hope, rebirth, transformation.'

There was a silence while each contemplated the intricate depiction of the great bird rising from the flames.

'And Torran came here with you?' Anne said at last, breaking the spell and turning back to Jana. She knew this, of course. But if she kept asking maybe the answer would change and he would have come and stayed, would, in fact, have just popped out and be expected to return at any minute. She ducked her head towards Maya, who was now fast asleep, curled like a cat in Anne's arms. The little girl's hair smelt of jasmine.

'Yes. He stayed with us for a few months. He went off, as he did, for a while and then came back for Christmas. He left in January. We haven't seen him since.'

'But he might come back again?' Anne kept her eyes on the crown of Maya's head. 'If he went and came back before, what's to stop him doing it again?'

Jana looked at her kindly but without the agreement Anne so desperately needed. 'It was different, this time. He left with most of his things. He told us he was leaving. Before, he would just slip away.'

Anne looked from Jana to Maeve.

'But he left the books,' she whispered.

'He gave them to me,' Maeve said. 'He told me he didn't need them any more, that he wasn't coming back this time. I'm sorry. I don't think he will.' She bit her lip and looked at her hands, hair tumbling over her face.

Anne couldn't remember the last time she'd felt so tired. She turned to Esther.

'So what now? Where on earth do we go from here?'

XLV

ESTHER

They spent three days at Shambala. Jana and Ace were generous hosts, plying them with wholesome food and good company. Esther and Dawa helped Jana in the garden and Ace in the
kitchen, neither of them any good at sitting back and relaxing.

Anne slept a lot and the tiredness behind her eyes began to
fade. Her wan cheeks filled out. She started to look more like
she had when Esther first saw her in Mussoorie, less than three
weeks earlier. And though there was something enchanted
about being there, the business of leaving Shambala and where
they would go next weighed heavily on Esther's mind.

She didn't see much of Maeve after the first evening. Taking
Maya to and from the local school took up much of her time, for it
was a round trip of over an hour and a half. The second day Maeve
didn't return in the morning but stayed at the school to teach an
English class to the children. Jana told Esther they'd thought of
home-schooling Maya, but Maeve wanted her daughter to have
the chance to socialise, to feel normal. As normal as possible in a
tiny mountain school where she was the only foreign child.

'I don't think Maeve regrets her upbringing,' Jana said, pinching out the new leaves on the stalks of her tomato plants. They
were in a large polytunnel in the sunniest part of the garden. 'But
I guess she found it hard to relate to people her own age when
she left. It was quite an extreme existence in the Sunshine Valley.
She always had people around, but they were older; they'd had
their lives before the valley. Maeve seems happy living here, but
I think she wants Maya to have the chance to feel happy living
among others too. This country is her home.'

*

'Will you ever go back?' Esther asked later, when they were sitting under the shade of a sprawling oak, its leaves beginning to brown and curl. Ace had brought them a tray of tea and flapjacks, sustenance as they fed a small bonfire with garden cuttings and burnable waste.

Jana looked at Esther over her mug. 'Go back where? The Sunshine Valley?'

'No, home home.'

Esther didn't even know where exactly they were from. Jana sounded German, Ace sounded English, but she wouldn't swear to either.

Jana smiled and then said slowly, as if explaining to a child, 'Esther, we are home.'

'I meant back to your native countries.'

Jana took a flapjack, the baked syrup glistening in the sun.

'Heaven,' she said, smiling as she chewed. 'I know what you're trying to say. But the truth is, we won't ever leave. This is our home. Ace and I were in our early twenties when we arrived in Kathmandu. We lived in the Sunshine Valley for over thirty years. Those people became our family. We left everything else behind.'

'What about your real families?'

Jana sighed. 'The Sunbirds are our *real* family. Maeve. Maya. Even Yatri.' She paused. 'But I understand what you're asking. You want to know if we left people behind – not knowing – like Yatri's parents.'

'Not just his parents. His friends, his family, people whose lives he's touched. His disappearance has been felt by a lot of people – it still is.'

Esther could hear her voice rising, and the bitterness in her words took her by surprise. But it was hard to like him right then, her baby cousin whom she barely knew. She thought of Robert, pacing the empty house at night, leaving the door unlocked in case his son's spirit came home.

And she thought of Iris – Robert's mother, her grandmother – who'd whispered in Esther's ear when it was clear she wasn't going to get better, that Esther was right, that Anne was to blame, that Anne wasn't fit to be a mother.

Not that she'd said that in her article. Not exactly.

Jana was watching her closely, eyes narrowed against the smoke.

'Life is always more simple and more complicated than that. Every one of the dropouts I've met in my years in India, every one, and there have been a great many, came with their own messy stories and circumstances. And in the beginning it mattered a lot. We were in the old mindset, where our attachments and perceived responsibilities towards others are paramount.

'But then you begin to see that there is another way to be. You can cut the ties of attachment. You can be free. You can be a Sunbird.'

Esther pictured her father, his grey flat where no plants would grow. What would his life be like if she didn't return? Her brother might visit once a year. The neighbours would probably check he was still alive, get the shopping in. But who would take him out for his lunch? Who would sit and do the crossword with him before he was too drunk to see straight? Who would make sure he ate? It was hard to imagine how she could ever feel free while her father sat alone in his Edinburgh flat. But maybe if she'd had the luxury of a functional family, she would have felt differently.

Jana's gaze had drifted to the trees, which grew close together at the bottom of the terraced patch. Esther wanted to ask her who she'd detached from in order to live the life she was leading, but something in the way Jana had spoken stopped her. They lived a charmed existence now, one worth making sacrifices for. Esther didn't know whether she envied or disapproved of them and their choices. But she knew she liked them.

And would she like the adult Torran too, despite everything? If they ever found him.

There was a squawk from above and two parrots took flight from the veranda as Anne appeared, gathering the clothes they'd hung to dry on the railings. She looked down at them, raising a hand before turning back to the house.

'She's looking better,' Jana said, motioning towards where Anne had been.

Esther murmured in agreement. Anne *was* looking better. But she was also retreating into herself again. And whenever Esther tried to bring up what they were going to do next, where they should go, Anne changed the subject. Dawa had another job starting soon and they'd agreed to leave the following day. But as far as the search went, this couldn't be it. Things couldn't just go back to how they'd been before; something had to change.

'Have you and Anne always been so close?'

The question hit Esther unexpectedly, the twist of something delicate and new. *Were* they close? She looked at her hands, rubbed at the ink smudge on her index finger. But the stain wouldn't shift.

'We've been through a lot together in the past few weeks. It's not always been easy.'

Jana nodded. She had an intense way of observing you, like she was checking what you really meant by reading your body language, the subtle movements of your face. It reminded Esther of Evie Sinclair.

'You lived with them for a time. As a child?' Jana held her gaze until Esther looked down at her hands again. She'd told them this much already.

'I had some troubles at home. My mum – Robert's sister – left, and my dad . . . Robert took me in for a few years. Anne wasn't happy about it. She never wanted me there. She was already pregnant with Torran.'

Esther glanced back up. Jana had her hands wrapped around her cup, still watching.

'Go on.'

'That's it. I moved home to dad's as soon as I could. When I was fourteen and could look after us both.'

'That's very young to be looking after someone, Esther.'

'I'm a journalist,' Esther said, pushing on. 'When Torran disappeared, I wrote an article about it, about all the disappearances in this area in the nineties. But he was the main focus. And that's why Evie approached me. Because she'd seen the article. I went to tell Anne and Robert, but Anne was out here already, and Robert didn't want to come. He asked me to come instead.'

Jana didn't ask why Robert hadn't wanted to come; she didn't ask about the article. She leant forwards to throw a flattened cardboard box on the fire.

'Still looking after people,' she murmured. 'Anne must have been happy to see you.'

The shadows were growing long in the garden; soon the sun would drop behind the mountains.

'No, actually.' Esther glanced at the veranda again, but Anne was nowhere in sight. 'She wasn't happy about that article I wrote; neither of them were.'

Jana raised her eyebrows, draining the last of her tea and putting the cup back on the tray.

'I always thought Torran had chosen to disappear.'

Jana nodded. 'A reasonable assumption.'

'Yes. But when I wrote about why he might have wanted to disappear, without telling anyone . . .' Jana hadn't asked, but it felt like a confession, and now that she had started Esther found she couldn't stop. 'I wrote things I probably shouldn't have. About his childhood, the isolated upbringing; Robert's obsession with his work; Anne's mental health; their lifestyle choices. The parallels with Anne's own life – Torran wasn't the first person in the family to walk out on his parents.'

She paused. Jana was shaking her head.

'What?'

'Why are you telling me this?'

205

Esther hesitated. A tiny bird perched on the tip of a pine tree was rocking backwards and forwards, looking down at them. Beyond the trees, the sky was fading to grey.

'I don't know.'

Jana's eyes were steady as she considered Esther.

'I think you do,' she said. 'I think you feel bad about what happened. What you did. How you made her feel. After she took you in. After she was a mother to you.'

Esther shook her head, reaching for a stick to nudge the cardboard closer to the flames.

'She was never a mother to me.'

Her words rose towards the bird, acrid as the smoke. And she felt an old, primal rage. Jana didn't get it; no one did.

'She didn't even try. She wasn't cut out to be a mother. Even her own son ran away from her—'

She broke off as Jana's attention shifted and she knew from the look on Jana's face that Anne was there. That she'd heard everything. Or heard enough.

Esther turned to see Anne standing behind her, face blanched, bending forwards slightly as if winded. And then she turned and walked away.

Esther found her in their room, folding laundry with an unnerving calm.

'Anne,' she said, but Anne wouldn't stop, wouldn't look at her. 'I don't know why I said that. I didn't mean it.'

Anne finished folding one of Esther's shirts and added it to the pile. She took another from the basket, her movements slow and methodical.

'You don't have to do that,' Esther said, trying to take the shirt, but Anne held firm, pulling it sharply from Esther's grasp. She continued folding. 'Anne, please.'

'It's fine,' Anne said quietly, taking the last piece of laundry from the basket. 'It's not as if you haven't said it all before.'

She lifted the clothes from the bed and put them in Esther's arms, avoiding her eyes.

'If we're leaving tomorrow, we'd better pack.'

Esther sat on the bed, still holding the clothes, as Anne retrieved their backpacks from behind the door. She thrust Esther's towards her, and a notebook fell from the top pocket, landing open on the floor between them.

Anne bent to pick it up, glancing down at the pages.

'What's this?' she said, as Esther threw the clothes aside and reached for the notebook. Not this, not now.

'Nothing.'

She tried to take it, but Anne wouldn't let go, her eyes fixed on the words.

'Anne—'

She shook her head, backing away and turning the pages slowly. Scanning the notes Esther had been making ever since Taigh na Criege: observations, thoughts, theories. Transcribed conversations. Scribbled by torchlight, under blankets, on the side of mountains, in all the moments she'd snatched alone.

'You're still writing about us,' Anne said. She scanned a few more pages. 'Of course you are.'

'No.'

'All this time.' The hurt on her face made Esther flinch. 'You never really came here to help.'

'It's nothing,' Esther said, trying not to sound desperate. 'Observations. A journal. Lists. It's nothing.'

'Don't, Esther.' Anne's voice was sharp, her face a picture of disbelief. Closing the notebook, she handed it back, and Esther saw how her hands shook. 'You promised. After all we've been through . . .'

Anne sank on to the bed, eyes fixed on the wall, her expression changing to that same look of defeat she'd worn on the steps of the Sunshine House.

'Why do you hate me so much? After everything we did for you.'

It was the self-pity, more than anything, the childish whine in her voice, the failure to cope with life like an adult, to ever take responsibility for anything. That bewildered, innocent expression of hers. As if she didn't know why bad things ever happened to her, as if she couldn't understand the part she played in her own life.

'What?' Esther said, unable to stop her voice rising. 'What did you do for me, Anne? What did you ever do? Robert did it all. You never wanted me there. You never made an effort. I hardly even existed to you.'

Anne's eyes widened.

'No. That's not true. I did my best. I tried everything to make you like me. But you never liked me. Nothing I did was good enough for you.'

'You didn't even see me. You were so wrapped up in Torran. I was invisible to you.'

'You made yourself invisible. You were always running away from me, hiding. Refusing to speak. You were difficult.'

'I was a child! You were the adult. You should have tried harder.'

Anne stood and took a step towards her, face flushed. In a voice as loud as Esther's she said, 'What would you have had me do, Esther? What would have been good enough? I wasn't your mother. I couldn't replace your mother.'

'Don't talk about her! I don't want to talk about her.'

'Esther.'

Anne reached a hand towards her, but Esther turned away, the anger leaving as quickly as it had come.

'Esther.' There was a new note in her voice, something broken and kind. Esther felt the tears that had been threatening. She turned back.

'I'm not crying,' she said, stupidly.

Anne almost laughed and then put a hand over her mouth, but Esther smiled, relieved. For a moment she thought Anne might hug her, but she stayed where she was.

'I'm sorry. About this.' Esther held up the notebook. 'About the article. About all of it.'

Through the window, smoke was still rising from the bonfire. Esther looked at the book in her hands and back to Anne. This couldn't end here; she needed more. They had to keep searching.

'I do still want to write about this,' she said, gesturing vaguely around them. 'All of this. But I won't. If you don't want me to.'

Anne held her gaze, her expression unreadable.

'I'd do it differently this time. I'd make it right.' It wasn't until she'd said it that Esther realised how desperately she wanted to make things right.

'I don't know if I even care any more,' Anne said, finally breaking eye contact.

Esther swallowed. 'About what?'

'What people think of me.' She looked down at her hands. 'But I did try, Esther. With you. With Torran. I did try.'

XLVI

BEFORE

They collect Esther on a wet, windless day, grim clouds pressing down on the block of flats where she and her dad are living. It's been eighteen months since her mother left. In Dundee, now, with a new man. Less than two hours away but she never visits and seldom calls. Gone is the little terraced house on the nice street where Iain had planted roses that climbed the walls. Her brother Callum has joined the army and Iain's shift patterns make it difficult for him to be there for eight-year-old Esther. At least that's what they tell themselves – and him; easier than getting into the drinking, the forgetfulness, the dirt that streaks the windows, the mould that creeps across the ceiling.

Esther doesn't make a fuss, which is a relief. She sits stony-faced in the back of the car, rain hitting the windows. Anne reaches for words of comfort, words of encouragement, but finds none. She is awkward in the face of this silent, serious child, and she looks to Robert to take the lead. But he is somewhere else entirely, eyes fixed on the winding road. He is on a book deadline, and she can almost hear the strands of story and character being woven together in his mind.

They stop to stretch their legs on the banks of Loch Lomond and Anne vomits in the trees. She is eight weeks pregnant. Esther walks to the rocky shore, eyeing a tree which grows from the water. One twisted branch resembles a small clinging bear, and Anne wants to point this out but her stomach heaves again and she closes her eyes.

*

On the ferry they buy Esther a hot chocolate and Robert rallies, pointing to the lighthouse, the castle, the sails of a distant boat. But Esther will not engage and Anne, bent double against the motion of the waves, feels a stab of irritation, of dislike, which she swallows down with the bile that keeps threatening to overwhelm her.

'It'll get easier,' Robert says mildly, as they sit by the fire that evening. A silent Esther in bed upstairs. Anne hadn't known if she was supposed to kiss her goodnight, if the door should be left open, if she should be reminded to pee before sleeping, if she needed help brushing her teeth.

Anne nods but she can't help feeling like she's already failed. Grasping in vain at the things she assumed would come naturally. So determined not to be as distant and exacting as her own mother, but not entirely sure how to be otherwise.

Robert is watching her and she wonders if he sees these failures too. He reaches a hand to her still flat belly and smiles.

'Thank you.'

She gives him a questioning look.

'For suggesting we take her. I know it's not ideal timing with the pregnancy and my deadline. But it means a lot to me. And it won't be for long. Lucy will be back.'

Anne bites her lip, because his beloved sister has been gone for too long with hardly a word, and because she is bone-tired and out of her depth and she suspects this shouldn't feel so much like drowning.

XLVII

ESTHER

After an early supper they spent the evening much as they had that first one, sitting by the fire in the round room, talking and drinking whisky while Ace strummed his guitar and Maeve read Maya her bedtime story. When it was finished, as had become her habit, the little girl crept over to Anne and curled up on her lap. Esther saw the softening of Anne's body as she wrapped her arms tightly around Maya, and turned her gaze quickly back to the fire before Anne could catch her looking. There was something unselfconscious in the way Anne was with Maya that Esther had never seen before.

She tried to concentrate on the conversation in the room – Ace and Dawa were discussing the route they would take back to Manali in the morning – but her mind kept running over the afternoon's argument. Snagging on Anne's face when she'd found the notebook. How the fear and anger Esther had felt gave way to relief. How Anne had looked at her, really looked at her, before looking away.

Before bed, she and Dawa went out to the veranda for a smoke. It was a clear night and they sat on the swing seat, leaning back to catch the shooting stars that fell like rain.

A meteor shower, Dawa told her. It happened every year around this time.

The air was sharp, and they sat close together, a scratchy blanket across their knees. It smelt like an old jumper, the sort Esther's dad would wear in the winter rather than turning the heating on. She'd grown used to these companionable evenings with Dawa, leaning in to an easy intimacy unburdened by the past.

He spoke softly as they gazed up at the sky. Telling stories of his village, near McLeod Ganj, the different communities and people – exiles, refugees and travellers who'd made those foot-hills home. About the glaciers which retreated every year, the creeping changes of climate on his beloved mountains.

'It's not just the people who need their stories shared. You should come – when all this is over.' He looked at Esther for a long moment and something subtle yet palpable seemed to shift between them.

But before she could respond the glass door opened and Ace stepped on to the veranda, pulling a chair to where they sat.

'Mind if I join you?' he asked, sitting down without waiting for an answer. He had a long wooden pipe that he smoked in the evenings, packed with Malana cream. He didn't approve of tobacco, or any other type of marijuana. Only Malana cream.

He lit the pipe now and took several long tokes, exhaling a series of smoke rings upwards. Esther watched as they quivered in the lamplight and dispersed.

'I have something to say.' Ace broke the silence, his voice more serious than might be expected after the whisky and the ganja. 'Just between us.'

Esther exchanged a look with Dawa, and she could feel him tensing as her pulse quickened; she'd known this couldn't be it.

Ace studied them for a moment more before speaking.

'I'm fairly certain Yatri is in a Buddhist monastery in Ladakh.' He took another puff on his pipe. Behind him, the tops of the trees swayed gently.

Esther let out the breath she'd been holding.

'What makes you say that?'

He blew another smoke ring towards the stars. 'Because he told me that was where he was going.'

'But I thought—'

'He told *me*. Not the girls.' Esther couldn't see Ace's expression in the shadows. 'He decided it was time to cut the ties, the attachments he felt towards us – especially Maeve and

Maya – and move on. He didn't want to tell Maeve because he knew she'd go looking for him.'

Selfish, so selfish. Esther didn't say it aloud, but her anger returned at the path of confusion and grief Torran left in his wake. How could one person hold their own needs and desires so high above everyone else's?

'Do you know which monastery?' Dawa asked. 'Ladakh is full of them.'

Ace was silent for a long time, his eyes on the night sky. Eventually he turned to look at them through the smoke.

'Yes,' he said, with something like reluctance. 'I think I do.'

XLVIII

ANNE

Anne carried a sleeping Maya to bed. Following Maeve to the room they shared, she placed her tenderly on the mattress. The child shifted in her sleep without waking. She was so beautiful, fair hair falling in ringlets around her face. The two women gazed down at her in the dim light. She would have been a good grandmother, Anne thought; it would have suited her better than motherhood, in many ways. Now she'd probably never know.

Maeve pulled a crocheted blanket over her child, running a hand through Maya's hair.

'She's exhausted,' she said, her voice a whisper.

'Long days and sea air,' Anne said. A favourite expression of Rob's.

Maeve gave her a bemused look.

'Well, mountain air, I guess.' Anne smiled and Maeve smiled back.

'I'm sorry he left you,' Maeve said and for a second Anne thought she was talking about Rob. 'You seem nice. But Yatri – he's on a spiritual journey. He's still searching and he can't let anyone hold him back.' She bit her lip, suddenly looking very young and very sad.

Anne tried to merge the image she kept close of her boy with the man Maeve had known. The man who'd lived in the mountains. Who was like a father. Who never stayed. And she wondered how he bore it, the weight of all the love they'd given him.

She put a hand on Maeve's arm and squeezed it gently. 'I'm sorry he left you too.'

*

Esther was waiting in their room, sitting up in bed, a woollen blanket wrapped around her shoulders. She started speaking as soon as Anne closed the door, her voice low and excited.

As she listened, Anne waited for her heart to leap, her pulse to quicken, the adrenaline of a new lead to kick in. But she was still thinking of Maeve, of the community Torran had found among the Sunbirds, of how he'd been happy and how he'd left. She sat on the edge of the bed and nodded when Esther asked if she was all right.

He'd been happy and yet he'd left them too. Perhaps she could find some solace in that.

They were ready to go before six, bags heavy with provisions Ace had packed for them. The sky was crimson as they hugged their hosts goodbye. Jana held tightly to Anne for so long that she eventually took a step back, breaking the embrace. There were tears in the older woman's eyes, a look that Anne couldn't read.

'I have something for you,' Jana said quietly, as if she didn't want the others to hear. From the pocket of her dress she took out Torran's battered copy of *Kidnapped*. 'Maeve agreed: it belongs to you.' She shoved it brusquely into the front pocket of Anne's rucksack before stepping back.

'Thank you,' Anne said. 'For everything.'

Jana shook her head. 'I should have got it to you sooner. Forgive me.' She looked like she wanted to say more, but Anne was already backing away, pulled by the impatience of the others waiting further along the path.

With a final wave, she turned and walked under the rhododendron arch, following Esther and Dawa back through the gate to the roughly paved track that led to Ramini and the main road back to Manali. Half listening to their conversation and half absorbed in the sky, the birdsong, the smoke that rose from chimneys.

As they reached a fork in the road, they startled a tribe of blue magpies, who took to the air, cawing. Anne watched them rise and tried to imagine the weightlessness of flight, the confidence to soar so high without fear of falling. The earth contracting as the sky explodes.

XLIX

ESTHER

From Ramini they took a taxi back to Manali – a mere two-hour journey, incredible after the days of walking they'd done. It was disorientating to move so fast, to see the houses and rivers and valleys rush by without having the time to take it all in.

Esther had expected Anne to want to set off for the monastery immediately. It was an overnight jeep ride to Leh, the capital of Ladakh, a region high in the mountains north of Manali, and from there another two hours' drive to the Likir Gompa monastery. But to her consternation, Anne wanted to wait, to spend a night at the Green Tara and set out the following day. Or the next. Her sudden lack of urgency reminded Esther of the moments before reaching the Sunshine House, of Anne falling further behind the closer they got.

In Manali, they sat outside a German bakery, waiting for Dawa to return from arranging a jeep to take him home. He would not be coming to Ladakh. He had jobs lined up in McLeod Ganj, and though he'd told Anne he would happily cancel them, she'd been surprisingly firm in her refusal. There had been no question of Esther not going, and Anne's assumption that they'd be travelling on together pleased Esther more than she cared to admit.

As they ate the flapjacks Ace had packed for them, Esther took out her *Lonely Planet* and began reading the introduction to Ladakh out loud. She could already picture the lunar landscape, the colourful Tibetan monasteries hewn from the mountains, the high-altitude sand dunes, Anne's reunion with Torran – and she was impatient to go.

'I was thinking I might stay, you know, after we find him.' Anne cut across Esther's reading. 'At least for a while.'

Esther put the book down. Anne hadn't been listening; she was jumping ahead. Too far ahead. Esther didn't want to think about what would happen when it was all over. Not yet.

She raised an eyebrow and Anne smiled, crumbling the flapjack between her fingers.

The sun was warm on their backs, two mugs of coffee on the picnic table before them. There were travellers at another table, studying a map and debating in low voices. One of them had dreadlocks so long they almost touched the ground.

'I was thinking I could help. The other families. It doesn't look like they've found that couple.'

It was true; there were posters all over town bearing the grinning faces of the young Americans who'd disappeared from Malana.

'Maybe I could set up some sort of support network, a charity or something.' She shrugged. 'It's just an idea.'

'It's a good idea,' Esther said cautiously.

'And I'd like to travel. Around India. We went to all these places, but we never really saw anything. So much looking and only seeing what wasn't there.' Anne paused, sipping her coffee, cradling the cup in both hands. 'I don't feel I've really embraced India. And now I think I'd like to.'

Esther looked across the road, towards the river that flowed through town, rickshaws and scooters and cars streaming over a wide bridge, beeping their horns, scattering chickens. The water moved quickly, dragging broken branches and plastic bags downstream. She felt the weight of the guidebook in her hands and wondered if she'd embraced India as much as she could have, what that even meant.

'You need to call Robert,' she said, glancing at Anne. But Anne didn't respond.

Turning her eyes back to the river, Esther saw Dawa's familiar figure walking towards them. She thought of the stories he'd told her about his community, the Tibetan refugee colony, the cottage industries, the grassroots initiatives for change, for sustainability. The resilience of a people in exile. She thought of all the other stories she could write.

Anne finished her coffee and stood up.

'I know I have to call him,' she said. 'So much has happened.'

Esther nodded, watching two pigeons snatch crumbs from beneath a table, picturing Robert halfway around the world. Waiting. The early morning light. The wind teasing the waves, the gulls circling overhead.

'It wasn't the same for him, you know,' Anne continued, her eyes following Esther's to the pigeons.

Esther looked over. 'What?'

'Being a parent. Fatherhood – it wasn't as stifling. It was the pleasant breeze that floats through a room. But for me, being his mother was oxygen, the very air I breathed. Only I was always drowning, and I could never get enough.' She turned to Esther and there was something pleading in her expression. 'It was like never being able to catch a breath.'

They said goodbye to Dawa beside the jeep as the driver loaded his bags and the camping equipment they'd taken with them to the Sunshine Valley. They were surrounded by other jeeps, drivers and guides leaning against their cars, watching with unmasked curiosity.

Anne offered her hand to Dawa and he took it in both of his.

'I can still come with you,' he said. 'I can stay with you until you find him.'

He glanced at Esther and she wanted to tell him yes. To stay. To come with them and finish this thing together. But Anne was shaking her head.

'I'll never be able to thank you enough,' she said. 'For everything. Not just for pulling me out of that river.'

Dawa laughed. 'It's been my great privilege, Anne. I would rescue you from a river any day. That one—' He nodded towards Esther. 'I'm not so sure.'

Anne tried to give him more money than the agreed fee, but he pushed it gently aside. Thanking him again, she put a hand to his cheek and held it there, before turning and busying herself with her pack. Unnecessarily adjusting a strap, giving them a moment of privacy.

Dawa looked at Esther.

'It feels too soon to say goodbye,' she said, not quite able to return his smile. Their shadows stretched long in the sun.

He stepped forwards until her nose was pressed against his jacket and his words were in her ear.

'I wasn't going to say goodbye. You come find me when all this is over, Esther. We'll find some other stories for you.'

She smiled then, though he couldn't see it. Feeling his arms tighten around her, thinking of how endings are also always beginnings.

L

ROBERT

Robert was walking Tessa and didn't hear the phone ringing unanswered through the empty house. Outside, the sea was a churning green, autumn creeping over the hills in whispers of orange and brown.

It rang again an hour later when he was shovelling seaweed into a wheelbarrow to spread on the garden: the blackcurrants, the rhubarb, the flower beds. It had been a long time since his heart had leapt at the sound but for some reason it did then, and without being conscious of dropping the wheelbarrow he found that he was running.

The ringing had stopped by the time he flung open the porch door, and he stood in the middle of the kitchen looking around as if for some clue as to who had been calling. His eyes fell on a photo of Anne and Torran on Inch Kenneth and he knew in his bones it had been Anne. He waited a moment more, listening intently to the ticking of the clock, holding his breath, trying not to disturb whatever forces might be at work in the magical ringing of the phone. But when the silence persisted, he exhaled and walked over to the Aga, lifted one of the hotplate covers and set the kettle on the hob.

He was just finishing his tea when the phone rang again. Anne's voice. So familiar and so strange. He gripped the receiver and listened with everything he had, as if attempting to untangle the syllables of a foreign language. He was standing in the hallway, staring at the pile of letters addressed to himself and Anne which he'd neglected to open. As his wife spoke to him over the buzz and echo of a noisy line, he looked at the letters of her name and marvelled at their simplicity.

And then, from all the words that were spoken: 'You need to come. We know where he is. This is it, Rob. I really believe this is it.'

He thought he could hear the smile on her face, and looking up caught the smile that was spreading across his own in the hall mirror.

'Rob? Are you hearing me OK? Rob?'

Lost in his own reflection, Robert turned back to the receiver in wonderment.

'Rob?'

'Yes . . . I hear you. I'm here.'

She laughed. 'Great. I thought I'd lost you.'

'You never lost me, Anne. Not for a minute.'

She laughed again, but he heard the unguarded joy falling away and he wanted to reach out and pull it back towards them.

'No,' she said, and she wasn't laughing any more. 'I meant on the phone, Rob. This doesn't change anything.'

Now he laughed. 'What are you talking about? This changes everything.'

There was a pause. Robert listened to the static and clicks on the line and, somewhere beyond, the sound of the wind.

'I think we're going to find him now.' Her voice was growing more distant, the connection breaking. 'You need to get on a plane. I'll send you the details.'

'Anne, listen. I've been thinking. A lot.' The line hissed and a rumble like low thunder filled his ear.

'I can't hear you, Rob. Let's talk when you arrive.' Her voice was thin and wispy as a sigh.

'All this time I thought he was dead,' Robert said to the click of the line being cut.

Robert will forget the conversation with Anne, the sounds drifting down the receiver from unknown Himalayan streets. He will forget the blood singing briefly in his ears and how his stomach dropped to understand the distance between them, as expansive as the horizons that filled his waking dreams.

But he will remember leaving the house and taking the path through the garden to the sea, the abandoned wheelbarrow and the impossible divide between the moment of dropping it and this. How his world shifted. A realignment of what he thought he knew and what actually was. Light-headed, light-hearted, so giddy he could laugh. Or cry. But he did neither, only continued walking like a man enchanted to the gate that marked the end of the land.

He will not remember the height of the tide or the angle of the sun, the length and depth of the shadows upon the sand. He removed his shoes and socks and left them by the gatepost, but he will not remember this either. Nor will he be able to say precisely how he came to be naked and walking into the sea, arms open to the icy grip. The tug of current, not strong, but insistent, pulling him towards the horizon. The water closing around his legs and torso and shoulders. The smoothness of the sand beneath his feet interrupted by the pain of embedded rocks, broken shells, the movement of something alive, disturbed by his presence.

He will remember his eyes closing only as the water rushed over them, filling his nostrils and ears, rejoining over the crown of his head. And he will remember picturing the sea's grey surface from above as something complete. Something unbroken.

LI

ANNE

There were murmurings among the travellers when they entered the common room of the Green Tara Guesthouse. A large group had gathered near the windows but a silence fell as they noticed Anne and Esther in the doorway.

Anne looked around for Dolma. She recognised a few faces from their previous stay, but her friend was nowhere to be seen. A whisper rippled through the travellers. *That's her.* She saw the exchanged glances and faltered.

'What is it? What's happened?'

Esther put a hand on her arm. A tall girl with a shaved head and a nose piercing walked towards them. She wore an expression that could mean only one thing.

'Are you the mother of the missing boy?' she asked. Her eyes were grey, like a winter sea.

Anne tried to respond but the room was rushing away from her.

'Get a chair,' someone said. There was a general shuffling, and an overstuffed armchair was thrust forwards. She felt Esther guiding her into it. Funny, the things you notice, she thought, gazing at the pattern of entwined vines and leaves. Where had this chair come from? How had it ended up with her now sitting on it, in this moment, at the end of everything?

People were talking again, but she wasn't listening, an insistent buzzing in her head. She traced the vines with a slow finger. They reminded her of a wallpaper she'd seen once in a catalogue and almost bought.

At least it's over now.

Esther was talking to the grey-eyed girl and another who had curly dark hair and silver bangles on both arms. Anne had never been the sort of person to wear bangles, but maybe she would try. She liked the way they jangled together, like laughter. Things would be different now, anyway.

And there were so many things she'd never done. Too many to list, but she started anyway: drugs, tattoos, piercings, full moon parties, dancing barefoot on the sand, riding a motorbike, cliff jumping . . . Ridiculous really. Had she ever truly lived?

Yes.

Standing at the top of the world looking down at the Sunshine Valley. The quivering of a purple sunbird in the trees. Torran laughing in the garden. Rob standing in the middle of a crowded auditorium. The vibration of bow on strings, the swell of music in the air. The beating of wings in her chest. This was it. She was free. She felt a rush that could have been flight or could have been falling, the thrill of the earth rising to meet her, the vastness of the sky. Joy and sorrow in equal measure.

'Anne!' Esther was kneeling before her. She was quite beautiful, really, in a strange sort of way. *If I'd had a daughter.*

'Anne, listen to me.'

She was aware of the others shrinking back, as if from a flame. They don't want to be here; they don't want to witness this pain. She wanted to tell them that it was all right. She would be all right. It was over; she was free. At last, an ending. All she'd ever wanted was an ending.

'It's not Torran. It's not Torran.' Esther was repeating the same phrase over and over and Anne stared at her, the words refusing to make sense. Until suddenly they did.

'What?'

The confusion in the room cleared. Esther took Anne's hands. 'Are you OK?'

Anne shook her head. 'Yes. What's happened?'

'The body of that American boy was found this morning. It looks like he was attacked.'

'And the girl?'

Esther sighed. 'No sign. They found some belongings dumped in a ravine not far from the body. But no money and no passports. It doesn't look good.'

Anne felt the weight return to her limbs. 'Would they have kept the girl alive?'

'It seems unlikely. She was probably killed as well and dumped somewhere, or made a run for it and got lost in the mountains.'

'And died.'

'Most likely. But you never know.'

'No,' Anne said, sinking back into the chair. 'You never know.'

She thought of the parents, and she didn't know who to feel worse for. The ones who were taking their child home in a coffin or the ones who might never take their child home. Who might spend the rest of their lives wondering and hoping and never knowing. The burden of a loss too great to bear, too precious to lay down.

Anne slept fitfully that night, and though morning brought birdsong, the heaviness in her body hadn't lifted. She lay in bed and watched the sun's first rays fan the ceiling like water, postponing the moment when she would have to rise, to shower, to dress, to go. Even though they were so close; because they were so close. Like staring directly at the sun, Anne found she couldn't quite look the moment of finding him square on.

The evening had been a chaos of rumour and news and plans jostling for attention. But Dolma, pragmatic as always, had taken Anne and Esther away from the shocked chatter of the common room and ensconced them in her private quarters. Esther had been the one to fill Dolma in on everything, while Anne sipped sweet chai, adrift in the aftermath of the last twenty-four hours, unsure what to cling to.

It was only as they were standing, preparing to retire, that Anne understood a plan had been made. Dolma would call ahead. Even monasteries at the end of the world had telephones these days, and she would go into Manali first thing in the morning to check the number at the post office. Anne felt dazed. It seemed improbable somehow, after such a journey, that everything could culminate in one simple phone call.

Esther didn't appear at breakfast, which was served in a hall adjacent to the common room now that the weather was cooler. Anne avoided the familiar faces and ate quickly. It was strange to eat alone, and she found she kept looking around for Esther, missing her lively chatter, the observations she threw out about everyone and everything.

When she'd finished, Anne put some fried bread and jam on a plate and carried it to Esther's room. She knocked softly and, when there was no response, pushed the door ajar to peer in.

Esther was on the bed, eyes closed, still wearing the dust-streaked clothes of the day before.

'Esther?'

She didn't reply but Anne saw her eyelids flicker. She looked startlingly fragile. Childlike in a way that twisted Anne's heart.

She walked over to sit beside her, suddenly afraid.

'Esther? Are you asleep?'

Esther mumbled incoherently before opening her eyes. She looked at Anne for a long moment without any sign of recognition.

'I don't feel very well,' she said eventually, her voice barely a whisper.

Esther had never been a sickly child. Anne could count on one hand the number of times she'd had to stay home in bed.

Anne put the plate down on a chair and placed a palm on Esther's forehead. She was burning up.

She'd been too dizzy to stand, she told Anne quietly, and her head was pounding. She felt light-headed but also like there was an unbearable pressure between her skull and her skin. She wanted to throw up. Her breathing felt tight.

'You've got a fever,' Anne said, rapidly running through and attempting to dismiss the more serious causes. But in this part of the world there were so many. And some could be deadly.

Anne fetched painkillers from her room, and a rehydration sachet, just in case. She mixed the powder with water from a bottle and handed it to Esther, along with the pills.

'You probably just need rest,' she said, trying to sound more confident than she felt; Esther looked diminished.

'I'm so sorry, Anne,' Esther murmured, eyes half closed. 'You should go today . . . Once we know for sure he's there . . . I'll be all right with Dolma till you get back.'

Anne was already shaking her head when, as if conjured by the mention of her name, there was a cursory knock at the half-open door, and Dolma entered. They both turned towards her.

'You're not well.' Her manner as she surveyed Esther was matter-of-fact. 'I will call for the doctor.'

Anne was perched on the bed, a hand on Esther's arm. She saw Dolma take this in for a moment before speaking. She could feel Esther's pulse beneath her fingers and tried to let it steady her.

He was there. He had to be there.

'I have news.'

She spoke with such tenderness that Anne knew before Dolma continued, and she clutched at Esther's clammy hand, willing the news to change, the outcome to be different. Searching Dolma's face for the smile that didn't come.

'I have spoken with Yongzen Rinpoche, from the monastery. I'm sorry, Anne. Torran was there, but he left. Not long ago. In the last week.'

There is always a moment when something is shattered beyond repair.

Esther drew in a shaky breath, and Anne felt the pressure of fingers on her own.

'OK,' she said, drawing herself up, casting around for a smile. 'I'm OK.' She wished Dolma would leave, that they would both stop staring at her with such concern. She had been here before. Too many times.

'Did he know where Torran was headed?' Esther's voice was breathless as she struggled to sit up against the pillows.

'No,' Dolma said, still looking at Anne. 'Rinpoche thought he was heading south. But he had no idea where.'

Anne left Dolma tending to Esther and returned to her room, ostensibly in search of her first aid kit and a thermometer. But she found herself motionless, staring at her rucksack. She had barely unpacked; it would be easier to go than to stay. As she returned her few belongings to her bag, she thought of the magpies the previous morning, swooping through the air as she watched from the ground. It would be a relief to get out of the mountains for a while. Robert would be here soon, and until then Dolma would take care of Esther. She was in good hands. There was no real reason now to stay.

She heard Dolma leaving Esther's room and waited until her steps faded away. She scribbled a note to Esther and slipped it under her door. She could hear Esther's breathing, laboured and tight, and she hesitated, opening the door slightly to peek in. But Esther was asleep, head thrown fitfully back against the pillows. Anne closed the door quietly and tiptoed away.

LII

BEFORE

Lying in the darkness of her childhood bedroom, Anne counts the headlights that flash across the ceiling. It's a quiet residential street in south London and sometimes the minutes stretch to hours between the yellow arches that fade to red as a car slips past.

She has finished her exams and knows she's done well. It's only four months until her eighteenth birthday and tonight she is about to rewrite her story. Come September, she will not take up her hard-won place at the Royal College of Music. Will not graduate and join the Royal Philharmonic Orchestra. Will not live the life her parents have dreamed for her. But she is not rebellious by nature and this single act of defiance will shape her in ways she cannot begin to imagine.

She doesn't think sleep will come but it does. She wakes before her alarm and for the beat of a second it is an ordinary day. She gets up and showers and brushes her teeth. She stands perfectly still in the centre of the rug and then puts the letter she has written under her pillow and walks out.

She lingers in the kitchen to say goodbye, but the significance of the moment is hers alone. Her father glances up from his newspaper and gives her a nod; her mother doesn't even turn from the sink where she stands washing the dishes, her Marigold gloves covered in bubbles. Anne wants to say something, but in the end words fail her.

The latch sticks briefly as she pulls the front door shut.

Robert is waiting in his old van, some belongings and her cello stowed safely in the back; by nightfall they will be in Scotland. The trees that line the street are dusty with blossom.

A blackbird calls from a gatepost. At the corner she turns and looks back up the road at her parents' house for the last time. A moment of hesitation. But there are no clouds in the blueness of the sky; she has no way of knowing that by the time she decides to call them it will be too late.

Her first sight of Taigh na Criege is the one she will remember when she is no longer there. Not a breath of wind; sunlight skimming the sea, pulling the green from the grass; birdsong.

She walks beside Robert, and he squeezes her hand as they approach the rundown farmhouse, the walled gardens, the tumbling sheds and outbuildings. She wants a moment to take it all in, this new life at the edge of the world. But Robert is excited. He wants to show her everything at once and can't stop talking, telling her what they will do and how it will be. And all the while she is trying to catch her breath.

They will spend the first night alone, whispering together in sleeping bags on the floor of what will become their bedroom. The window is open and they will hear the sea sing its lullaby to the shore.

Robert's friends will come the next day with his stuff, with furniture and tools, and they will begin rebuilding, stripping and transforming the summer house of his childhood into their new home. Their great adventure.

But they are children playing at life, and it will take much longer and be much harder than either of them can imagine now, as they stand hand in hand in the sun, watching the starlings who have nested in the roof streaking across the open sky.

LIII

ANNE

At the Manali bus station Anne scanned the boards, the familiar destinations and the ones she'd never heard of. Still, after all this time. She felt the rush of possibility. Thought of all the places Torran might have gone. Of Liam's beach in Goa. Her hotel room in Mussoorie. Taigh na Criege.

Rishikesh. A holy town straddling the Ganges, somewhere she'd always wanted to return to. As good a spot to start as any. She bought her tickets without another thought. The overnight bus to Dehradun and then the Noon Express AC to Haridwar. Perhaps she'd find that bookseller Liam had told her about, get something new to read. Then a short local bus ride from Haridwar to Rishikesh.

She boarded the bus as the sky began to darken, the propulsion of the journey in her veins. The thrill of moving forwards. She thought of how close they had been, of how close she might still be. But was she running towards him or running away? Was she still searching? She thought of Robert, arriving to find her gone, to find Esther abandoned. What would they think and would she tell them where she was?

She wanted to move, but the bus idled, waiting for the last passengers to board. A Tibetan woman who could have been Anne's age or could have been much older was holding things up, blocking the doors as she hugged a younger woman goodbye. They were so similar they could only have been mother and daughter. The younger woman, trapped in the tight circle of her mother's embrace, was casting apologetic looks at the people trying to board around them, rolling her eyes affectionately.

But Anne saw how she leaned in to her mother at the last moment, how all the weight left her body as she kissed her goodbye.

Above the crowded station a monkey was running on all fours along an electrical wire, one baby clinging to its front, one to its back. As Anne watched, the baby on the back slipped and began to fall, little arms flailing in the air. Without breaking stride the mother caught it, threw it deftly over her shoulder, and carried on down the line as if nothing had happened.

Smiling, Anne turned to ask Esther if she'd seen, but of course the seat beside her was empty, and she stared at the space where Esther should have been. She felt the vibration of the engine as the driver revved it impatiently. People were shouting farewells. They were about to leave. And all at once Anne was standing, pulling her rucksack from the overhead rails, pushing past passengers as she moved against the tide to the front of the bus. Coming face to face with the daughter just as she broke free from her mother's arms and climbed the stairs. Seeing Anne, the woman stepped back down to let her off.

'You're going the wrong way, aunty,' she said, with a smile.

Anne looked around for the woman's mother, but she'd melted into the crowd. She opened her mouth to tell the woman . . . something. That there was no right or wrong way, perhaps; that sometimes to move forwards you have to go back. But it all sounded ludicrous and, anyway, the woman had gone, was aboard and the doors had closed and the engine rumbled, and Anne watched as the bus reversed out of the bay and drove away.

She stood in its wake and for a moment imagined herself on it still; imagined the sleepless night, the sunrise in Dehradun, the Noon Express to Haridwar. Dizzy at the divergence of two ways, neither right nor wrong.

It was dark by the time she returned to the Green Tara. Dolma was emerging from Esther's room and didn't blink at seeing Anne, rucksack on her shoulders, walking down the corridor towards her. Anne wanted to say something, to try to explain, but couldn't find her voice.

Dolma's face was kind as she wordlessly handed Anne the note she'd slid under Esther's door. She put a steadying hand on Anne's shoulder before continuing down the hall.

Esther was still asleep. She lay with hair splayed around her head in an auburn crown, a fine sheen of sweat across her brow. The room was full of shadows; through the window an almost full moon was rising.

Anne left her rucksack leaning against the wall and pulled an armchair close to the bed. She tucked the sheets around Esther, placing a hand briefly on her hot forehead. Esther stirred, muttering something she couldn't quite make out. Anne brushed the hair from Esther's cheek. And when she was sure she was still asleep, Anne took Esther's pale hand and felt the fingers curl and tighten around her own.

When the moon had risen high in the sky, Anne turned on the small bedside lamp and looked around for something to read. She didn't think sleep would come, and she didn't want to leave Esther. Not yet. She thought briefly of the shelves of books downstairs in the common room, left behind by other travellers. And then she remembered Jana shoving *Kidnapped* into her bag just as they were leaving, and went to her rucksack to retrieve it.

A slim paperback edition, it weighed almost nothing. She'd bought it for Torran as a going-away present, half hoping it would serve as a reminder of all he was leaving behind. She'd read it to him so many times when he was a child.

Back in the armchair, she flicked idly through the pages and it fell open in her hands where the spine had broken. She looked down and her heart turned over.

There, tucked between the end of one chapter and the beginning of the next, was an envelope. Her name. Robert's name.

Their address. Ink faded. Envelope creased and stained but unopened. She turned it over and over again. But however she looked at it, the writing remained unchanged. The unmistakable scrawl of her son's hand.

LIV

ROBERT

Evie was sitting on the bench in Princes Street Gardens when Robert arrived. She wasn't the only woman sitting alone, but he knew instinctively that it was her. And he had the feeling she knew he was approaching, even though she didn't turn her head.

'Evie?'

'Robert.' Her eyes were a striking blue against her white-blonde hair. She reached a hand towards him and rather than shaking his she simply took it in her own and pulled him to sit beside her on the bench. She patted their entwined fingers with her other hand, the way his grandma would, smile never wavering.

They sat in silence. Before them, a young mother was push-ing a pram up and down the path, exhaustion etched in every line of her face, but she smiled as she walked past and Robert had a sudden vision of Anne standing in the doorway of his study, a screaming Torran in her arms, and the regret of it almost winded him. As if reading his thoughts, Evie nodded and patted his hand again, and he thought about how he should feel awkward by this uninvited intimacy and yet all he really wanted to do was lay his head in her lap and cry.

'You leave this afternoon?' Evie said.

'Evening flight to London and on to Delhi tomorrow morning.'

Evie sighed and it was a wistful sound. 'Not a day goes by that I don't think about boarding a plane and going back.'

As she spoke she looked up at the sky as if to find the plane that would take her there. 'I thought Scotland was home, and

237

the whole time I was in India I knew I'd eventually come back. But now it's the opposite: I can't imagine dying here, and isn't that the final test?'

Robert cleared his throat. The young woman had sat down on a nearby bench with a book in her lap, one hand pushing the pram back and forth, back and forth. Above them the castle was a dark outline cutting the sky like a child's stencil.

'I was in India when my mother died,' Evie continued. 'She was young enough that it was a shock, when I finally returned. Losing a parent isn't something you can truly comprehend until it happens. I always thought there would be time.'

Robert turned at the quiver in her voice.

'For what?'

She glanced sideways at him. 'To make amends: she never knew what happened to me. How happy my life was. She died not knowing.'

'I'm sorry,' he said, thinking of his own mother. Thinking of Anne's parents, both killed in a car crash not long after she'd run away with him to Scotland.

'It was my own fault.' Evie squeezed his hand and then withdrew hers and folded them together in her lap.

Robert leant back against the bench. 'Thank you for agreeing to speak to me.'

'Of course.'

The leaves were turning, orange bleeding into summer's green. Robert knew he had a right to be angry, to demand answers, but he felt strangely detached, like the leaf that at any moment might break free and flutter to the ground or be swept away on a current of air.

'Why didn't we hear about you?' he said. 'Turning up after all those years. That's a newsworthy story.'

Evie nodded. 'It should've been. I'd no official papers, just enough money to get to Delhi, to throw myself at the mercy of the British embassy. I'd last been registered in Nepal so they had no record of me ever entering the country. But it was

September 2001 and by the time they'd got round to interviewing me, the planes were crashing into the Twin Towers; within a week India and Pakistan were threatening nuclear war and nothing else was newsworthy after that.'

Robert grunted at the inevitable memory of where he'd been: the static of his portable radio and the unreality of it as he shovelled compost with the hens, the sea blinding in the sunshine. Anne just gone.

He looked at Evie. 'When did you leave? Anne was travelling to India . . .'

To his surprise, she was already nodding.

'You knew?'

'I didn't know. But I had a feeling. They put me on a plane two days later. The airport was chaos: so much security, flights cancelled, people everywhere. I saw a woman who looked like Yatri. She was searching, looking at every single person. I remembered her because there was a bit of a scene. She took someone's arm, just to turn him around to see his face. A simple mistake. But he was on edge, probably trying to smuggle something out of the country. He didn't want to be noticed, anyway.'

Robert could picture it well. He'd been through it enough times – the quickening of his pulse as he recognised something familiar in a stranger's step.

'She caught my eye. But I didn't know who she reminded me of until after and then it was too late – and what would I have told her? It was only when I found the article.' She looked at Robert. 'I recognised her and Yatri in the photos. And I recognised you – he's so very like you.'

It was an offering which he accepted, closing his eyes briefly to find his son's smile where it always was, a constellation in the darkness.

'We used to tell ourselves there was virtue in our choice,' Evie continued. 'That we were walking the truer path. You must remember those years of revolution and love. The great rebellion against what had come before. It wasn't just that we were young; the world was young too, reborn after the war and out of its infancy. But still young enough to be malleable; to be whatever we wanted to make it.'

'"The arrogance of youth".'

'Perhaps. When I realised I couldn't change the whole world, building our own seemed like a good substitute. And what a world it was.'

Evie's voice had turned wistful and the part of Robert that was forever young felt that longing too. He thought of the van he'd once intended to drive to India, long sinking into the grass behind Taigh na Criege, useful parts repurposed, rainbows and peace signs faded and reproachful as tattoos on aged skin.

'I called my parents before I left,' Evie said, cutting across his thoughts. 'From Kathmandu. Told them what I was doing, though not where I was going. We couldn't tell anyone that. And though it helped them for a while, it wasn't enough. It was never going to be enough. People say they just want to know you're all right. But then they don't hear from you for a while and they start to wonder if you're still all right – they need constant reassurance. I understand that now, but I didn't then.

'I never asked Yatri if he'd told you he was going. It was easier to just assume. But when I read the article – knowing what my family had been through – I wish someone wiser than me had told my parents I was OK, and told them often. That I was living the best years of my life.'

'Was he happy? At the Sunshine House?' Robert thought of his son in those last months – years, if he was honest – restless for adventure, bored with school. The hint of disdain for the quiet life his parents had chosen. But weren't all teenagers like that? He ran his hand over his face and rubbed his chin, trying to ease the tension in his jaw. 'Did I encourage him to dream too big? Teach him to be too independent? Give him more freedom than he knew what to do with?'

Evie shook her head. 'I never had children,' she said. 'But I know what it is to be young and searching. And it's not always about where you've come from – what you're leaving behind. Some of us are just all forwards motion, looking for something so intently we forget to remember. To look back over our shoulder and see the people who love us, waiting. I don't know at what point I started looking back, but for me it was too late. The things I thought were just behind me had slipped away.'

'It's been seven years.' Robert's voice was louder than he intended and he felt Evie flinch. A man walking a dog on the path glanced over before quickly looking away. The park was filling up. Office workers coming out to eat their lunch, pale faces turning towards the light like sunflowers. Robert looked at his watch. It was time to go.

Evie started to speak as he stood.

'I'm sorry.' Her voice was small. 'Seven years is a long time.' She put out a hand and he took it, squeezing before letting go.

He was already walking away when she called out to him. Robert stopped, seeing the trail of a plane cutting through the sky just before he turned.

Evie was standing by the bench. She was looking past him, eyes following the plane's arc. The woman with the pram had gone.

Robert glanced up at Princes Street, at the buses and cars and people, and mentally traced his journey – the suspended hours of flight, the cool of the mountains, and Anne, waiting for him. Waiting for him with Torran. His happy ending.

'I'm sorry,' Evie said again, and he was just about to tell her there was nothing to be sorry for when she continued. 'There's something else I need to tell you.'

LV

August 1997

Mum and Dad,

I've started to write this letter a thousand times and I never seem to get anywhere. I want to tell you everything that's in my heart but I don't know how and so I will say this:

I love you both. You were good parents to me and I tried to be a good son to you.

I know my decision to stay on in India will be hard for you to understand, and I wish I could tell you where I am and what I am doing, but that would put others at risk. So I will tell you only that I am happy, that I am following my true path.

During my time in India I've come to realise that that is all we can expect or hope for in this little life of ours: to be true to ourselves; to be brave enough to live the life we were born to lead.

I believe this is the life I was born to lead and to be free I need to break away from my old life, my old way of being. I don't expect you to understand why, but I hope you will understand.

Know that I love you both and I pray that in letting me go, you too will be able to find your path to freedom and truth.

Namaste
Torran

LVI

ESTHER

As she read Torran's letter, Esther felt the weight of Anne's eyes on her face. She scanned it quickly, glancing up at Anne, sitting straight-backed in the armchair by the bed. Her hair was swept back, neat as ever, her salwar kameez uncrumpled, though Esther knew she'd spent the night there. She'd woken from feverish dreams, convinced Anne had gone, not just from the room but from her life, and she'd stared in terror at the darkness until a cloud had slipped from the moon and she'd seen Anne's steady outline beside her. A book in her lap and a single sheet of paper in her hands. Esther had tried to ask what she was doing but she'd been fighting against a sleep that wanted to drown her.

And now it was dawn and she was, miraculously, still alive. The fever had broken and, though weaker than she'd ever felt, she'd been able to sit up against the pillows, to accept a few sips of the chai Dolma had brought before slipping quietly away, as if sensing the things that needed to be said.

Esther turned the paper over and then turned it again, in case there was something on the other side, in case there was something she'd missed. She reread it. Slowly. Searching for the missing piece that would make it all OK.

'It's not enough, is it?' Anne was still watching her. 'After everything. It's something. But it's not enough.'

She'd told Esther how she'd found it between the pages of *Kidnapped*, how it hadn't been there when she'd looked at the book that first night at Shambala. How she assumed Jana must have had it all this time. Perhaps Torran had given it to her to post, and she never had; perhaps Torran had written it and decided not to post it, and Jana had discovered it among his things after he left. Anne told Esther she'd spent the night thinking about this, about the letter and what it said and what it didn't, and also about how she had finally come to read it when it had almost been kept from her.

'But why wasn't it sent? If you and Robert had got it seven years ago . . .'

Anne sighed. 'Then what? We may have slept a little easier, for a while. I don't know if it would have made much difference in the end. He would still have been gone.'

Esther frowned at that. Anne reached over to take the letter delicately, almost reverently, out of her hands. The paper looked older than it was, like an ancient prophecy, lost and rediscovered centuries later, its true import lost in antiquity.

'Of course it would have made a difference,' Anne said after a moment, looking down at the letter. 'But would I change it? I don't know. If I went back and changed that, everything else would change.'

'We wouldn't be here now.'

'No, we wouldn't be here now.' Anne folded the letter carefully and put it back in its envelope. 'And you wouldn't be at death's door.'

Esther laughed. 'I think I'm going to pull through.'

Anne smiled, but her eyes were serious. 'I'm glad.'

Esther spent most of the morning dozing, sensing Anne's presence and meekly accepting the painkillers and fluids she'd been instructed to take. The doctor had not been unduly concerned when she visited the previous day. She'd told Dolma that as long as the fever went down within twenty-four hours and there were no further symptoms, Esther should recover in a few days.

Anne stayed by her side, reading *Kidnapped* aloud when Esther was awake and humming softly when she drifted off. She had a beautiful voice and it mingled with Esther's dreams, stirring memories of Anne singing Torran to sleep, perhaps even singing a young Esther to sleep; the echo of a moment she couldn't quite reach.

At midday Esther sat up and looked over at Anne, still clutching the envelope in her hands, eyes fixed on the thangka of the Wheel of Life that hung on the wall above the bed. The endless cycle of death and rebirth and suffering. *Samsara.* The same Wheel of Life that had hung on the wall in the Sunshine House.

'I should be on a bus to Haridwar right now,' Anne said, eyes still on the thangka. 'I almost left yesterday.'

Esther swallowed, her throat thick and her mouth dry. There had been moments during the worst of the fever when she'd woken to find Anne gone, Robert sitting beside her, telling her about the garden, holding a baby Torran in his arms. Liam and Dawa playing chess in the corner. Tomato vines climbing the walls. She swallowed again.

'Where were you going to go?'

Anne shook her head. 'It's over now.'

Esther felt a shiver of unease. Anne's voice was calm laced with what could have been sorrow or could have been relief.

'It's not over,' Esther said, gathering her strength and pushing an optimism she didn't feel. 'Far from it. We know he was at the monastery just days ago, we know he's heading south. He can't have gone far; someone will have seen something. And Robert will be here soon. We're closer than ever.'

But Anne was shaking her head. 'He doesn't want to be found, Esther. He never wanted us to come looking for him in the first place.' She tapped the envelope against her palm and then placed it between the pages of the novel, as if to mark her place, closing the book with a snap.

'It's over.' Anne spoke gently, as if she was talking Esther off a cliff edge.

Esther held her gaze. 'But Robert's coming,' she said, and she could hear the note of pleading in her voice. 'What about Robert?'

245

What about me? she wanted to add. *How could you think of leaving without me?* What was she supposed to do now?

Anne was looking through the window, eyes narrowed against the sun. 'It's time for us all to move on. When you see him—'

'No,' Esther cut in, pushing herself to sit taller, feeling the old frustration flair. 'He's coming here for you, Anne. As much as Torran. You have to see him. You have to talk to Robert.'

Esther crossed her arms, feeling the room swell and settle as her eyes began to ache. A wave of exhaustion crashing over her. Anne was still staring through the window and Esther bit down on her irritation.

'You're right,' Anne said at last, and there was no resentment in her voice. 'But not here – I don't want to stay here any longer than necessary. Aside from Dolma and the Green Tara, I can't bear Manali. Robert and I have had the worst moments here. We can meet him in Rishikesh in a few days, when you're better. I'll call and leave a message at his hotel. He should be landing soon.'

The tension in Esther's body eased and she sank back on her pillows, eyelids heavy.

'Good,' she said. Sleep was tugging at her thoughts and she allowed Anne to help her shuffle down, closing her eyes as Anne arranged the covers around her. Tucking her in. She tried to ask why Anne wanted to go to Rishikesh and not meet Robert directly in Delhi. She thought to challenge her on not just waiting for Robert to join them in Manali. But it occurred to her, as she fell into sleep, that Anne was stalling, postponing something she wasn't quite ready to face.

LVII

BEFORE

Robert is freedom, excitement, possibility; all the things missing from Anne's life. He offers her a different story from the one her parents have always told her, and she keeps this new story to herself, to be read by torchlight under covers. Robert is working in a bar now, but he has big plans. He is a writer and before that he will be a traveller; he is going to India in his van and he wants her to go with him. She knows she will not go; she has no interest in places so far away. But she lets him believe she might. He loves to talk about the places they will visit and the adventures they will have; he is a storyteller, after all. And she loves to listen, to see herself as the heroine of such epic tales. She can lose herself in his stories the way she would lose herself in her music, and this shift in allegiance is so subtle that by the time she realises it has happened, it's too late.

And by the time Robert understands that she has no desire to go to India, he is so in love with the stories he has woven of their life together that it is too late for him as well.

LVIII

RAJESH

Rajesh Kapoor was sitting on the Noon Express AC (not working) bus to Haridwar, fanning himself with a rolled-up *Hindu Times*. It was twenty-three minutes past one and they were still sitting in the station at Dehradun. The midday sun was slowly but surely sending the temperature in the bus to unbearable levels. The man across the aisle had already removed his shoes and shirt. The white vest he wore beneath had several holes around the armpits. Rajesh checked his watch again and rolled his eyes. His sister would be annoyed; his mother would worry.

The driver's door opened, and a harassed-looking man clambered up behind the wheel, ignoring the shouted complaints of the passengers and mopping the sweat from his brow with a blue flannel. He turned the key in the ignition and for a moment the engine revved but then it abruptly stopped. He tried again with the same result. Rajesh and the man in the holey vest exchanged exasperated glances.

And then two things happened at once: the driver got the engine going and someone jumped on board just as the doors were closing, thrust his ticket stub at the surprised conductor and started walking down the aisle looking for a seat.

Rajesh turned his face to the window, hoping the new passenger wouldn't sit beside him. He was a Westerner, one of the hippie dropout types, hair pulled back in a messy ponytail, clothes baggy and unwashed, Jesus sandals on his feet. As he approached Rajesh could smell him, the cloying smell of sweat and socks.

The man sat down beside him, and, really, it was too much! Rajesh shifted in his seat, leaning as far towards the window as he could, not wanting to taint his neatly pressed slacks and crisp white shirt, the unofficial uniform of all the young men at the RJV College of Computer Sciences. He pushed his glasses up the bridge of his nose and continued to stare determinedly out the window, as if the road he had travelled on a regular basis for the past three years was suddenly of great and pressing interest.

The entire journey should have taken less than two hours. But half an hour out of Dehradun the bus shuddered violently and the engine made a spluttering sound before stopping altogether. The driver swore and a communal moan ran through the bus as the vehicle came to a halt at the side of the road. The bus driver and the conductor muttered among themselves and then got out to open the bonnet.

Rajesh Kapoor tutted loudly and looked at his watch. The hippie next to him leant back against the seat and closed his eyes, an idle smile on his face. Rajesh frowned at him before turning back to the window.

After a few minutes the conductor got back on the bus.

'Everybody off,' he said, in several dialects. There was another collective groan as the passengers began disembarking. The hippie next to Rajesh didn't move.

Rajesh looked at him closely. He was sitting very still. Too still.

In a sudden panic, Rajesh prodded him in the ribs and the man's eyes flew open.

'What the—?'

Despite himself, Rajesh grinned at the hippie. 'I thought you were dead.'

The guy sat forwards, rubbing his ribcage.

'I was asleep.'

'You look dead when you sleep.'

'Thanks.'

The hippie looked him in the eye and started laughing, and Rajesh found himself laughing too.

'Everybody off!' The conductor was shouting at them from the front of the now empty bus.

'What's he saying?' the hippie asked.

'We have to get off. This bus is broken.'

They sat on the side of the road in the shade of a eucalyptus tree watching the bus driver, the conductor, several passengers and half a dozen men who had appeared from nowhere, puzzling over the bus's engine. A boy sidled over with a bucket of half-melted ice and glass bottles of Fanta and Cola. Rajesh bought one for himself and one for the hippie and they sipped them in companionable silence. The hippie didn't smell so bad in the fresh air.

'Where are you going?' Rajesh asked after a while.

'I was in the far north,' the hippie said. 'But I had to leave. Some people were looking for me.'

'And you didn't want to be found?'

'Not now, no. It's not my time, man.'

Rajesh pondered this for a moment. He wondered if the hippie was being chased by the police and felt a secret thrill. Perhaps he was a drug lord who had been hiding out in the hills. He imagined the look of horror on his mother's face when he told her he'd bought a drink for a wanted man.

The hippie took another sip of his Fanta as he gazed along the road. There was a lot of traffic: white Ambassador taxis, oxcarts, buses, brightly painted trucks. And on the opposite side, a steady stream of men in saffron robes, some walking in groups, others alone, all carrying a stick over one shoulder with small water-pots hanging from each end.

'Who are those people?'

Rajesh looked over at them too. 'Devotees of Shiva. They're going to the Ganges in Haridwar and Rishikesh to collect water. They will carry it back to their villages and pour it on Lord Shiva in their temples. It is for the festival of Kanwar Yatra.'

The hippie nodded as if he had been expecting Rajesh to say this.

'I knew there was a reason I was going to Rishikesh,' he said, still nodding slowly to himself. 'It all makes sense now.'

Rajesh frowned. He glanced down at his watch. They were already three hours behind schedule.

'You really don't need to worry about the time,' said the hippie.

'I actually do. I have my sister waiting to pick me up. And my mother has made lunch.'

The hippie smiled. 'Time is irrelevant, friend. It keeps moving whether or not we worry about it.'

Rajesh's frown deepened. The man was clearly an idiot. Too many drugs, most likely, or too much time in India. He'd heard it wasn't good for foreigners to stay too long. Some article in the *Hindu Times* about a thing they were calling 'India Syndrome', when Westerners were unable to handle the intensity and spiritual richness of India and lost their marbles, started thinking they were Buddha reincarnated, or God.

Over by the bus there was a commotion. A man had arrived on a motorbike with a box of tools and a can of petrol. There was much discussion as he got to work.

'I might join them,' the hippie said, standing up.

'Do you know something about engines?' Rajesh looked at him doubtfully.

The hippie smiled. 'No.'

And he turned and stepped straight on to the busy road.

Rajesh jumped to his feet as a speeding motorbike carrying two men and three children swerved around the hippie, horn blaring. Unperturbed, the hippie continued across the road at a leisurely pace while the honking traffic moved around him.

When he got to the other side he turned and waved at Rajesh, shouting something which was carried away by a bright green bus whizzing past.

'What?' Rajesh yelled, cupping his hands around his mouth to make the sound travel.

'Thanks for the Fanta,' the hippie called through a break in the traffic, and then he turned to join the procession of pilgrims walking along the road.

LIX

ESTHER

It was another three days before she had recovered sufficiently to undertake the long journey south. They spent them quietly, Esther lying propped up on the pillows, fading in and out of sleep while Anne continued to read to her. *Kidnapped*, and, when that was finished, an interminable Stephen King that Anne had found in the common room and which seemed to amuse her for reasons she didn't share. Esther complained that they'd never finish, that it was too heavy to carry with them. But Anne only laughed and kept right on reading.

And as Esther grew stronger and spent more time awake, Anne read less and dozed more. Purple blanket across her knees, head lolling against the armchair while Esther wrote. Not about Torran or Anne or their journey, for now; she wrote down the stories other people had told her: Dawa, Danny, Ace and Jana.

Dolma brought tea twice a day and the three women drank it together, speaking softly of other things, of other people and other lives, dancing around the edges of everything that had happened.

On the morning of their departure Esther woke to find Anne standing before the open window, face illuminated by the early sun. The room was freezing. Esther pulled on a jumper, still watching Anne. She was luminescent, skin bathed in amber, dark hair loose, for once, and hanging down her back. Esther remembered seeing her that first morning in the restaurant of the Hotel Clarks in Mussoorie, how she had worn defeat in the lines of her face.

'I always thought this would end in one of two ways,' Anne said, without turning. Esther saw that Torran's letter, which

Anne had kept tucked in *Kidnapped*, was lying unfolded on the chair. 'That we'd either find him – alive or dead – and we'd know what happened, or I'd live suspended forever. Never knowing. I thought there was no other way to find an ending. For this to stop.'

Esther waited, but Anne had fallen silent. 'And now?' she prompted.

'He doesn't want to be found. He doesn't want *me* to find him. Can you write me a better ending, Esther?' There was a wry note in her voice, but Esther could hear the sadness as well.

'I never wanted him to come to India. I thought he was too young. Too impatient. I worried he'd never get round to university. That he'd end up like me: throwing his life away over a romantic idea.'

'You didn't throw your life away.'

She shrugged. 'I could have been someone. I was a musician.'

'I know.'

A pause. 'But you're right. I don't know why I still say that. I don't believe it any more. Maybe I never have. It's just that being a wife and a mother wasn't what I expected it to be. It wasn't enough. But would anything have been?'

Anne turned and her eyes met Esther's. 'How do you know when a story is finished?'

Esther stared back at her, trying to understand what Anne needed her to say.

'If we leave aside the fact that a story is never really finished?'

'Yes, leaving that aside.'

'I guess when there's been enough of a change. When you can draw a line and say "Things are different now".'

Anne looked at Esther for a long moment and then nodded, turning back to the window, her attention caught by something beyond.

'Do you hear that?' she said, motioning with her head, and Esther rose to stand beside her, shivering in the damp air. Anne had her purple blanket wrapped about her and she put an arm around Esther's shoulders, drawing her closer, cloaking them both.

The morning was alive with the chatter of birds in the garden.

'You see that?' Anne said, indicating a tiny green and blue bird with a shock of red across its head. It was balancing on a huge white flower with a yellow stamen, dipping its beak into the petals and chirruping. 'A blue-throated barbet. And over there? Those are whistling thrush.'

'I'm glad one of us was paying attention to Dawa.'

Anne smiled. Dawa had tirelessly identified every bird they'd encountered during the trek to the Sunshine House.

'What about that one?' Esther asked, pointing to a small bird with an orange beak watching from a nearby tree.

Anne laughed. 'That's a blackbird, Esther.'

They fell silent, listening to the chatter of the birds, the rustle of the leaves, the tuneful song of the blackbird. Beyond the rooftops of Manali, the far mountains stretched forever, layers of blue upon blue.

'Sometimes I wonder if this could be enough,' Anne said quietly.

'What?' Esther was already turning, letting the blanket drop from her shoulders as she glanced at her watch, thinking of the journey ahead.

'Just this.' Anne motioned to the view before them. 'The sun rising above the mountains; the birds singing. Life. Just as it is.'

The bus arrived in Rishikesh shortly after nine that evening. Robert stood apart from the crowd of waiting relatives and porters and general onlookers, his hands deep in his pockets.

The night was warm and chaotic with the rumble of traffic and honking horns, the chatter of crowds milling about and the profusion of music tumbling from shops and restaurants.

Esther was the first to reach him and he gave her a tight hug. He smelt of Taigh na Criege: woodsmoke and salt and that other unique scent every house – every family – has of its own.

She stepped back and saw Anne standing with their bags. Robert walked towards her with tears in his eyes and Esther turned away.

The lights of the ashrams and guesthouses on the opposite bank were reflected in the river. A long suspension bridge stretched across, lit up like a fairground. There were people everywhere, many wearing saffron-coloured clothes. Some kind of festival was taking place.

'It's a festival of water,' Robert said as he led them over the dangerously crowded footbridge. 'They call it Kanwar Yatra. Something to do with Shiva. All these people come to gather holy water and take it home.'

'Yatri?' Anne said, raising her voice over a group of pilgrims who were singing bhajans as they stepped off the bridge.

Robert leant towards her. '*Yatra*. It means journey, I think.'

'It's so close to Yatri,' Anne said, in a quieter voice.

'What?' Robert frowned and leant in again.

Anne shook her head. 'Nothing.'

With the festival on it was lucky Robert had found them somewhere to stay. The Dharmsala Guesthouse was a few kilometres upstream in the area around the Lakshman Jhula bridge, a less chaotic part of town which also straddled the Ganges on both sides. They squeezed into the back of an auto-rickshaw, Esther and Anne clutching their packs on their knees, Robert half hanging out the side. No one spoke as they sped through the darkness. A long-tailed monkey sitting on the road jumped up and disappeared into the night.

At the guesthouse, Anne followed Esther into the bedroom Robert had reserved for her. She put down her pack and sat on the bed.

'I'm staying here with you,' she said. And Esther was too tired to argue.

LX

ANNE

Anne was awake before dawn; somewhere an ashram bell was calling in the day. She rose with a fully formed plan and got dressed quietly. In the bathroom a dozen cockroaches the size of small mice scurried under a bucket, but she barely noticed them as she splashed cold water on her face.

She was about to slip from the room when Esther stirred, turning and sighing in her sleep, and Anne stopped. She watched her for a long time, seeing the child, as she always did, but also seeing the woman, who had come all this way. Who had stayed.

Anne leant down and shook her shoulder lightly. Esther murmured and opened her eyes, taking a while to focus on Anne, frowning in the weak light. Anne had opened the curtains and although it was still dark, the sky was edged with blue.

'What's happened?' Esther mumbled.

'Come with me,' Anne said, gathering Esther's clothes and dropping them on the bed.

Outside it was cool and damp. Across the river, a gong summoned devotees to prayer and the thin, wavery voice of a man singing bhajans followed them down the street.

They walked upstream until the town was behind them and the sun's rays crept over the horizon in golden arcs. The river ran quickly here, trees replacing the buildings on its banks.

At a small shrine to Parvati, Anne left the path and led Esther towards the crescent bay of a broad bend in the river, where the current was tamed by boulders stretching from the land like a protective arm.

Anne had been here before, once, in the early days of the search. She'd sat on a rock and watched the river and wept. Fear had taken hold and she couldn't see how she could bear it. But she'd also been numb, unable to accept that it was happening – and happening to her.

Both herself and outside of herself.

She saw the figure of a woman now, by the water, and half expected to find herself still there. Still weeping. Still numb.

But the figure moved, not a ghost or a memory but a woman in an orange sari. And she was not alone.

On the rocky shore a group of six women in bright saris and salwar kameez were standing with their toes in the water, clutching each other and laughing.

Anne stopped and Esther paused beside her.

This wasn't what Anne had expected; she'd imagined going into the water alone. Or if not alone then with Esther. A moment of ceremony, of closure, of peace. Bathing in the Ganges was supposed to wash away your sins.

Esther glanced uncertainly at her. 'Do you want to leave?' she said. 'It feels like we might be intruding.'

But the longing to shrink back into the trees, to disappear, did not come.

Anne began walking again, towards the shore, where the women had stopped their slow descent into the water to look back at them, hands raised in greeting, wide smiles catching the dawn. Anne waved back and the next moment the women were coming towards them, laughing and calling. Reaching to help her, to hold Esther; everyone talking at once, everyone moving as one, as hands and hearts and voices carried them to the river.

They all stumbled in, sliding on the rocks and gasping at the icy water. Fingers reached for balance while eyes and smiles flashed as shrieks of laughter were offered up like prayers, until, one by one, each woman fell silent, turning towards the rising sun and slipping beneath the water.

Anne looked at Esther.

'On the count of three?'

Esther was staring at the river. They were now up to their waists, and Anne thought she was about to change her mind. Esther's teeth were chattering; she'd only just recovered from being ill.

'Unless you'd rather not?'

But when Esther looked up a sly grin was spreading across her face.

'"The only way is straight in without any fuss",' she said, in such perfect mimicry of Robert's mother that Anne burst out laughing.

Around them the women were emerging from the water, wading towards the shore, wringing out saris, talking softly together.

Esther held out a hand and Anne took it in hers.

'On the count of three.'

The women had brought breakfast and, when everyone had dried off and changed, they handed round chapatis and sweet biscuits, pouring chai into plastic cups from an enormous thermos.

'Good?'

'So good.'

A large, round-faced woman gave Anne a dimpled grin as she handed her another chapati.

'But where are our manners?' she said, looking in mock horror at her friends. 'We haven't even told you our names.'

After everyone had introduced themselves, amid smiles and the passing round of more biscuits, a woman asked about their husbands.

'No husbands,' Anne said quickly, wiping crumbs from the front of her top. She didn't look at Esther, but she felt her glancing over.

'Better, no?' said the oldest of the group, a white-haired woman wearing a sari of the most dazzling yellow. Everyone laughed.

'You're not married?' Esther said to the women, clearly surprised. 'None of you?' They all shook their heads.

'Not married,' a tall, elegant woman confirmed. 'We are the Early Morning Swimmers' Club but we could just as easily be the Unmarried Women's Club.'

'*Haan*, or the Retired Ladies of Delhi Club,' put in a short woman with a mouth full of biscuit.

'Or the Hindu Feminist Club,' said the woman with the dimples. 'But it's too tiresome to put oneself in just one box, yes?'

'Do you swim every morning?' Anne asked, still feeling the thrill of the ice-cold water, her body lighter than air.

'Oh yes, we always swim daily when we're here; it's excellent for the circulation, you know.' The woman took a bite of her chapati and chewed it for a moment before adding, 'And the soul.'

It was still early when they returned to the guesthouse. They climbed to the rooftop restaurant and drank coffee as they waited for Robert to join them. Anne could feel the weight of the coming day and tried to remember the lightness of water.

Upstream, a rubber raft was making its way down the river, its occupants crying out as they bumped across a series of rapids, droplets gleaming on raised paddles.

Anne cleared her throat. 'I've been thinking about what you said. About the end of a story. About change.' Esther turned to look at her. 'I've been looking back for seven years at all the things I did wrong. Looking for the thing – that one thing I could point to and say, *This is it. This is why he left us.*'

Esther shifted, fiddling with a sugar sachet. The raft had reached the relative calm in front of their guesthouse and the people on board waved as they drifted past. Anne raised a hand in return, squinting against the light that bounced off the water.

'But there was no one thing,' she continued, determined, for once, to say what needed to be said. 'No one reason. Perhaps there never is. It was everything and it was nothing. I could have done better – we all could – but we could also have done a lot worse.

'When something like this happens, everything seems pre-ordained, like it was always hanging over us and we were just too blind to see it. Every memory is tainted. But there were so many happy times. And sad times. And just ordinary times. And they all added up to something, and here we are. And I can't go back, and I don't think I would now, even if I could. I don't know who I'd be, without all this.'

Esther's eyes were on the raft as it meandered downstream.

'But how do you let it go?' she said. 'All the things that happen to you? You can't stop people letting you down. You can't be grateful for that.'

'I'm sorry we let you down,' Anne said. 'I wasn't there for you in the way you needed me to be.'

But Esther was shaking her head. 'I was just so angry with Mum – for leaving. And with Dad for not being able to look after me. But the past can change, can't it? If you let it. The colours shift. The knots untangle. I remember those small kindnesses, how hard you tried. Those things I'd forgotten, or didn't want to remember. And I know I made a lot of that time you almost left in the article, but it was just one thing. And you never would have gone through with it.'

Wouldn't she?

She'd driven to the ferry terminal and parked in the queue. She was early and the horizon was wide open. The sea a silver knife. As the ferry rounded the headland she'd felt something tightly coiled spring free. And she could have cried with relief.

But then a rap at the window had made her jump and a familiar face peered in, a neighbour from two farms over. She'd panicked, waving distractedly and manoeuvring the car out of the queue, back to the road, back to Taigh na Criege. Back to her family and the only life she had.

261

The moment of possibility, the moment of unbounded freedom, already consigned to memory.

Anne looked at them now, the memories she'd been combing over, spread before her in a vibrant tapestry, the sun picking out the golden threads, and she wanted that to be her past – shifted, untangled, golden – she wanted to take it, but she wanted to let Esther keep it more.

'No,' she said. 'Of course not. I couldn't have left; I knew you and Torran needed me.'

Esther gave her such a grateful smile that Anne reached over and tucked a strand of hair behind her ear.

'All the adults who were meant to look after you let you down, one way or another. But it wasn't your fault. You're so much more than what happened to you, Esther. And you're not responsible for your parents' choices.'

Esther was twisting the sugar sachet round and round, her eyes fixed on the movement. She didn't stop until it tore and a cascade of white granules formed a pyramid on the table. When she eventually looked up at Anne, her eyes were glistening. But something had lifted, and Anne understood there was nothing more that needed to be said.

When Robert finally joined them, Esther quickly gathered her things and stood to leave. She told them she needed to call her father; that they must want some time alone. There was so much to catch up on. She smiled brightly, glancing between them, her hand resting lightly on Anne's shoulder. Something hopeful in her face.

Watching her go, Anne felt a pull on her heart and had to resist the impulse to call her back.

Robert sat in the seat Esther had just vacated. Anne could feel the tension in him as he looked at her with his smile in his eyes. That exact mixture of uncertainty and hope that took her back to before everything, and she faltered now as she had then. The weight of his love, his expectation, his needing. And still, as she met his gaze, she saw that other self: the woman he'd always believed her to be. The woman she'd always assumed she wanted to be.

'You're different,' he said.

She looked at his hands, clasped together. The golden band of his wedding ring. It had been his grandfather's.

'It's been a long time, Rob.'

His gaze shifted towards the river. 'I wanted to come. I tried to come. But the days kept passing.'

Anne slowly let out the breath she had been holding. On the riverbank pilgrims were gathering water.

'Three years.'

Robert sighed. She could feel his regret like a physical thing, a heavy rock he was trying to hand to her. But she didn't want to take it.

'I know. I let you down. I let you both down.'

Anne wondered if he meant her and Esther or her and Torran. Or all of them.

Robert turned his palms upwards. He needed her to say something, but she didn't know what. She didn't know how to be around him any more.

'I really thought we were going to find him,' she said at last. 'We were so close.'

Robert drew himself up, stretching out the cricks in his shoulders. Shaking his head. She wondered if he looked older. If she did.

His hair was longer than it had been in over twenty years, the curls more pronounced. Like when they'd first met. And she thought to ask whether this was intentional, or if he just hadn't got round to cutting it. She ought to ask about Tessa, about the garden and the chickens. His family. But these were questions for another time. He seemed more like a stranger than ever and yet so unbearably familiar. She clasped her hands on the table, trying to centre herself as the worlds collided.

'We just need to regroup,' Robert said, bending forwards to catch her eye. 'Formulate a plan. We're so close. I'm sure if we—' But he stopped as Anne shook her head. 'What?'

She hesitated. There was so much to say and she didn't know where to begin. The words forming a mountain between them, one she didn't know if she could cross. She thought of Liam; she thought of Torran's letter; she thought of Esther. The moments that were hers alone and those she owed him.

'Anne—'

'It was so beautiful,' she said quickly. 'The Sunshine Valley. The house. I can see why he loved it – I can see why he stayed.'

Robert smiled but his eyes were wide. He turned his hands over again, curling his fingers inwards, pulling the skin tight. With the instinct of a lifetime, Anne reached across the table to take his hands in hers, and as she uncurled his fingers she felt the tension ease. His eyes met hers. Perhaps it was never too late.

LXI

BEFORE

When does a person begin? Anne sees him from the stage. He is one of the first to enter the auditorium and take his seat. He doesn't wear a coat, but he has a long scarf wrapped several times around his neck, a scarf which will one day hang forgotten in the cupboard of the house by the sea where they will raise their child.

There is no lightning bolt. No shock of recognition as she looks at him. Of course there isn't; this isn't a fairy tale, and he is a stranger. But she notices his curly hair, falling almost to his shoulders, unruly in a way her mother would disapprove of. She notices that he has a concert programme in his hands, but he doesn't look at it. He is looking instead at the people milling about, at the ornate ceiling of the concert hall, half smiling at some thought of his own. She notices the kindness in his face, how he is tall but bends to fit the space, like a tree.

And then the lights dim and the conductor enters, and she forgets him completely. Forgets the audience, forgets the world, becomes the music.

It is only when the lights come back up and she is standing to bow with the rest of the orchestra that her eyes return to his face. He is standing, in the centre of the auditorium, clapping enthusiastically. A little too enthusiastically, perhaps, for a mediocre midweek performance from a youth orchestra. But it makes her smile, and as she takes a final bow and looks up once more she finds herself caught in the directness of his gaze. And that is the moment. That is the beginning of everything.

LXII

EVIE

After her partner Isaac died, in the summer of ninety-six, Evie Sinclair headed south. She had no official papers and little money, but wanted to see something of India before she left. If she left. Recently Scotland had been calling her; she'd lain in the grass of the valley and traced the trails of aeroplanes across the sky, imagined them touching down on the cold tarmac of home. Because Scotland was still home, even after all this time.

She travelled to Goa, to the beaches, and let the changes of the world wash over her. It had been twenty-one years since she'd spent more than a few days away from the valley and when she smelt the sea again she cried, understanding the losses as well as the gains of the life she had chosen.

By Christmas she was restless and headed south. To Kanya-kumari, the very tip of the country, where three seas met to wage war around a rocky island. She spent New Year on the beach with her feet in the water, jasmine garlands woven in her braids. She hadn't had a proper conversation in weeks and for the first time in her adult life she was lonely.

After the fireworks and cries of celebration the night was quiet once more, and Evie walked barefoot along the sand, watching the waves court the moon's reflection. A set of foot-prints emerged before her and she followed them until she reached a cluster of boulders where a young man was sitting with his elbows on his knees, staring out to sea.

He turned when he heard her approach and smiled, the moonlight reflecting on the white of his teeth.

'Happy New Year!' he said in an accent not dissimilar to her own.

'And to you,' she replied. 'Happy Hogmanay!'

The boy's smile widened. 'You're Scottish,' he said, offering a hand to pull her on to the rock.

'Yes, I guess I am.' She sat down beside him. They were silent, listening to the waves against the sand. After a while, Evie felt the boy's eyes upon her.

'Have you been here long?' he asked.

'Almost thirty years.'

He whistled softly.

'Well, not here. But in India. In the north.' It still felt strange to explain herself like this. She habitually avoided the endless questions of travellers and never told them the truth. But that night she was unguarded, the story of her time in India and all that it had meant yearning to come out.

'What have you been doing for the last thirty years?' the boy asked. He sounded genuinely curious.

Evie tried to think of a way to explain what her time at the Sunshine House had been. 'I was just living, I guess. The best way I could.' She smiled at the boy and he smiled back, apparently satisfied with this explanation.

'And now?'

She looked at the sky and the sea, one fractionally darker than the other, separated by the faint line of dawn. 'Now I don't know.'

The boy pointed to the black mass of rocky island not far from shore. 'Have you been across?' And then he continued without waiting for an answer. 'I went there today. The building is a memorial to some Hindu philosopher who sat on that rock and reached enlightenment. Do you believe in enlightenment?'

He wore an expression she couldn't quite make out.

'That depends on what you mean by enlightenment.'

He tilted his head. 'Well, that's the question, isn't it? The more I learn, the less I know.'

'So you've come here to learn?'

'To India? I came here to volunteer, to help.' He shook his head and laughed self-deprecatingly. 'As if anything I did could really help. The children at the school where I was teaching – they were disabled and the stories . . . I heard one of them had been discovered chained like an animal in their home. And the idea that their disabilities were punishments for things they'd done in their past lives.' He shook his head again. 'Not the teachers, they were more *enlightened* than that, but the local community . . . It shocked me. Perhaps more than it should.'

The light on the horizon was bleeding across the sky, deepening the shadows, revealing the shape of things.

'And the poverty and the suffering,' he continued. 'It's one thing knowing about it, isn't it? But seeing it, smelling it, tasting it. There's too much. It's just too much.' He held her gaze. 'Your eyes are blue,' he said at last, and turned back towards the ocean.

Evie thought of Siddhartha, the young prince whose father had protected him from all the bad things in the world. How, when he was eventually confronted with pain, old age and death, he left his princely life in search of a way to end all suffering – in search of enlightenment.

She put her hand on the young man's arm. 'It's not up to you to fix the world.'

He nodded, a half-smile loosening the tightness in his jaw.

'I know,' he said, somehow managing to look both older and younger. 'I just need to find a way to live in it. The best way I can.'

The sun's red orb rose with little fanfare. A gradual lightening of sky and sea, a smudge of pink across a dark canvas. And in the liminal light of night and day the boy lay on his back and closed his eyes. Evie watched as his face relaxed.

'Tell me a story?' he said.

So Evie took the salt air into her lungs and told him about a valley hidden deep in the Himalayas, filled with sunshine, inhabited by a group of ordinary people who had found an extraordinary way to live. Who had become Sunbirds.

As she spoke, she watched the sun clear the sea and begin its ascent and knew that same sun was cresting the mountains above the valley, as the inhabitants of the Sunshine House stirred into life. And she knew she would go back.

The boy smiled as she spoke, but softly, as if in sleep, and when she at last fell silent he was so still that she thought he must have drifted off. But then, eyes still closed, he murmured, 'It sounds too good to be true.'

Evie laughed and he opened one eye and squinted up at her. 'It is.'

They walked together back to town, the shops and restaurants just opening, the streets still being cleared of debris from the night before. The boy was tall beside her, and Evie knew that people would assume he was her son, and this thought nudged at a regret she refused to acknowledge. They'd had a good life together, she and Isaac, a complete life.

At the door to her hotel, she turned to the boy, who looked older in the daylight – he was a grown man, after all. He was restless now, his gaze roaming the street, hands pulling at threads on his shirt, pushing at the hair that fell over his eyes.

'Where have you really been all these years?' he said. 'An ashram? I've been thinking of joining an ashram. Or a monastery. Or . . . I might just go home.' He shifted his weight, eyes on the ground. 'I've been feeling . . . lost. No, not lost. Disappointed.'

'Disappointed?'

He made an impatient sound. 'I'm still looking. I thought I would have found it by now. But I don't even know what I'm looking for.'

She had planned to stay longer but, that afternoon, boarded a bus heading north. The decision made, she wanted only to get back to the valley and the Sunbirds. She would return to Scotland eventually; she knew she would. But not yet.

She sat by the window and watched the world: men tying suitcases and rucksacks and crates and mysterious bundles to the roofs of buses; a boy selling chai, hefting a brass kettle almost above his head to pour it out; backpackers squinting over tickets; the multitude of onlookers and commentators and hawkers who existed in every public space in India. And then she spotted him, the young man from the beach, standing between her bus and the next, and a moment later he saw her too. He grinned and motioned for her to open the window.

'I went back to your hotel, but they said you'd left.' He rose on tiptoes, his fingers gripping the window frame, his eyes searching. 'I just wanted to say goodbye.'

She smiled. 'Are you staying for long?'

He looked over his shoulder as the bus behind him started to reverse out of its bay. 'I might go home.'

Evie shook her head. 'Don't go home yet; there's still so much—' Her words were drowned by the bus's engine choking into life.

'What?' he said, leaning further into the window. Up front the doors were closing, the driver shouting something while simultaneously fiddling with his radio. Evie motioned helplessly at the boy – it was too loud; they were leaving.

She sat back with a final smile, expecting him to let go of the window frame, but instead he reached for her, said something she couldn't make out.

'What?'

'The valley.' He had his hand on her sleeve, his eyes fixed on hers.

'It was just a story,' she said as the driver turned down the radio enough that they could hear themselves once more.

'No.' He took her hand, his fingers squeezing hers. 'I need that valley.'

For a moment she wavered, seeing in his eyes herself as a young woman and the incredible gift Lorrie had given her, all those years ago. But things were different now; time was running out.

Evie squeezed his hand and gently let it go. 'We all need that valley. But it doesn't exist. I'm sorry.'

She willed the bus to start moving but instead the engine cut out and the driver jumped off and disappeared – fate sometimes nothing more than timing and luck.

'OK.' The boy had his hands up in surrender. 'OK – I get it.' He looked her straight in the eye. 'But if it did exist, where would it be?'

LXIII

ESTHER

She spent the day alone, wandering the streets, half-heartedly scanning the faces of passing travellers. Rishikesh was hot and grimy, a world away from the tranquillity of the mountain villages. Yet even here, beyond the colourful ashrams and endless hotels, the mountains rose in jagged, tree-covered peaks, so small and tame after the lofty Himalayas, toy mountains behind a brightly painted toy town.

On the riverbank saffron-clad pilgrims gathered to fill their water jugs. Esther stopped to watch a half-naked child being dunked in the river by his father, laughing wildly, willing and resisting at the same time. Her own father was on her mind. She should call him; she should arrange her flight home. But she was thinking of Dawa as well, of the stories he'd told her, the places he'd spoken of. There was still so much to see.

She was turning back towards the guesthouse when a familiar face in the crowd made her stop suddenly, pulse racing. For a second she thought it must be Torran and in the same instant she realised it was Liam. She started to call out but he was gone, swept up in the urgent stream of people and scooters and rickshaws and animals. She hesitated, considering chasing after him, but already doubting herself. It could have been him; it could have been anyone. Because of all the places in all the world, why would he be here?

When Esther got back to their room Anne was already there. She turned from the mirror to greet her, eyes gleaming in the half-light. She was wearing a dark green dress Esther had never seen before. It was loose but more fitted than the salwar kameez she usually wore, tapered in at the waist, the skirt fuller and falling to skim her knees. Golden threads caught the light when she moved.

'You look beautiful,' Esther said, sitting on the bed, deciding in that moment not to mention seeing Liam. If she'd seen him.

Anne turned back to the mirror where she was pinning a string of jasmine blossoms around her head like a crown, their sweet scent filling the room. She smiled at Esther in the glass.

'There's a full moon celebration on the beach. I think we should go. I think it will do us good.'

The party was in full swing by the time they arrived. Flames from the bonfire leapt high, sending sparks to join the stars. The moon was low and bloated, its light picking a path across the river.

There were people everywhere, on the sandy stretch of riverbank and the giant boulders that guarded the bay. Round the fire, people played music: guitars, ukuleles and cajon drums. An old woman with long white hair crouched over a harmonium; a sunburnt man in Bermuda shorts beat a tambourine against his head. There were a few young Indian faces, but most of the people were foreigners. Despite Rishikesh's no-alcohol policy, bottles of beer and rum had been procured and were handed around along with chillums and loosely rolled joints. English mingled with Russian and Hebrew, French, German and Spanish, and other languages Esther didn't recognise. Laughter rang high over everything. Someone had brought portable speakers and soon the musicians were competing with the relentless beat of house music. People were dancing, silhouetted against the moon. A firework exploded in the sky.

Esther looked for Robert and Anne, but they'd disappeared. A girl sitting on a sarong near the fire pulled Esther down beside her. She looked vaguely familiar, but Esther couldn't place her face.

'Come join us,' the girl said with a grin. One of her front teeth was missing. Someone handed Esther a plastic cup of rum mixed with something sweet and sickly.

'You look familiar,' she said to the girl, leaning forwards so she could hear her. 'Have we met before?'

The girl looked at her closely. 'I don't know. Possibly. In another life.'

Esther raised a sceptical eyebrow and the girl laughed, taking a long toke on a glass chillum. Another firework exploded overhead. Esther drained her cup and someone immediately handed her another. The girl pulled her back to lie beside her so that their heads were almost touching.

'Man, I love India,' the girl said.

Esther looked up at the night sky, the planets and stars, watchful and senseless as they'd always been, yet beautiful too.

'I have to go back next week,' the girl continued. 'But sometimes I think I'll just stay. People do, you know. I met this guy in Goa who's been selling coconuts since the seventies. He's from Madrid. When he left, Spain was still a dictatorship. He said people have told him it's been over for thirty years, but he doesn't care. He's happy selling his coconuts and partying on the beach.'

Esther could feel the sand vibrating with the beat of the music.

'It's just one endless party here.' The girl laughed. 'It's going to be hard to go back to the real world.'

Esther let her thoughts drift as the girl continued talking about the all-night raves on Anjuna beach, the illegal trance clubs in Hampi, the international party boats in Kerala. Yet another side of India that Esther hadn't seen. Yet another reason foreigners came and returned and kept coming. Or never left.

She remembered Ace talking about his time in Rishikesh in the late sixties. How he found himself sitting on the banks of the Ganges one morning watching Paul McCartney strum his guitar, the lyrics of 'Blackbird' taking shape before his eyes. John and George meditating on a rock beside him.

The story seemed too fantastical to be wholly true. A meeting, perhaps, of memory and desire in a country that has as many faces as gods, that can mean anything to anyone. But that was when he'd known, Ace had told her, that he was a Sunbird. That he was never going home.

LXIV

ROBERT

As the night wore on the moon climbed higher in the sky, extinguishing the surrounding stars. The crowds thinned, the batteries in the portable speakers died, and the airwaves were reclaimed by the musicians around the fire.

Robert followed Anne to a rock, away from the dancing and the flames, her cool hand holding his. They sat side by side, bodies touching, hands still clasped. Like two pieces of a jigsaw, Robert thought, those ones for small children. Ever since Torran's birth he'd imagined them that way: a three-piece puzzle. But maybe he'd been wrong, maybe they'd always been a two-piece – the easiest to put together.

He was teasing the metaphor to its conclusion when Anne shifted and the night air slipped between them.

'Curtaingate,' she said, a smile on her lips.

Robert chuckled, letting go of her hand to pull her back to him. And to his relief she stayed, head resting on his shoulder.

'His first great vanishing act.'

'I've been thinking about that lately. The whole time it took us to find him – what, less than an hour? I was terrified, but at the same time, on another level, I didn't really believe he'd gone. I didn't believe anything truly bad had happened.'

Robert remembered the panic in Anne's eyes as they'd searched the theatre for their six-year-old son, the concern on the ushers' faces, the nervous glances exchanged as time passed and Torran didn't materialise. 'No, I didn't either. But people don't, do they?' He touched his face briefly to the top of her head.

Anne was silent for a moment. 'When we pulled back that curtain and found him – his little face pressed up against the window, staring out at the Christmas lights – I was so angry and so relieved. I wanted an explanation and an apology, but he just looked at me with those big green eyes, completely oblivious to what he'd put us through. And you said, "Just leave it, he didn't mean it. He wasn't doing it to worry us." And you were right, he just wanted to look at the lights, he didn't do it to upset us.'

He couldn't remember saying it, he remembered only the relief as he ushered his wife and son outside. His puzzle once more complete.

Over by the fire more people were dancing, throwing their shadows against the rocks. Robert scanned the faces again, just in case. He glanced down at Anne, expecting her to be doing the same, but she was looking at the sky.

'Remember how he used to follow you everywhere?' she said, sitting up so that his arm fell from her shoulder. 'Your little shadow.'

Robert sat up straighter too. 'But remember how much he needed you? When he was little and no one else would do? Long before he was my shadow, he was yours.'

Anne turned towards him, angling her body so that her face was half hidden by the night, her eyes bright reflections of the moon. 'It was too much. And then it wasn't enough. I kept waiting for the happy medium.'

'That's usually the part that comes later. When they're fully grown.'

'Maybe. Maybe that's what we've lost. But it's never truly equal, is it? The love between us.'

Anne took his hand again and turned to look at the dancers. Watching her profile, Robert had the uncanny feeling of sitting on a train when it starts to move, only to realise it is the train on the parallel track that has departed, and you haven't moved at all.

'I thought for a long time that he was punishing me.'

It took a moment for her words to make sense to him. 'Anne – there was nothing to punish you for.'

She looked back at him. 'He was different afterwards. He became *your* shadow. And all this time, I thought if I couldn't have him back – if he wanted to stay here – at least I could ask for his forgiveness. If we found him. But it isn't his job, is it? To forgive us. We can't put that burden on him.'

Robert shook his head. 'My love. There's nothing to forgive.'

She looked at him for a long moment and something in her face troubled him. The music was getting louder, more drums, people singing. Wood was thrown on the fire and the flames rose higher.

'All my life, I've felt like water.' Anne's eyes found the river. 'The way it's transparent but also reflective. He saw right through me and yet everything he did was reflected on me, like being nothing and everything at the same time. There and not there.' She turned his hand over in hers, opening the fingers one by one and pressing her thumb against his palm. 'And you were the earth – so solid, so stable. Somewhere safe to land. But his actions were never a reflection on you. It was all me. I was always trying to expand, to fit around, to fill the empty space.' She closed his fingers again, one by one. 'It's impossible.' He tried to keep his expression open, to look like he understood what she was saying. 'I've always found that.'

'I only ever wanted things to be easy for you. For both of you. All of you. Esther too.'

'We should have tried harder with Esther. I should have. But you should have too.'

Robert nodded. 'She turned out all right, though.'

'More than all right,' Anne said. 'Although I think that was despite us rather than because of us. But it's been good. Having this time with her. And we had a good life. I can see that now.'

Robert took her hand again, holding it tightly in both of his.

'We can still have a good life. We can still find Torran – we're so close, Anne. I know we are.'

She looked at him, half smiling and half frowning, and something in her eyes made him clutch tighter and keep talking.

'Or we can leave. We can go home and wait for him there. We can start again – we can do things differently. It's not too late.'

Tears were filling his eyes, pushing Anne's face out of focus as she leant in and kissed him, and he couldn't tell if she was crying too but for a moment there was only her, the overwhelming sense of her. And then she was drawing away, standing, pulling him up with her.

'Shall we dance?' she said, brushing the sand from his shirt and then pausing, reaching a hand to the side of his face. He could feel the tremor in her fingers. But it was too dark to see the green of her eyes and the moment weighed on Robert, heavy with a significance he couldn't grasp.

Beside the fire was a confusion of bodies and sound, shadows flung across the rocks and the river rushing on and on. Robert hovered by Anne, unable to lose himself in the dancing but unwilling to leave her side. She was swaying beside him, eyes closed, arms awkwardly searching for the rhythm. He tried to remember the last time he'd seen her dance but the images that came to him – summer ceilidhs, her favourite song on the kitchen radio, their wedding – felt insincere, like memories of photos rather than the moments themselves.

He turned to scan the crowd for Esther – it had been some time since he'd seen her – and his eyes snagged on someone in the shadows, at the edge of the dancing. It was impossible to tell, from this distance, in this light, with the crowd of moving bodies between them, but, as he craned his neck and moved to the side, he caught sight of the man again and adrenaline flashed through him.

'Anne!' He tried to grab her hand, but she was really dancing now, the swaying turned to steps, her arms high in the air above her head. She moved gracefully in time with the bodies around her, music vibrating the air.

Robert whipped back to find the man again, the man who was even now turning away towards the road above the beach, who was the right height, the right build, the right age, the right rightness, who must – yes, he was sure of it – be his son.

'Anne,' he said again, seizing her wrists and glancing over her shoulder at the man as she finally turned to him and opened her eyes. 'I've seen him – he's here! We have to go.' But Anne just stared at him, incomprehension on her face. 'Come on.'

He was already moving, pushing through the crowd, desperately trying to keep his eyes on his son as he pulled Anne behind him. But she shook him free, and he was forced to stop. Turning, he tried to convey the urgency, but she was shaking her head. She was speaking but he couldn't hear her above the music and the press of people laughing and singing and he looked back to where Torran had been and he was gone and when he turned again to Anne she was gone too and for a split second Robert faltered.

And then he was running, weaving through the dancers, around the fire, past the musicians, over the sand and across the rocks towards the road where – yes! – he could see his son up ahead, making his way carefully through the moonlight.

LXV

NOW

Anne is dancing. And the music doesn't just fill her ears, it fills her body and her soul. She sees the flames across the rocks, the faces, the shadows. She hears the urgency of the river and the silence of the stars, hears the music like she has never heard music before. Her body moves of its own accord: she is a bird cruising the airstreams; the seaweed pushed and pulled by a relentless tide; the bow dancing across the strings. She is the colours of the setting sun: blood red and daffodil yellow. She is every moment of every day she has ever lived: the twitching watchfulness of the purple sunbird, the aching expanse of mountain upon mountain, the burnt-out heart of the Sunshine House. Crackle of fire, rush of river, song of blackbird. She is nothing: she is everything.

Arms in the air, feet tracing circles in the sand, she moves like the reeds that are bent forwards and back by the wind. Forwards and back, yet they never break. Again, she rises, again, again. She is the moon laying a path across the waters of the bay. The reflection of light. The memory of water.

She closes her eyes and everything ceases, moment upon moment upon moment retract to nothing. She is.

She is.

And she is falling. Falling through a night of stars, falling past the hands that reach and the eyes that haunt and the mountains that watch and the seas that circle. And the fall is longer than she ever imagined, longer and more beautiful, and without end. The arms of the earth hold her. She is lying in the sand, lying in the sand with eyes open wide. And she is laughing.

LXVI

EVIE

It had been a confession of sorts. Telling Robert.

Evie had thought a lot about redemption since her return to Scotland. About personal responsibility. About freedom. About choice.

She hadn't just found that article while clearing out her parents' house, as she'd told Esther; she'd found boxes. Boxes and boxes in the spare room which had once been her childhood bedroom. Filled with newspaper clippings and magazines, not only thirty years' worth of missing foreigners in Asia but reference books and travel guides, mountaineering manuals, every single edition of *Lonely Planet* for India and Nepal.

Her quiet, conservative parents who had never left Britain. Who had never come looking for her. Who had never stopped searching. All those years.

She'd lain on the floor, surrounded by the proof of their love and their pain, and let night fall. When she could no longer see, she'd pulled herself up and turned on the light. She'd made a cup of tea with three sugars and returned to the boxes, taking the first magazine that came to hand.

And there was Yatri, smiling up at her.

Almost three years to the day after leaving the Sunshine House, and less than forty-eight hours after meeting Yatri's father, Evie Sinclair boarded a flight back to India. As the plane broke through the knotted grey, she gazed wide-eyed at the blue. And the bird that had been singing outside her body these past years settled inside her once more. She was going home.

LXVII

ESTHER

The sun woke her, streaming in through half-closed curtains. Esther lay in bed looking at the ceiling, the fan slicing through the humid air with a dull whirr, the tiny copper stain of human blood where a mosquito had been flattened. From beyond the window, the urgency of the river rushing by, the sound of a gong, the hum of traffic. She rolled over and saw the other side of the bed was empty, stretched out a hand and felt the coldness of the sheets.

Head fuzzy, she sat up, fumbled for her water bottle, took a long drink, and tried to remember when she'd last seen Anne. She'd probably stayed in Robert's room, that was all. But Esther felt a rising panic in her chest.

She dressed quickly and walked down the hall to knock on Robert's door. There was no answer and she knocked again, louder, resisting the impulse to pummel her fists on the wood. She checked her watch; it was after eight. They'd probably gone to the roof terrace to have breakfast.

Stopping by her room to grab her money belt, she saw with relief that Anne's backpack was still there where she'd left it, leaning against the wall beneath the window.

Robert was sitting at the same table as yesterday, coffee cup in hand, staring at the mountains. He raised his eyebrows and smiled when he saw her.

'Isn't Anne with you?' she said, before he could speak.

He frowned. 'Not since last night. But I left quickly – I thought I saw Torran.'

Esther stopped short. There was a beat as all the possibilities jostled in her mind.

'I really thought it was him.' From his rueful expression it was clear he'd been mistaken. 'As if it could have been that easy. I forgot what it was like to be here – always chasing shadows. I lost Anne when I went after him – she was dancing. It was so loud; she mustn't have understood what I was saying.'

'Anne was dancing?'

Robert almost laughed at the look on Esther's face. 'I was surprised too. But I assumed she'd come back with you?'

Esther shook her head and neither of them said anything. Robert stood up.

'There are still some revellers from last night on the beach.' He nodded downstream to the sandy bay where the party had been, the fire still smouldering, a few figures lying beside it on the sand. 'She probably just stayed out to watch the sunrise.'

They walked side by side, scrambling along the rocks and over boulders, trying not to betray their fear. Robert talked about his plans for the day; he wanted to put up posters, start knocking on doors. He needed to reply to a message he'd received at the guesthouse; a student called Rajesh Kapoor thought he might have spoken to Torran on a bus. Robert's single-minded energy and determination after everything seemed futile. But perhaps he was using it to shore himself up, to stop the fragments of his life from splintering.

Anne wasn't there. They could see that even before they reached the remains of the fire. A young Australian couple Esther had met the night before were sitting against a rock and seemed to be the only people awake. The boy nodded at Esther and the girl waved sleepily.

'Great night,' the boy said.

'Have you seen Anne?' Robert broke in before Esther could say anything. 'My wife. The tall woman with the black hair?'

The girl nodded. 'Yeah, she was beautiful, man.'

The boy grunted in agreement.

'She *is* beautiful. Have you seen her?' Robert's eyes were already scanning the riverbank, the footbridge, the opposite shore.

'I spoke to her last night,' the girl continued in a dreamy voice. 'She's beautiful inside and out.'

Esther could see the effort it was taking Robert not to lose his patience.

'Please,' she said, crouching down in front of them. 'We can't find her this morning. Have you any idea where she might have gone?'

'You're talking about that tall woman?' a voice cut in from behind her. Turning, Esther saw a middle-aged woman with short hair and several facial piercings.

'Yes,' Robert said.

The woman came over to them. 'She was here all night. We were talking about a lot of things. Fascinating conversations. Watching the stars. She left just as the sun was rising.'

'Did she say where she was going?'

The woman shook her head.

'Was she alone?' Esther asked, and Robert shot her a quizzical look.

'Yes. She had a bag with her. Like a daypack? She headed off down the river and I saw her crossing the bridge. I remember because she stopped halfway across and looked back for a long time, like she'd forgotten something.'

Esther and Robert exchanged a look, trying to make sense of it. Esther didn't know Anne had another bag, and she certainly hadn't seen her with it the night before.

'Was she going to look for her son? Torran?'

The woman squinted at Esther and wrinkled her nose. 'I don't think so. We talked a long time and she never mentioned having a son.'

That evening Esther and Robert sat on the ghats by the Ram Jhula bridge and watched the river sparkle like the Milky Way, carrying its prayers into the night. They were crudely made offerings: a tinfoil boat harbouring a tealight, a handful of rice, a flower, captained by a small figurine of Shiva, Ganesh or Kali. Pilgrims and tourists paid a few rupees to set them upon Mother Ganga, brave little lights on their perilous journey south.

They'd spent the day searching for Anne, but there was no sign of her. Back in the hotel Esther had looked through Anne's stuff. Her passport and money were gone, along with a few clothes and her toothbrush. She'd left Torran's copy of *Kidnapped*, his letter still tucked between the pages, the picture of Torran from the Sunshine House and the book she'd been reading, her bookmark a third of the way through.

When Esther went to Robert's room to tell him, he stood very still for a long time, one hand on the top of his head as if trying to hold his thoughts together. She wanted to put her hand on his arm, to say something comforting, but there were no words and after a while she left, closing the door softly behind her. She heard a single wordless cry as she walked back down the hall, and then silence.

Later, on the ghats, Robert told her he wouldn't notify the police. Not yet. He wanted to give Anne time. She might just need to be alone for a while, to come to terms with everything. He would keep searching for Torran, and Anne would come back when she was ready. Esther didn't tell him that she thought Anne had left for good.

'I keep wondering if maybe she saw him.'

Esther looked over at Robert, his face half in shadows, half in light. 'Torran?'

'Aye,' Robert said. 'Maybe he *was* there last night. Maybe I was just chasing the wrong man. Maybe she followed him. Or maybe she heard something. I mean—' He drew the printout of Rajesh Kapoor's email from his pocket. 'This man thinks Torran was heading here. Maybe she did see him. Maybe she's with him now.'

He looked up at the starless night.

'She took her passport. She packed a bag. She knew she was leaving.'

Robert kept his face turned towards the sky.

'At least when I thought he was dead I had some kind of peace.' He spoke as if to the darkness. 'An ending. But now . . .' He trailed off, letting the unfinished thought float away with the river.

From behind them came the sound of chanting, voices gathered in harmony, notes swelling the air. A man with a popcorn stand shouted to people as they passed. A horn blared.

'We'll meet with Rajesh Kapoor tomorrow.' Robert's voice was stronger, renewed with purpose. 'Put new posters up, go round the ashrams. Someone will have seen something. We may even find him before Anne gets back.' He stopped talking when he saw the expression on Esther's face.

'What?' he said.

'It's time for me to go.' Her words sounded all too familiar. She thought of that morning at Taigh na Criege, sitting in the early sunlight and agreeing to come. The geese vanishing into the sky. She saw herself there, but it was like looking at a picture of someone else.

'You're leaving too.' Robert nodded as he spoke. 'Yes, of course. You should go home.'

'So should you. I don't think you're going to find them right now. Torran doesn't want to be found – Anne was sure of that.'

Robert looked at the printout in his hands, though it was too dark to read it. Esther saw a muscle in his jaw tighten and then release.

'She didn't say that to me,' he said.

'Didn't she?' Esther wondered what Anne had actually said and what Robert had heard.

He cleared his throat, shifting beside her. 'Sometimes I wonder what our lives would have been if she'd left all those years ago.'

Esther shook her head. 'She never would've done that. She'd never have left us.'

'Wouldn't she? Your mother did.'

'Yes,' Esther said, thinking for the first time of how it had affected him, losing the sister he was closest to. 'But Anne isn't Mum.'

Robert gave her an appraising look, emerging momentarily from his own pain. 'You're not angry with her any more.'

'Who? Mum? Or Anne?'

'Maybe both.'

Esther looked away. 'Maybe.'

She sensed, rather than saw, a shadow of a smile cross his face.

'It was good for you to come, then? To India.'

She shrugged but smiled too. 'Mum didn't exactly disappear. We do know where she is at least.'

'There's more than one way to disappear.'

'True.' Esther glanced at him, and his face was pensive again. 'But Anne never would've left when we were young. I hope you know that. Sometimes we just have to take ourselves to the very edge and lean over, knowing we'll never jump.'

Robert was silent, watching the river's current send waves across the steps.

'I know,' he said at last. 'I just wish I'd been better. Done more. Seen what was happening. How difficult it was for her. For you.'

A few steps below them a Japanese man was strumming a guitar, black hair falling over his eyes.

'Are you still going to write about it? Torran. The missing people in the Kullu Valley?'

Esther raised an eyebrow. 'I thought we agreed I wouldn't.'

He gave her a sideways glance. 'You never had any intention of sticking to that agreement.'

She smiled, relieved at the lack of rancour in his words. 'No comment.'

Robert's gaze drifted to the guitar player, singing softly as he strummed. All you need is love.

'Maybe you should,' he said, after a pause.

'Maybe I will.'

'But do us justice this time, Esther. Get us right. Torran. Anne. Me.'

There was a sadness in the names of those he loved the most. Perhaps there always would be. And Esther remained silent because she knew that his version of his family would never be hers. But that there was a moment where they would always meet, the line in the sand that marks the turning tide, the moment of simultaneous movement in opposing directions. The staying and the going. All at once.

'I'm glad you were here with her,' Robert said, following his own thoughts. 'It should have been me. But maybe it was meant to be you.'

After she'd phoned the airline to change her flight, Esther called her father. He answered on the second ring, but she had to wait several minutes for his confusion to lift. And even once he realised who she was, it lingered at the edge of his words. She started to tell him she'd be home in a few days but he interrupted with the news that her brother had been to visit. That there was talk of him quitting the army and moving back to Edinburgh; his girlfriend was pregnant.

Just before she said goodbye his voice cleared and the fog lifted.

'You don't need to rush back on my account,' he said, but she could hear the hesitation. 'Especially now. If your brother is going to be nearby.'

'We can't rely on Callum, Dad.'

He started coughing and she held the receiver away until he'd finished.

'Maybe not, sweetheart. Maybe not. But I've been all right.'

She listened to the bright buzz of daytime television from her father's flat and imagined what she would do if she allowed herself to believe him.

After she hung up, Esther sat in the glass booth and looked at the phone. No one was waiting to use it and Robert was sitting at one of the computers in the back of the shop, writing an email to Rajesh Kapoor. A solitary ant was climbing the glass and she resisted the temptation to reach out and squash it beneath her finger.

In her pocket was her notebook and folded within the pages was the piece of paper Dawa had given her with his phone number written neatly across it. She thought of Anne, imagined her dancing on the sand the previous night, a smile spread wide across her face. And though she understood that Anne had to go, she was hurt she hadn't told her she was leaving.

Esther sat for a moment longer and then picked up the phone again and dialled a number she still knew by heart. The electronic sounds repeated themselves faintly in her ear as the call was connected and the phone began to ring, the line suddenly clear as a bell.

Twelve rings and the answering machine clicked in and there was Anne's voice. Her voice but not her voice, different in some indefinable way. Esther closed her eyes and listened.

LXVIII
BEFORE

When the night begins to fade, Anne rises. She retrieves her bag, not exactly hidden but stashed safely between two boulders. The voices around the fire have fallen silent; she feels the coming of the light pulsing in her veins.

There is nothing left to do but walk. She follows the path that leads to the Lakshman Jhula bridge, where a white cow, long horns painted and garlanded with flowers, lifts its head from a grassy verge, dark eyes turning towards her and then away. She is halfway across the bridge before she stops, as if at the sound of her name, to look back.

She knows there is a part of her which will remain. With Robert, with Esther, with Torran. The Anne they carry with them; the Anne who stays. But things are different now. And this is the gift we give our children. The letting go.

Below her on the shore a lone pilgrim stands, feet in the water, hands raised to greet the sun.

Enough. It is enough.

She turns and walks towards the opposite bank and the future is as open as the sky. The sun is rising over the mountains. And the birds are singing.

Acknowledgements

Thank you –

to my late father, Jeremy, for being proud enough of me in the first twenty-one years of my life to last me for a lifetime. You always said I'd be a writer, and now I am.

to my mum, Dorothy, for introducing me to the wonderful, wild places of this novel and for your unwavering belief in me.

to my agent Jo Unwin, for seeing straight to the heart of this story and for loving it, for championing it and me tirelessly with such humour and grace. To Donna Greaves for pouring so much energy, care and editorial insight into it – this novel would not be what it is without you. And to Daisy Arendell for expertly completing the JULA dream team.

to the foreign rights team at C&W, particularly to Kate Burton, for being passionate champions of *Sunbirds*, and for your amazing deal-making.

to Jocasta Hamilton for snapping the book up and making it all happen in record time; to Becky Walsh for editing with sensitivity and precision; to Hilary Hammond, Corinna Zifko, Katharine Morris, Alice Graham and everyone at John Murray Press for all their hard work in making the dream a reality. And to Sara Marafini for the beautiful cover design.

to my teachers and fellow students at Manchester Metropolitan University's Writing School, where I completed my first draft of this novel as part of an MA. Also to Emylia Hall at The Novelry, Rebecca Nouchette and Hamish Wilson at the Garsdale Retreat, Charlie Haynes at Urban Writer's Retreat, and the many friends and writers I met along the way.

to my first ever reader and editor Lizzie Corsini, for getting me over that finish line, and to my other early readers: Rhiannon Brislee-Young, Fiona Johnston, Nancy Karamichou and Catherine Brislee, for all the feedback and encouragement. With an extra special shout-out to Rhiannon for the unfailingly wise counsel and the eleventh-hour punctuation, grammar and sense-checking.

to my best girl Anna Knight, for more reasons than there are words, but not least for being blonde so that we can be best friends for ever. And to my writing wife Kate Billington, for spotting the mistakes everyone else misses and for your constant support and enthusiasm. You have both contributed so much to this novel and I cannot thank you enough.

to Antonia Munoz del Moral, Sally Miller, Judy Gibson, Ruth Herbert and my Croft family, my Findhorn cheerleaders Clark Heijbroek, Rolf Adkinson and Jannike Liebwerth, to Wendy Cartwright, Daniel Kirk, Jimmy Maverick, Talitha McQueen, Samantha Tring. Thank you for all the book chat, the life chat, the ribbons, the encouragement, the commiserations, the celebrations, the childcare and the love.

and, most importantly, to my family: to my beautiful boys Finlay and Emilio, and to Luis, without whom there would be no book. Thank you for making all of this possible.